PENGUIN BOOKS

Kevin Brooks was born in Exeter, Devon, and he studied in Birmingham and London. He has worked in a crematorium, a zoo, a garage and a post office, before giving it all up to write books. Kevin is the award-winning author of six critically acclaimed novels and lives in Richmond, North Yorkshire. *Being* is his first novel published by Penguin.

Praise for *Being*:

'He's an original. And he writes one hell of a story' – Meg Rosoff, author of *How I Live Now*

'Violently enjoyable' – *The Times*

'A gut-wrenching thriller . . . so powerfully evocative that it is like sitting in a private cinema of the mind' – *Telegraph*

'Original in its premise and captivating in its delivery. A gripping read' – *The Big Issue*

'Sharp and precise . . . a meditation on the nature of humanity' – *Sunday Times*

'An exciting on-the-run thriller . . . you'll be gripped' – *Flipside*

Books by Kevin Brooks

BEING
BLACK RABBIT SUMMER
CANDY
KISSING THE RAIN
LUCAS
MARTYN PIG
THE ROAD OF THE DEAD

Kevin BROOKS Being

PENGUIN BOOKS

PENGUIN BOOKS

Published by the Penguin Group
Penguin Books Ltd, 80 Strand, London WC2R ORL, England
Penguin Group (USA) Inc., 375 Hudson Street, New York, New York 10014, USA
Penguin Group (Canada), 90 Eglinton Avenue East, Suite 700, Toronto, Ontario, Canada M4P 2Y3
(a division of Pearson Penguin Canada Inc.)
Penguin Ireland, 25 St Stephen's Green, Dublin 2, Ireland (a division of Penguin Books Ltd)
Penguin Group (Australia), 250 Camberwell Road, Camberwell, Victoria 3124, Australia
(a division of Pearson Australia Group Pty Ltd)
Penguin Books India Pvt Ltd, 11 Community Centre, Panchsheel Park, New Delhi – 110 017, India
Penguin Group (NZ), 67 Apollo Drive, Rosedale, North Shore 0632, New Zealand
(a division of Pearson New Zealand Ltd)
Penguin Books (South Africa) (Pty) Ltd, 24 Sturdee Avenue, Rosebank,
Johannesburg 2196, South Africa

Penguin Books Ltd, Registered Offices: 80 Strand, London WC2R ORL, England

penguin.com

First published 2007
Published in this edition 2008
5

Text copyright © Kevin Brooks, 2007
All rights reserved

Set in Sabon
Made and printed in England by Clays Ltd, St Ives plc

British Library Cataloguing in Publication Data
A CIP catalogue record for this book is available from the British Library

ISBN: 978-0-141-31910-0

www.greenpenguin.co.uk

1

It must have been around nine thirty in the morning when the waiting-room door opened and the sandy-haired man with the clipboard came in. My appointment was at nine, so I'd already been waiting a while, but I wasn't really that bothered. I suppose I was feeling a little bit anxious, and there was something about the hospital gown I was wearing that made me feel weirdly uncomfortable, but I wasn't pacing around the room or chewing my fingernails or anything. I was just standing at the window, gazing out at the hospital grounds, trying to convince myself that everything was going to be OK.

It was just a routine examination.

All they were going to do was stick a tube down my throat and take a good look inside my stomach.

What was there to worry about?

'Robert Smith?' the man at the door said, glancing up from his clipboard.

I don't know why he asked, I was the only one there. But I suppose he had to say something.

I looked at him.

He nodded at me. 'This way, please.'

I followed him out of the waiting room and he started

leading me down a long white corridor. I wasn't sure what he was – nurse, administrator, some kind of assistant – but he was wearing a hospital tunic with a name badge pinned to the pocket, so I guessed he knew what he was doing. He walked briskly, with busy little steps, and as we crossed the polished floor, it was a struggle to keep up with him. Too fast to walk, too slow to run. I scampered along behind him.

'Dr Andrews will be performing your endoscopy,' he told me, glancing over his shoulder. 'He's very good.' He smiled reassuringly – a quick professional smile. 'There's nothing to worry about. It'll be over before you know it.'

I gave him a look – half-smile, half-shrug – just to let him know that I *wasn't* worried about anything, but he'd already turned his attention back to his clipboard and was marching away down the corridor.

I wiped my sweaty hands on my gown and carried on following him.

At the end of the corridor, just as we reached a pair of green curtains set in the wall, he stopped quite suddenly and spun round to face me. I scampered to a halt in front of him.

'Uh, sorry about this,' he muttered, peering at his clipboard. 'I just have to . . . um . . . sorry, I just remembered something.' He frowned to himself for a moment, then looked up and smiled tightly at me. 'I won't be a minute.'

'Uh . . . OK,' I started to say. 'What shall I . . . ?'

But before I could finish, he'd turned round and walked away, leaving me standing there in front of the green curtains, nervously fingering the hem of my gown, not knowing what to do.

I crossed my arms, uncrossed them, put them behind my back.

I shuffled a little.

I looked around.

I kept still and stared at the floor.

I could hear muffled sounds from behind the green curtains. Low voices, medical mutterings, the scuffle of small movements. Adjustments. The ring and tink of instruments. I listened hard, trying to make sense of it all, but none of it meant anything to me. They were just hospital noises.

I rubbed my eyes.

I scratched my neck.

I shuffled some more and carried on staring at the floor.

I looked down at the floor again.

Time passed. Seconds, minutes . . .

Nothing happened.

The hospital moved all around me. Porters, nurses, patients, doctors, men and women in suits. Everyone was busy.

I stood there waiting.

When the sandy-haired man eventually came back, he was carrying a large brown envelope in his hand.

'Sorry about that,' he said, slightly out of breath.

I looked at him, wondering if the envelope had anything to do with me. But if it had, he wasn't telling.

'Right then,' he said, whipping back the green curtains, 'let's get started.'

*

The little room beyond the green curtains wasn't really a room at all. It was more like a short white corridor. A chamber. A halfway place. An anteroom, perhaps . . . whatever that is. It was a small place, functionally cramped and quietly busy. Machines, doctors, nurses, trolleys. Monitors, instruments, bottles, tubes.

The machines hummed and whirred.

The doctors and nurses muttered gently.

It was a place of confidence and no emotion. Everyone knew exactly what they were doing. Everyone except me.

The air smelled of metal and clean hands.

Through a narrow opening at the far end of the corridor, a darkness glowed with a hidden light. Rinky-tink sounds drifted down from the darkness, and I knew that was where I was going.

Into the darkness.

It all happened so quickly.

So fast, so final.

'Lie on the trolley, please.'

I felt really awkward, clambering on to the trolley. I felt stupid and clumsy and useless.

I clambered.

I sat.

I lay down.

Now I was lying on my back, staring up at a strip light on the ceiling. The light was sterile, penetrating.

I blinked.

Swallowed.

Waited.

Nothing was happening.

When I raised my head to see what was going on, I saw a man in a green tunic removing a plastic syringe from a hygienically sealed packet. Dr Andrews, I presumed. He placed the syringe on a dull metal worktop. It rolled a little. He steadied it. He said something to a nurse. (What did he say?) She nodded and turned away. Somewhere behind me, someone was humming a tune – *hmm hmm hmm*. Shoes scuffed softly on the white-tiled floor.

My neck was stiff.

A nurse came over and put a blood-pressure cuff on my arm. I smiled at her. She looked at a monitor, read out some numbers.

Dr Andrews said something to her.

She nodded again.

She asked me to open my mouth.

I opened my mouth.

She told me she was going to spray something into the back of my throat, to numb it. 'It won't hurt,' she said. 'Don't breathe or swallow while I'm spraying.'

I nodded.

She sprayed.

It felt cold.

'You can swallow now,' she said.

My throat felt numb and it was hard to swallow, but I did my best.

Dr Andrews had a needle in his hand now. A shortish needle attached to a small pink tube. He moved up beside me and took hold of my hand.

'All right?' he said.

'Uh-huh.'

He started rubbing gently at the back of my hand, peering at it, looking for a vein. Talking. Rubbing. Talking . . .

He was talking to me.

'. . . just a very light anaesthetic, Robert, a sedative really. It might knock you out, but don't worry if it doesn't. It's not unusual to remain conscious throughout the examination . . .'

I tried to listen as he explained the rest of the procedure, but I couldn't seem to concentrate. I was too self-conscious, too aware that I was *supposed* to be listening. As he carried on talking, his voice calm and confident, I realized that my sense of touch was unnaturally heightened. I could feel everything – the firmness of his fingers on the back of my hand, the padded metal of the trolley, the dry spit glued to the corners of my mouth. The only thing I couldn't feel was the back of my throat.

'All right?' the doctor said.

'Uh-huh.'

I watched intently as he slid the needle attachment into a bulging vein in the back of my hand.

Ting – a tiny pain, sharp and bright.

I closed my eyes for a moment, then opened them again. The doctor was holding the syringe in his hand now. Studying it, checking it. It looked so small. A tiny plastic tube of almost clear liquid . . .

I wondered how it worked. A tiny plastic tube of almost clear liquid . . . how did it work? How did it do what it was meant to do? What was in it? Was it pre-filled? I didn't see the doctor fill it. Or did I? I didn't know.

Absently, as if he'd done it a thousand times before, the doctor did something to the syringe – shook it, knocked it, jiggled it – and as I watched him, I wondered why the syringe was in two parts. I knew it didn't matter, but I couldn't seem to stop thinking about it. *Why is the syringe in two parts? Why is the needle separate from the body of the syringe? Why is the syringeless needle inserted into my vein and* then *attached to the body of the syringe?*

The question grew to hide my anxiety as the plunger was depressed and the anaesthetic was injected into my blood.

I felt it – that sharp, alien, liquid pressure . . .

Why is the syringe in two parts?

Some reason, I was thinking.

Some medical reason . . .

And then I wasn't thinking at all.

2

nunuuuuuuunuuuuunnununnunsaasaaa tah
thhahh ah hta ta and th tht its ah impimpimperative thath
ahahuntil we know no one professorcasing must know do
you understananand? of course. cooper. sir. tell hayes to
get the names. sir. whoelse apart from usnandrews?
anynursenstaff? no therewas nothing to be seen. no.
nothingImean not anything physical.   On a screen. On
tape. It was on the screen. Right. So who else? Carlingle,
the assistant. Kamal here, the anaesthetist. Kamal

Voices.

You know we cant keephimunder much longer you know
just wait. Wait. Professor? What do you think?   Cooper.
Sir. Wheres Ryan? Anyminute, sir.   see those pictures
again.   Christ. What is that?   What the hell is that?

Shit

Rubber and gas. Tubes.

Voices.

8

Shit.

What the hell is that?

Clean rubber. White gas. The taste of plastic tubing, deep in my throat. Scratchy and hard. The taste of chemicals. What is this? This shouldn't be happening. This shouldn't be. I'm lying on my back with my eyes closed. A white sheet covers my body. Beneath the sheet I'm naked.

Pins . . .

Needles in the back of my hand.

Tubes, tubes . . . thin wires taped to my chest. I'm breathing through a tube . . . rubber and gas. Hiss of breath. Breathe. Some kind of mask.

My eyes won't open.

Wait a minute, wait a minute . . .

Move.

Fingers, toes, arms, legs, hands, head – nothing. I can't move. I'm unable to move.

Paralysed.

This is wrong. This is very wrong. This is a bad situation. Wait a minute, wait a minute, wait a minute . . .

What is this?

Where am I?

Voices.

Where's Ryan? Anyminute, sirhe's coming now

Who are these people?

9

What *is* this?

A door opens. Someone enters the room.
I hear voices again.

Morris.
Sir. This is the consultant – Professor Casing.
Ryan. Is that him?
Yes.

The voices move closer. I can sense people standing beside
me now. I can't see them. My eyes are closed. I'm nothing
– a petrified container. All I can do is lie still and listen.

What have we got?
Robert Smith. Sixteen years old. Suspected ulcer.
Referred by his GP for an endoscopy. That's a –
I know what an endoscopy is, Morris. What happened?
Professor?

A man coughs, clearing his throat.

At nine forty-five this morning, the patient was anaes-
thetized and taken into the examination area where Dr
Andrews began the procedure.
Was he conscious?
The anaesthetic we use is very light, not much more
than a sedative, but it's often enough to render the patient
unconscious.
So he wouldn't have known what was happening?
We think not.

You've kept him unconscious since?
We thought it best.
Good. Go on.
As you know, endoscopy is a fairly straightforward procedure. A flexible fibre-optic tube is inserted into the patient's mouth and eased down into the gastrointestinal tract. The endoscope sends images to a video screen, allowing us to visually examine the oesophagus, the stomach, parts of the small intestine and so on.

A short pause.

In this case, the images from the endoscope . . . the images displayed on the video screen were . . . not normal.

Silence.
   Not normal?

Can you show me?
   Kamal?

A button clicks, something hums.

This video shows the results of a normal endoscopy.

Hmm . . .

That's the oesophagus . . . just there, look. You can see it quite clearly as the endoscope travels down. Now . . . into the stomach. There. See how it looks? That's how it should look.

OK.
Now.

Click.

This is what Dr Andrews saw.

Silence.
  Hmm . . .

What the hell is that?
  That, Mr Ryan, is the inside of this boy.
  Christ . . . it looks like some kind of plastic.
  This tubular area here is very short, no more than ten centimetres. Look.
  Shit. What was that? Rewind it.

Click. Whirrr. Click.

What is that? Look at that.

Silence.

See there? And there? That blackened area? And here.

Click.

These silvery filaments . . .

Click.

Watch there.
    They're moving.
    Watch.
    Christ.

Silence.

That's it.

Click.
    The humming stops.
    Another long silence.

It couldn't be an instrument malfunction?
    Everything's been checked, double-checked. There's nothing wrong with the instruments.
    Is this the only copy of the tape?
    Andrews made a duplicate. Hayes has got it.

Silence again.

After a while I become aware of someone leaning over me. Studying me. A man. I can feel his breath on my face. The dark smell of a man. He breathes in deeply, holds it for a moment, then breathes out again. When he speaks, I can feel the heat of his whispered words on my skin.

What the hell are you?

Nothing, I want to tell him. I'm nothing. I'm just a kid with a bad belly. I'm Robert Smith. Whatever you think this is, whoever you are – you're wrong. Listen, there's been a mistake. Listen to me, look at me. I'm awake. I'm conscious . . .

I want to scream.

But I can't open my mouth.

I can't move.

I used to dream. When I was a little kid, I used to dream of a whirling wind that spun me around inside myself and sucked me down into terrible places. I never knew what the terrible places were, but I knew they were going to kill me. And I didn't want to die. I didn't want to go to those terrible places. I just wanted to wake up. I knew that if I could wake myself up, I'd be all right. I *knew* that. And I knew what I had to do to wake myself up. I had to move. Move anything. A finger, a hand, a leg. Anything. Just move it. Move. Move. Move.

It was impossible then, but I always managed to kill the dream.

But this was no dream. This was nowhere near a dream. This was the worst thing imaginable. Worse than that: it was real. I was lying on a hospital bed, paralysed and mute, and unknown people were saying unknown things about me.

Silvery filaments?

Some kind of plastic?

It couldn't be real.

But it was.

I can still hear the voices.

. . . and I want the immediate area quietly secured and Andrews and Ingle, get them debriefed and confined until further notice. I want his medical records, clothes, finger-prints, history . . . everything. I want to know everything about him. Was anyone with him when he arrived?

No.

What about his parents? Where are they?

He's a looked-after boy –

A what?

He's an orphan. Abandoned at birth. He's lived in Homes or with foster parents all his life. For the last year or so he's been with a couple called Young. Peter and Bridget Young. We haven't been able to contact Mrs Young, but we've been in touch with the husband. He's been told there were minor complications and the boy needs to stay in overnight.

What did he say? Did he want to see him?

He's on his way now.

Sort it out. Go.

Sir.

The door opens quietly, then closes again.

Someone locks it.

The man called Ryan carries on talking.

Why didn't this show up on the X-rays? Was he X-rayed?

Four weeks ago. Here.

Flip flap – the plastic flap of an X-ray film.

Are these normal?

Perfectly.

This is him?

Yes.

You're sure?

Yes.

Flip flap. Silence.

Right . . . we need to do it now.

I don't understand.

Open him up.

I can't –

You have to.

No, listen –

No, you listen, Professor. You're doing it now, and you're doing it alone.

But –

Now! Do you understand? You cut that thing open now.

The shock of the words takes a moment to sink in – *cut that thing open* . . . that's what he said . . . *you cut that thing open now* – and then it hits me. Panic. Terror. Physical horror. Shit, they're going to cut me open. Right now. Cut me open. They're going to CUT ME OPEN . . .

I have to *do* something.

I have to move.

Anything. A finger, a hand, a leg. Anything. Just move it . . . move move *MOVE!!*

I can't move.

I breathe in, trying to steady my heart, breathing the taste of gas. Rubber. Gas. Tube.

Breathe slowly.

Don't panic.

Think about it.

Think.

Think.

Think.

Listen.

Concentrate, listen.

Silence. A background hum. Something ticking. A faint solitary beep. No voices. For a moment, I think they've gone . . . but then, from across the room – *snap* – a rubbery snap, and the murmur of voices again.

This is ridiculous, Ryan. I can't operate without consent. What if he dies? What if –

I'll clear it. It's cleared. I can take care of it. Listen, you're not doing anything – OK? It's just a minor emergency operation. You had to do it. These things happen, don't they?

Yes, but –

We have to know. We have to find out. There's no choice. We have to find out right now.

I don't understand –

Click.

Do you understand this?

A threatening silence.

All right. But only –

Only an exploration. That's all we need.

A heavy sigh. Then another sharp snap, the snap of a surgical glove.

Put this surgical mask on, Mr Ryan. I'm going to need some help.

The fear is killing me now, overpowering my mind. I can't think. I *have* to think. I have to move. Move move move. I'm *trying* to move myself – trying, forcing, straining, struggling – I'm doing everything possible to think myself into moving my body. But it's useless. There's no connection between mind and flesh. Nothing. My body just lies there, inanimate. It's just a thing. A container. I'm still conscious of it, conscious of its unconsciousness, but I can't do anything with it.

Kamal, how is he?

Tick tick.

The same. Steady.
  I need you there, Ryan.
  All right.
  Don't touch anything, just do what I say. Kamal?
  OK.
  OK.

A chill tingles my skin as the sheet is lifted from my stomach. I can feel the cold white air. I'm naked. Out in the open. Exposed. I can hear a distant whistling sound inside my head, a scary white noise. The sound of fear. I want to clench something, but I don't have anything to clench *with*.

Membraned hands touch my skin. Soft. Then a little harder. Kneading, probing.

Words.

It feels all right ... a little unusual. Here, I think. Something ... maybe.

The whistle of fear intensifies, then suddenly stops. All at once my head is soundless. Empty and dead. And in the inner silence, I can hear the inaudible sound of a scalpel being plucked from a silver tray.

I'm going to cut here.

No ...

Fingertips ... then the flat of a hand on my skin.

Oh no.

No ...

The slice of the scalpel is quick and tight. At first I feel nothing, just the silent peeling of skin and fat, opening up like a blood-red smile ... then suddenly the pain cuts in.

It hurts.

Oh, it *hurts* ...

IT HURTS.

So sharp it's dull, like cold, like ice ... burning hot ...

It hurts it hurts it *HURTS* ...

And there's nothing I can do to stop it.
Somewhere in the screamless distance, the voices continue.

Hold that, Ryan, just there. Let me clear that.
What is it?
I can't make it out. Just a second.

Pain and pressure . . . pressure and pain . . .

I don't understand it.
What's that brown stuff?
Hold that away.
Look at that. Jesus!
There's some kind of . . . like a shell. Hard, pliable. A
plastic. I think it comes up to about here.

A sudden searing pain rips through my belly . . . it's too
much too much too much too much . . .

What's in there? What's underneath it? Is that liquid?
Wires? They look like moving wires.
This . . . I can't get through it. It has – look – patterning.
Like bone structure. Outlines. It could be some kind of
shield. That might explain the X-rays.
A shield? A body shield?
Perhaps . . .
Get in underneath it.
I can't without –
Just prise it up, for Christ's sake.
Pass me that.

It was then, just as the tip of a broad-bladed instrument touched something under my skin . . . it was then that I felt my fists clench. Out of sight, beneath the sheet . . . I felt them clench.

And unclench.

I felt the movement.

Movement.

I could *move*.

And in that same miraculous instant, I was suddenly seeing a face. Above me. Behind me. Hovering over my head. Brown eyes, olive skin, a slight beard showing beneath a surgical mask. Kamal, the anaesthetist. I could see him. My eyes were still closed, but I could see him. It wasn't possible, but I didn't care. I could see him.

I could see all around me.

The pain had gone.

How?

How had the pain gone?

How could I see all around me?

There shouldn't have been time to think about it, no time to take anything in . . . but somehow there was. There was all the time in the world – and I took it all in:

A small white windowless room.

White white light.

Machines and monitors.

Silver cutting instruments laid out on a tray, like an exhibit of lunatic cutlery.

A metal table covered with papers and tapes and photographs.

A white door guarded by a thickset man in a suit.

And there, standing over me, two masked men, peering intently into the meat of my belly: Casing and Ryan. Professor Casing was the narrow-faced one, the one in the white coat and glasses. Ryan was tall and severe, dressed in a plain black suit. He had silver eyes, a grey face, coal-black hair. An automatic pistol was clipped to the back of his belt.

They were looking at me, looking inside me, and now I was looking at them. I didn't know how, but I was looking at them.

Look.

Shit, look what they've *done* to me. What have they done? My poor belly . . . white and flat with a slash of red and – shit! – what *is* that? Look – a gaping slice, like a bad clown's grin, fastened back with tiny black clamps, and inside me . . .

Oh God, the things inside me . . . the things I saw. Unknown things. Terrible things. Black and brown things, red things, silver things . . . creamy-white shapes of living metal or plastic or God knows what . . . all of it moving like a blood-dark shimmer inside me.

I couldn't think about it then. It was just too much. There wasn't time. The frozen moment was nearly over – all the time in the world was fading.

And I was moving.

I was *moving*.

As Casing dug a spatula into my guts, and Ryan leaned over to get a better look, something electric shifted inside me – and I moved, faster than I'd ever moved before. Jerking upright, tearing the mask from my mouth, ripping the tube from my throat . . . I didn't know what I was doing.

But something inside me did.

With tapes and wires snapping off all around me, I saw myself snatching the pistol from Ryan's belt and jamming the barrel against his head, and then a voice hissed out of my mouth.

'That's enough,' it said – a cold dry whisper.

3

Ryan barely reacted to the sound of my voice, he just turned slowly and looked at me, his eyes calm and still. But Casing was shocked beyond words. I'll never forget the look on his face – it was the horrified look of a man who's just seen a monster. A pale naked monster.

As he stood there staring at me, his eyes aghast, I glanced at the spatula still poised in his hand. The blade was smeared with a scrape of washy brown liquid.

A scrape of something.

A scrape of me.

There wasn't time to think about it. The big man by the door was moving towards me now, pulling a pistol from inside his jacket. He was huge – thick and heavy – with a large bull head and sharp little eyes. I looked at him for a moment, wondering how a man that big could move so fast, then – without taking my eyes off him – I jabbed the gun against Ryan's head.

'Stop there,' I said, 'or I'll kill him.'

The big man hesitated for a moment, then stopped. He was halfway across the room.

'Drop the gun,' I told him.

He looked at Ryan.

'Do what he says, Cooper,' Ryan told him.

The big man's eyes never left mine as he stooped down and placed his gun on the floor.

'Turn round,' I told him. 'Stand against the wall.'

My voice was unfamiliar. Dry and weak, a croaky whisper. And the words – *stop there or I'll kill him . . . drop the gun . . . turn round . . . stand against the wall* – they were ridiculous. Like something out of a stupid spy film. I couldn't believe what I was saying.

I couldn't believe any of it.

It couldn't be real. These people couldn't be real. Real people don't do this. Real people don't have guns. Real people don't really do these things. They just don't. And what about me? How could I be doing this? How could I be sitting here on a hospital trolley, all naked and bloody, with my belly cut open and a gun in my hand?

How could any of it be real?

I glanced down at the mess of my stomach, and I knew that it *was* real.

It hurt.

Hurt is real.

I had to get out of there.

'You,' I said to Casing, 'pick up the gun and give it to me.'

He stiffened for a moment, his eyes twitching in fear, then he slowly bent down, picked up Cooper's gun and cautiously handed it over.

'Get over there,' I told him, waving the pistol at the far wall. 'Away from the door. Face the wall.'

I waited until he was facing the wall, then I turned my attention to Ryan. All this time, he hadn't moved. He was just standing there – controlled and serene – his eyes fixed steadily on mine. I still had his pistol held to his head, and now I was vaguely aiming Cooper's gun at his belly, but it didn't seem to bother him.

He just looked at me.

And I looked at him.

Then he spoke.

'Robert,' he said, slowly and calmly, 'I'm going to take this surgical mask off. Is that all right?'

I nodded.

He carefully reached up and lowered the mask from his mouth, revealing a clean and confident smile. It didn't surprise me. Without the mask, he looked like what he was. I had no idea what that was, but he looked like a man who never let go. A hard man. A big man. He wasn't *big*, but he was big. Big as a shiny black wall.

'Why don't you put the guns down, Robert?' he said. 'Just put them down, and then we can talk.'

'Shut up,' I told him.

He raised a sleek black eyebrow, then lowered it. 'What are you?'

I looked down the gun barrel into his eyes. They were silver, like silver moons. Or brand-new coins.

The room was white.

The gun was black.

My fingers were pale on the trigger.

'What *are* you?' he said again.

That's the question.

That *is* the question.

*

When I told Ryan to shut up and lie down on the floor, he didn't move for a while, he just stood there, staring into my eyes. He didn't look at the gun in my hand, but I knew he was wondering what I would do if he went for it. Would I pull the trigger? Would I shoot him? Could I do it?

He knew that I could.

He could see it in me.

It was there.

With a slight nod of his head, he slowly lowered himself to the floor.

'Face down,' I told him. 'Hands out to the side.'

He did as he was told.

Keeping both pistols levelled at his head, I glanced at the anaesthetist behind me. He was wearing a green V-necked tunic over a thin white T-shirt. His eyes were scared.

'Kamal?' I said to him. 'Is that your name?'

'Yes.'

I nodded at Ryan. 'Can you put him to sleep? Anaesthetize him?'

Kamal hesitated, his eyes glancing quickly at a pack of plastic syringes laid out on a metal tray.

I said, 'I'll kill him if you don't.'

Kamal carried on looking at me for a while, and for a moment I thought he wasn't going to do anything, and I started wondering what I was going to do if he didn't – shoot him? shoot everyone? – but then I saw him take a deep breath, and he nodded, and I watched with relief as he reached for a syringe and moved out from behind his machinery.

'Will that do it?' I asked him, gesturing at the syringe in his hand. 'Will that knock him out?'

27

He nodded again.

'Do it,' I told him.

As he crouched down beside Ryan and started rubbing at the back of his hand, a sudden spasm of pain ripped through my stomach. I put down Cooper's pistol and pressed my hand against the wound. It felt sticky, and when I looked down I saw a thin dark liquid – red-black and brown – oozing between my fingers. I clutched myself harder.

Kamal was fiddling about with the syringe now, tapping it, studying it.

'Come *on*,' I urged him. 'Just stick it in.'

He glanced at me with mild disapproval, started to say something, then changed his mind and inserted the needle into the back of Ryan's hand. Ryan flinched slightly, then almost immediately went limp.

The room was still again.

White and silent.

Just the sound of anxious breathing, the hum of monitors, a faint hiss of gas.

It's strange, but when all this was happening, it didn't seem to have any immediate presence. I knew it was happening, and I knew it was real, and I knew it was scaring me to death, but I couldn't see it at the time for what it was. It was just stuff that was happening: sounds, movement, words, feelings, intent. The ingredients of an event. That's all it was.

An event.

I just lived it.

It was automatic.

But now, as I'm playing it over in my mind, as I'm looking back at the things that happened, and the things that I did . . . now it's *everything*. There's nothing else at all. It's the only thing in the world, the *killingest* thing in the world. And even though the memory of it is nothing more than that – just a memory – it's still enough to leave me broken and exhausted.

Kamal was just looking at me now, standing over Ryan's unconscious body, waiting for me to say something.

'Is that it?' I asked him, glancing at Ryan.

Kamal blinked. 'Yes.'

'How long will the anaesthetic last?'

He shrugged. 'Half an hour.'

I looked over at Casing and Cooper. Casing was still facing the wall, but Cooper was looking over his shoulder at Ryan. He didn't like what he saw, and as his face darkened and he looked over at me, I picked up his pistol.

'Come here,' I told him.

He turned slowly and started moving towards me, walking like a big bad dog – *pad pad pad* – his dumb lips snarling. When he was halfway across the room, I told him to stop, but he didn't. He just kept on coming – *pad pad pad* – lumbering towards me, getting bigger and bigger with every step. I raised both pistols and told him to stop again, but I knew he wasn't going to. His eyes were cold, he'd had enough. My hands gripped the guns and I levelled them both at his head. I looked down the barrels, watching him get closer and closer – five steps away, four, three, two – and then, just as he was reaching out for me, I hit him, hard and fast, cracking both pistols into his face – *crackcrack*. His nose broke and he doubled over, moaning in agony. I hit him again, hammering both barrels into his head, and the big man dropped to the floor and lay still.

I've always been stronger than I look. A lot stronger. A creepy guy in one of my Homes tried messing around with me once and when I hit him, I nearly killed him. Broke his nose and his jaw, fractured his skull. And I only hit him a couple of times.

'Casing,' I said. 'Come over here.'

The surgeon turned away from the wall and hesitantly crossed the room.

'Stand there,' I told him, indicating a spot about half a metre away from me.

Casing moved, stopped, looked at me.

'Closer,' I said.

Casing moved a little closer. He was petrified. Shaking. I could smell his fear – sour and stale – and the smell of it gave me confidence. He was more frightened of me than I was of him.

'All right,' I told him, 'listen to me. Are you listening?'

He nodded.

'OK,' I said. 'I'm going to lie down on the trolley now. I'm going to put down one of these guns, but I'm keeping the other one right here.' I poked Ryan's pistol into Casing's belly. 'I'm going to lie down, and you're going to sew me up. I want this hole in my belly stitched up. Do you understand?'

He nodded.

'Say it.'

'I understand.'

'Good.' I put down Cooper's pistol, placing it on the trolley beside me, then I gave Casing another short jab in the belly. 'If I think anything's wrong – *any*thing – I'll pull the trigger. All right?'

'Yes.'

'OK – get what you need.'

With shaking hands, Casing plucked a small box from the instrument tray, opened it up and removed a pre-threaded needle. The blue-black thread trembled in his hand as he held out the needle for me to see. I nodded at him. Then I glanced at Kamal. He was standing over the two unconscious bodies with his hands behind his back.

'I don't want to hear you move,' I warned him. 'OK?'

He didn't answer, just bowed a little.

A final look at Casing, then I leaned back slowly and lay down on the trolley. The pain in my belly reared up, raw and hot, and I couldn't stop an animal sound escaping from my lungs, a low growl of agony. I was beginning to feel weak now. The bright light above me was burning into my eyes . . . the gun in my hand was getting heavy. I felt faint. Dizzy. Sick.

'Go on,' I said to Casing. 'Do it.'

Once again, I felt those latexed fingers taking hold of my flesh. And then the pain as the needle started stitching. Pure and sharp – jab . . . pull . . . jab . . . pull . . . jab . . . pull . . .

I moved to the rhythm – clench . . . grip . . . moan . . . hiss. Feeling the pain. Forcing myself to feel it.

31

Feel it.

Don't think.

Just feel it.

I had to feel the pain to stop myself thinking. I didn't want to think. What's happening to me? What's going on? What am I? No, I couldn't allow myself to think those things, not then. It would have killed me. All I could do was swallow it up, stick it in a hole in the darkest corner of my mind and try to ignore it.

But it was still there.

Dazzling in its horror.

If I'm not normal – what am I?

The answers were unthinkable: robot, automaton, android, cyborg, beast, machine, alien – no no no no no no no no . . . get those things out of your head . . . get them out, get them out, GET THEM OUT!

Just feel the pain.

See?

How can you feel the pain if you're anything but a sentient being?

How can you *be* anything else?

You have lived. You have hurt and bled. You have seen things and heard things and felt things and done things. You have considered yourself. You have a self. A mind, a body, a consciousness. You have memories. You remember things.

Memory is life.

You have lived.

You are alive.

You eat, you drink, you breathe.

You shit, you piss, you fart.

You hurt.

What else can you be but human?

'That's it. Done.'

I didn't know where I was for a second.

Tink. The needle dropped into a metal tray and the tiny sound brought everything back into focus. Professor Casing – anxious eyes and bloodied hands. Kamal – waiting calmly, quiet and still. And me. They were both looking at me. I sat up slowly, with just a slight groan, and looked at my stomach. It was ugly. Badly stitched and smeared with strange colours – yellowy-black, dirty red, pink and brown. But the wound was closed. The horror inside me was hidden away.

I gestured for Casing to move back, then I swung my legs round and stepped off the trolley. As my feet hit the floor, my legs gave way. Liquid pressure burst behind my eyes. I leaned on the trolley and sucked in air until the waves of dizziness subsided.

I was naked.

I could feel the cold metal of the pistol resting against the bare skin of my thigh.

I looked at Casing. 'Get Ryan's clothes off,' I told him. 'Shirt and trousers, jacket, shoes, socks.'

As Casing knelt down beside Ryan and started wrestling with his clothes, I glanced over at Kamal. He was younger than the others – mid-twenties, maybe. He was quite tall, thin and lean, with a long head, a slender body and loose limbs.

'See all that stuff?' I said to him, indicating the papers and photographs and videos on the metal table. 'Find a bag for it.'

33

As he moved over to the table and started scooping all the papers and stuff into somebody's old brown briefcase, I closed my eyes for a moment and tried to think. Clear your mind, I told myself. Think. Reason. Put things in order. Forget all the unknown things, forget all this madness . . . concentrate on what you know. What do you know? What do you remember?

I pictured myself leaving the house that morning . . . putting my coat on, shutting the front door, walking down the street to the bus stop. It was Monday morning, eight o'clock. The skies were grey, the wind was cold . . . everything was perfectly normal. Bridget was supposed to be driving me to the hospital, but her sister had got sick at the very last moment, so she'd had to rush off to see her, and Pete had already left for work . . .

'It's all right,' I remembered myself saying. 'I'll get the bus. I don't mind.'

'Are you sure?' Bridget had said.

'Yeah.'

'Well, OK . . . but make sure you get a taxi back.'

I remembered it all – waiting for the bus, getting on the bus, sitting on the bus . . . getting to the hospital, showing my appointment card . . . walking down the endless corridors, following the signs . . . putting on the hospital gown, sitting in the waiting room . . . standing at the window, gazing out at the hospital grounds, trying to convince myself that everything was going to be OK . . . it was just a routine examination . . . all they were going to do was stick a tube down my throat and take a good look inside my stomach . . .

What was there to worry about?

I opened my eyes and looked down at Ryan. He was almost naked now, only his underwear left. Silk boxers. In the cold light, his skin looked hard and white, like white plastic. Casing was standing over him with his clothes in his arms, looking bemused and out of place. *I'm a surgeon*, the look on his face said, *I don't* carry *things*.

'Bring them here,' I told him.

He shuffled over to me, dropped the clothes on to the trolley, then backed away. I looked across at Kamal. He'd finished putting all the papers and stuff in the briefcase and was standing there looking at me. I told him to leave the briefcase on the table and sit on the floor.

'And you,' I told Casing, 'get back over there and face the wall.'

I started dressing in Ryan's clothes. Trousers, white shirt, socks, jacket. They were all a bit too big for me, but it felt good to be clothed again. It gave me a sense of security. Cloth against skin. It made me feel human.

I stepped into the shoes, glanced up, then knelt down and tied the laces. I stood up and stamped my feet, then went over to where Kamal was sitting cross-legged on the floor.

'How do I look?' I asked him.

He gazed up at me. His mouth was thin-lipped and slightly crooked, and he had small milky-white teeth.

'Fine,' he said.

I told him to get up.

He rose in one lithe movement.

I said to him, 'Get Casing's coat and mask and bring them over here.'

As Casing removed his white coat and mask and handed

them to Kamal, I looked down at Cooper and Ryan, wondering who they were, what they were. What could they be? Police? Government? Some kind of . . .

No.

There wasn't time.

I stopped thinking.

Kamal was approaching me now, bringing me Casing's white coat and surgical mask. He stopped in front of me, and I reached out to take them.

Then someone knocked at the door.

4

Knock knock knock.

'Hello?'

Knock knock.

'Sir?' A woman's voice. 'Sir? It's me – Hayes. Let me in.'

For a moment or two I just stared at the door, hoping stupidly that if I didn't do anything – that if I didn't move or make a sound – everything would be all right. The knocking would stop. Hayes would go away. Everything would go away.

But then Hayes started rattling the door handle, pushing and shoving against the locked door. 'Sir?' she called out. 'Mr Ryan . . . are you in there? What's going on?'

And I knew that nothing was going away.

I pointed the pistol at Casing. 'Answer it,' I whispered. 'Get rid of her.'

'How?' he asked.

'I don't care – just do it.'

He stared at me for a second, then started moving towards the door. I followed him across the room and stood with my back against the wall. He looked at me again. I levelled the gun at his head.

'Don't do anything stupid,' I warned him. 'If she gets in here, you're dead.'

He blinked once, took a deep breath, then unlocked the door and opened it a little way. 'Yes?' he said confidently, peering through the gap.

'What's going on?' I heard Hayes say. 'Where's Ryan? I need to see him.'

'Not now,' Casing told her, his voice spiked with arrogance. 'We're busy.'

'I need to talk to him about –'

'We're *busy*,' Casing snapped. 'Come back later.'

Hayes didn't say anything for a moment, and in the silence I imagined her mind ticking over – assessing what Casing had just said, wondering if she should accept his authority or not. As I kept my eyes fixed on Casing, hoping his confidence would hold up, I could feel something inside me – my heart? – pumping hard.

Then I heard Hayes say, 'Tell Ryan that Morris is with Peter Young. Tell him it's under control. And give him these.'

I held my breath as Casing nodded and reached out to take something from Hayes, and I listened hard, willing her to turn round and leave. I heard the scuff of a shoe . . . a single step . . . a slight pause . . . then the slap of busy footsteps disappearing down an empty corridor.

I breathed out.

Pete's here, I thought to myself for a moment. Pete's here, Pete's here, Pete's here . . .

But I knew it didn't mean anything.

Pete was nowhere. A million miles away.

Casing closed the door and passed me a tattered brown

folder. His arrogance had gone again now. His eyes were full of self-pity. 'Your records,' he said wearily.

I took the folder from him and put it in the briefcase with the rest of the stuff.

'Lie down on the floor,' I told him.

He looked at me.

I stared back at him.

He lowered himself to the floor.

I turned to Kamal. 'Anaesthetize him.'

While Kamal crouched down and stuck a needle in the back of Casing's hand, I put on the surgeon's white coat and hung his surgical mask round my neck. A dull pain gripped my stomach for a moment, like the jab of a short blunt knife. It didn't hurt very much, but it felt really weird – as if it didn't quite belong to me. It felt like someone else's pain . . . but inside *me*.

I didn't want to think about it.

I closed my eyes. Breathed in, breathed out.

I was so tired now. Drained and exhausted. I didn't want to do this any more – acting tough, ordering people around, trying to keep control . . . it was too hard. I didn't want to do anything. All I wanted to do was sink down to the floor and go to sleep. Go to sleep, wake up in the morning and start all over again. But I knew I couldn't. I had to get out of that room. Get out. Get out. Go somewhere else. If I didn't, I might as well be dead.

And I didn't want to be dead.

When I opened my eyes again, Kamal was standing over Casing's unconscious body, looking at me.

'Have you got a car?' I asked him.

'Yes.'

'Where is it?'

'In the car park.' He waved his hand. 'At the back.'

'How far is it? How do we get there from here?'

'This is the basement,' he explained. 'There is a back exit, a fire door. The car park is just outside.'

'Can we get out without being seen?'

He shrugged. 'I don't know. I don't know who is here. These people . . . I don't know.'

I really didn't care any more. I just wanted to go. Get out of that room. Go somewhere else.

I grabbed the briefcase from the table and took one last look at the scene I was leaving behind: three unconscious bodies, a trolley, machinery, instruments . . . madness. I went over and emptied the tray of scalpels and needles into the briefcase, then beckoned Kamal to the door.

'We're going to walk out of here,' I told him. 'You and me . . . we're going to walk out to the car park, get in your car and drive away – OK?'

He nodded.

'You go first,' I told him. 'Walk in front of me. Not too fast and not too slow. Don't say anything to anybody. The pistol's in my pocket. I'll use it if I have to – all right?'

His brown eyes looked back at me. 'I understand.'

'OK,' I said, gripping the pistol and nodding at the door. 'Open it.'

I watched him as he cautiously opened the door. He moved very slowly, as if this might be his very last moment, and just for a second I thought it might be mine too. We could both see it happening – the gunshot, the scream, the rush of armed guards – and we both stopped breathing as the door inched open . . .

But nothing happened.

No sound.

No movement.

Kamal paused for a second, breathing out quietly and steadying himself, then he breathed in again, opened the door a bit wider and peered outside. He looked left and right, then left and right again.

'Is anyone there?' I asked him.

He shook his head. 'No one. It's empty.'

'OK, let's go.'

I followed him out into a low arched corridor. A bare light hung from the ceiling, showing white brick walls and a grey stone floor. The air was chilled. To our left, the corridor ran straight for about fifteen metres, then turned a corner. To our right, ten metres away, another corridor crossed at a junction.

'This way,' Kamal said, moving off to the right.

I closed the door and followed him. At the junction, we turned right again into another brick corridor that led us down a gentle slope past several closed doors. 'What is this place?' I asked Kamal.

'Mostly storage rooms,' he said. 'The laundry. There is a boiler room somewhere, I think.'

His voice was soft and precise, tinged with an accent I couldn't quite place.

We walked on.

My legs didn't feel too steady, and I was leaning slightly to one side to ease the pain in my stomach. The hard soles of my shoes – Ryan's shoes – were slapping unevenly on the sloping stone floor. *Sallap slap sallap slap*. Ahead of me, Kamal was walking quietly.

'How much further?' I asked him.

'Not far.'

We'd almost reached the end of the corridor when a porter pushing a laundry basket came round a corner. A hefty blond-haired man with a stubbled jaw, he was smoking a cigarette and kicking irritably at one of the basket wheels, trying to make the trolley run straight.

'Don't stop,' I whispered to Kamal. 'Just keep walking.'

When the porter looked up and saw us – doctor and anaesthetist – he snatched the cigarette out of his mouth and hid it behind his back. Kamal nodded his head at him, and the porter returned a false grin. I couldn't do anything. I just stared straight ahead, trying to look like a doctor, my hand sweating on the grip of the pistol in my pocket.

The laundry basket squeaked and rattled as the porter passed us by.

At the end of the corridor, Kamal turned left and led me up a short flight of steps. At the top of the steps was a door.

Kamal stopped.

'Is this it?' I asked him.

He nodded. 'The door leads out to the car park.'

I looked at the door – it was closed, barred. FIRE/SMOKE DOOR, it said. DO NOT BLOCK OPEN.

'Is it alarmed?' I said.

Kamal looked at me.

'The door,' I said. 'Does it have an alarm?'

He shook his head and shrugged. 'I don't know.'

I thought about it for a moment, but quickly decided it didn't matter.

'Open it,' I told him.

It was dark outside. Early evening. The darkness surprised me. A light rain was falling – misty and black, like spider silk. We were standing at the edge of a small rectangular courtyard at the back of the hospital. The main hospital building – a towering monolith of concrete and glass – stretched up into the night sky behind us. There were office buildings either side of us and an area of open ground in front. Soft white lights glowed in the distance.

As we moved out into the rainy night and headed across the courtyard, a pigeon flapped in the dark, then settled again.

I followed Kamal down a path that ran alongside the rain-snaked windows of empty offices. Through the windows I could see desks and computers waiting for the next day to begin.

It was Monday evening.

The next day was a long way away.

Nothing happened as I followed Kamal into the car park. The rain fell silently, the sky was black, the air smelled faintly of smoke. It was hard to believe that anything was wrong.

I took the gun from my pocket and held it down at my side.

'Which is yours?' I asked Kamal, scanning the cars.

'The white Fiesta,' he said, reaching into his pocket for his keys.

We walked across to the car and stopped beside it.

'Open the passenger door first,' I told him.

He opened the door, then walked round to the driver's side.

'Open it and get in,' I told him.

As he opened the door, I leaned inside the car and placed the briefcase on the back seat. I took off the white coat and stuffed it behind the passenger seat, put the gun in my jacket pocket, then got into the car. A blunt pain gripped me again for a second and I could feel something cold dripping beneath my shirt. The pain eased as I slumped into the seat.

The car was a mess: books, CDs, newspapers, empty Coke cans, sweet wrappers, all kinds of rubbish all over the place. The floor was littered with empty cigarette packets and the dashboard ashtray was heaped with cigarette ends.

'You can smoke if you want,' I told Kamal.

He looked at me, then reached into his pocket and brought out a packet of Marlboro. He lit one, breathed in hungrily, then offered the pack to me. I shook my head. He dropped the cigarette packet on to the dashboard shelf.

'All right?' I said to him.

He nodded.

'Take off your tunic,' I told him.

He hesitated for a moment, then rested his cigarette in the ashtray, pulled off his tunic and dropped it on the floor behind the seat. I looked at him. He wasn't an anaesthetist any more, he was just an olive-skinned guy in a thin white T-shirt.

I gazed through the windscreen. The cold darkness of the hospital grounds stretched out in front of us – lawns, slopes, curves, ribbons of roads cutting through the geometry of buildings . . . all of it veiled behind a silver-black mist of rain.

I glanced at Kamal. He was shivering.

I took the gun out of my pocket and rested it in my lap.

'Start the car,' I said.

We pulled out of the car park into an unlit section of twisty little lanes. The lanes led us out on to a broader road that curved around to the front of the main building. As we drove past the entrance, I caught a brief glimpse of myself in the reflective glass doors . . . and just for a moment I was me again.

I was Robert Smith.

A kid with a bad belly.

I could see myself approaching the entrance that morning – clutching my appointment card, gazing idly at my reflection in the glass doors . . . a rain-flecked face, pale and lean . . . dark hair, dark eyes . . . a tallish kid in a coat.

I wanted to wind down the window and shout out to the memory of myself – *Don't go in there! Turn round and go home! For God's sake, don't go in there!*

But I didn't.

And I don't suppose I would have listened to myself anyway.

We drove on.

There were no barriers to negotiate, no gates or anything, just a dark empty driveway winding through the hospital grounds. At the end of the driveway, Kamal slowed the car and pulled up at the hospital exit. The engine idled,

45

the windscreen wipers clacked, the rain pattered comfortably on the roof.

'Where to?' Kamal asked me.

I looked at the clock on the dashboard. It was half past six.

Where to?

I wanted to go home. There was nothing I wanted more. I wanted to go home to Bridget and Pete. But I knew I couldn't. Whatever was happening to me, I had to assume it wasn't a mistake. I had to assume that Ryan and the others were part of something big. Some kind of authority. Big, organizational, powerful, official, resourceful. Some kind of law enforcement. Security services. Government. Police. What else could they be, with their guns and their secrets and their suits? They had to be part of something. And soon they'd be everywhere. Looking for me. They *would* be looking for me. Not yet, perhaps. But soon. They'd be everywhere. Every place I'd ever been and every place I could possibly go. They'd be watching and waiting.

I couldn't go home.

'Do you know where Sainsbury's is?' I asked Kamal.

He gave me a puzzled look. 'Sainsbury's?'

I nodded.

'Yes,' he said, 'I know where it is. Why do you ask?'

'That's where we're going.'

5

It was still raining when we got to Sainsbury's. A lorry had broken down near the entrance, backing up the traffic, and as we crawled our way towards the car park, I gazed around at the rain-blurred faces and figures in the cars all around us. I saw heads and hands, tapping fingers, impatient eyes. I saw men, women, children, sitting in cars, going nowhere in the rain. Going shopping.

It was all very normal.

But it didn't seem to have anything to do with me any more.

To take my mind off it, I started searching through the pockets of Ryan's jacket. There wasn't much in them: two keys, a penknife, a slim leather wallet. The wallet contained two credit cards – American Express and Visa – some cash, an ID card and a handful of business cards. The photograph on the ID card showed a blank-faced Ryan staring at the camera. His eyes were cold and intelligent. He was wearing a white shirt, black tie, black jacket. His hair was slicked back over his high-crowned skull, and the harsh photographic light made his skin look deathly.

I held the card in my hand and stared at him: a man at one with his demons.

The only information printed on the card was his name – *David Ryan* – and a number – *1191212*.

The business cards didn't tell me much either. Just the name again – *David Ryan* – and beneath that, in small black print, a telephone number.

I put the cards back in the wallet and counted the cash. Three twenties and a five.

'Where do you want me to park?' Kamal said.

I looked up. We were entering the car park now. 'Over there,' I told him, indicating a row of empty spaces next to the recycling bins.

He pulled in and turned off the engine and we sat there for a while in silence. Kamal lit a cigarette. I wound down the window. The rain-rush of distant traffic rolled quietly in the air. I could smell petrol fumes, fresh bread, recycled waste.

'Who's Ryan?' I asked Kamal.

He didn't look at me. 'I don't know.'

'What *do* you know?'

'About what?'

'Anything. What happened at the hospital?'

He thought for a moment, resting his hands on the steering wheel. His fingers were long and delicate.

'I know very little,' he said quietly. 'I spent the morning in surgery. A coronary artery bypass.' He drew on his cigarette and breathed out slowly. 'I received a pager message from Professor Casing's secretary –'

'Who *is* Casing? What does he do?'

'He's a consultant surgeon. Gastroenterologist. The message said that I was to go to his office immediately.'

'And?'

'I went.'

'What did Casing want?'

'There was an unusual case, an emergency. That's all he would say. He needed an anaesthetist.'

'Why you?'

'I'm a good anaesthetist.' He shrugged. 'There was no one else available.'

'What about Ryan and the others? Morris and Hayes, Cooper . . . ? How did they get there? Who called them?'

'I know nothing about them. When Casing took me down to the basement theatre, he told me there were security implications. Nothing else. I don't know who those people are. They said nothing to me. I don't know where they came from.'

'What about Casing? Would he know who they were?'

'I would think so, yes.'

I looked out through the windscreen. A short slight man in a hooded parka was walking his dog along the grass verge in front of us. The dog was black, bouncing in the rain.

'Look at me,' I said to Kamal.

He turned and looked me cautiously in the eye. His face was ageless. Innocent and wise, like the face of a boy-king in a leather-bound storybook. I could have been mistaken, of course. I could have been seeing things that weren't there. But I don't think so. There was something there, I was sure of it. Something in his eyes. Something that didn't belong in a white Fiesta in a Sainsbury's car park on a wet November evening.

49

I rubbed my eyes. Dry stuff stuck to my fingertips. I looked at it – yellow, brown. Eye-snot. I held out my hand to Kamal.

'Look,' I told him.

He gazed at the crusty yellow smudge on my finger.

'I have bits of crap in my eyes,' I told him. 'I'm just the same as anyone else.' I wiped my finger on the car seat. 'I'm the same as you, Kamal. I'm not a monster.'

The clock on the dashboard ticked wearily, like it was too much hard work. Kamal said nothing.

What *could* he say?

'I was conscious,' I told him. 'When Casing was cutting into me, I was conscious. I could feel it. The pain. It hurt. It still hurts.'

Kamal looked at me. 'I'm sorry.'

I gazed out through the side window. A blonde-haired woman was walking past, pushing a well-packed shopping trolley. Two small children were walking behind her, skipping and kicking at puddles. The woman flicked her ponytail from side to side and talked at the children without knowing what she was saying. I watched her as she loaded the shopping into the back of a 4x4. One, two, three, four bags. She got the children into the car, left the trolley where it was and drove off.

Kamal said, 'You were anaesthetized.'

'I know.'

'You shouldn't have woken up. It's impossible.'

'I know.'

'You were anaesthetized.'

'I *know*.'

What else could I say? He was right. It was impossible.

'I need some money,' I told him.

He pulled a wallet from his pocket and handed over a couple of £5 notes. 'That's all I have.'

I folded the money into my pocket. 'Give me your wallet.'

He hesitated briefly, then passed me the wallet. I looked inside. Driving licence, credit cards, Switch card, hospital ID. I glanced at the Switch card. His full name was printed as MR KAMAL RAMACHANDRAN.

'What's the cash card number?' I asked him.

He could have lied to me, but I knew he wouldn't. I had a gun in my hand. I was unpredictable. I was alien and monstrous. He wouldn't lie to me.

'Four five one four,' he said.

'Cash limit?'

'£250.'

'Thank you.' I put the wallet and the gun in my pocket. 'Get out of the car.'

As we walked across the car park towards the bright lights of the supermarket, I buttoned my jacket to hide the dark stains on my shirt.

'Don't do anything and don't say anything,' I told Kamal.

He nodded.

We entered the supermarket.

It was a big store: food, clothing, toys, stationery, a pharmacy, all kinds of things. The aisles were wide and not too busy. I didn't hang around. I just grabbed stuff and threw it in a trolley: trousers, shirts, a jacket, a coat, underwear, shoes, chocolate bars, pies, pre-cooked chicken, paracetamol, Coke, a bottle of water, a bottle of vodka, a cheap rucksack, a road map.

At the till, Kamal smiled as he handed the checkout girl his card.

'Cash-back?' she asked him.

He looked at me. I nodded. He turned back to the checkout girl.

'Fifty, please,' he said.

I folded the clothes into a carrier bag and put the cash and the rest of the stuff in the rucksack. On the way out, we stopped at a cashpoint machine and I took out another £250.

Back in the car, I uncapped the bottle of water and took a long drink. I ate a Mars bar, then another, then four paracetamol washed down with more water. While I was doing this, Kamal sat motionless in the driver's seat, staring through the windscreen.

I unwrapped a pork pie and thought about what to do next.

I had to be alone now.

I had to hide.

I had to rest.

I had to find time to think.

I had to be alone.

I told Kamal to start the car.

We drove in silence for a while – the small silence of a small car on a big wet road – and I looked around at the passing blackness. There wasn't much to see. A flat, almost barren landscape of endless roads and long curved lines of orange lights receding perfectly into the distance. Kamal drove calmly, his keen eyes flicking constantly between the mirror and the road. Traffic was steady. It was seven thirty, Monday evening.

'What do you think Ryan will be doing now?' I asked Kamal.

'Looking for you.'

'Looking for us, you mean.'

'Yes.'

'What would you do if you were me?'

'If I were you?'

'What would you do?'

As he thought about it, a thick spray of rain from the wheels of a passing lorry doused the side windows of the car, causing us to lurch slightly to the left. Kamal adjusted the steering wheel and let the lorry pass. I peered through the rain at a passing road sign: CHELMSFORD 15, LONDON 40.

'I think you have two choices,' Kamal said. 'Either you trust me, or you kill me.'

It was a good answer, an honest answer.

Two choices.

Trust or kill.

I let the silence hang in the air.

'If I were you,' Kamal continued, 'I would trust me.'

I smiled at him. 'Why?'

'Because you don't want to kill me.'

'I don't want to trust you either.'

'It's the better option.'

'Is it?'

'I think so.'

'You would.'

'I do.'

I drank some more water and opened the road map in my lap.

Did I trust him?
   I did and I didn't.
   I didn't have much choice.

'Take the next left past the bridge,' I told him.
   We veered gently off the main road and followed a downward bend towards a dark roundabout surrounded by pine trees. I studied the map.
   'Take the second turning at the roundabout,' I said. 'It should be the next left after that.'

The car park at Heystone railway station was a small concrete field dotted with potholes. It was empty when we got there. No cars, no people, nothing much to look at – a broken fence, a ditch full of ditch things, tall trees slanting in the rain.
   My stomach hurt.
   I checked the timetable outside the station – there was a train to London in twenty minutes, a train to Ipswich in twenty-five. I told Kamal to park at the far end of the car park, away from the station lights.
   London, twenty minutes.
   Ipswich, twenty-five.
   London?
   Or Ipswich?
   It didn't really matter. As long as it was somewhere else.
   I took the pistol from my pocket and told Kamal to

give me the car keys. He removed them from the ignition and dropped them into my palm.

'And your phone,' I told him.

He pulled a mobile phone from his pocket and handed it over. I put it in my pocket.

'Look at me,' I said to him.

He didn't move.

'Look at me, Kamal.'

He turned his head and looked at me.

'Listen,' I said. 'My name's Robert Smith. I'm sixteen years old. This morning I went into the hospital for an endoscopy. When I woke up, I was lying on my back in a strange room. I was blind and paralysed. Conscious but unconscious. I was surrounded by men with guns. A man in a white coat cut my belly open and there were unhuman things inside me.'

I paused, trying to remember, trying to forget.

Kamal just stared at me.

'That's all I know,' I told him. 'I don't know anything else about it. I don't know why . . . I don't know what it means. I don't know who those people are. I don't know . . . I can't explain anything. All I know is that I have to get away. I can't let those people find me again.'

The clock ticked, the rain tip-tapped.

My bladder ached.

'What do you want me to do?' Kamal said.

'Give me an hour or so. Just sit here and wait.'

'I'll have to answer their questions. Ryan will want to know everything.'

'Just give me an hour, hour and a half. Then you can tell him whatever you want.' I pointed at the station entrance. 'There's a phone box over there. You can ring the hospital. Tell him . . . tell him . . .'

'Tell him what?'

I shrugged. 'Tell him what you like. I don't care, tell him anything.'

Kamal smiled. 'I'll wait here for as long as I can. You have my word.'

'Thank you.'

I put the pistol back in my pocket and picked up the briefcase from the back seat.

'Where will you go?' asked Kamal.

'I don't know.'

I dropped Kamal's wallet and car keys into the rucksack and zipped it up.

'Well . . .' I said.

Kamal held out his hand. 'Good luck.'

I looked him in the eye as we shook hands and I wondered briefly if I'd ever see him again, but somehow I knew that I wouldn't.

I stepped out of the car and buttoned my jacket.

I breathed the air.

It smelled of wet fields and iron.

I leaned into the car to say goodbye, but a sudden searing pain knotted my stomach and I closed the door without speaking.

Goodbye, Kamal Ramachandran.

Thank you.

I'm sorry.

I slung the rucksack over my shoulder and headed towards the station.

*

I didn't trust him. I learned a long time ago not to trust anyone. I *couldn't* trust him. He'd do whatever he thought was best for him.

Was he good?

Was he bad?

What did he think I was?

Good or bad?

It didn't matter.

Trust, faith, good, bad . . . none of it matters. All you ever do is what you have to do. Follow your desires, fulfil your needs, escape from pain. That's all there is to it. Kamal would do whatever he had to do, and it wasn't worth thinking about.

The telephone box was at the bottom of a slope at the station entrance. I went inside, took Ryan's penknife from my pocket and sliced through the telephone cord.

Inside the station, the ticket office was closed and the toilets were locked. I walked out on to the platform. A cold wind was blowing, whipping close to the ground, whistling around the empty buildings. The station clock said 20:04:42.

I sat on a bench and crossed my legs.

I wondered what I looked like. A reasonable tramp? A drunk in an ill-fitting suit? A scarecrow? An outlaw? It didn't matter. There was no one there to see me.

I looked around. The rain was coming down harder now, gleaming white in the stark station lights, making everything look harsh and unreal: the dull silver shine of the tracks, dirtied with wads of waste tissue; the sprawling yellow weeds dripping in the lowlight of arches and walls; red doors, blue doors; the sand and scrap of the station fringe.

I wondered if it was all an illusion. The rusted railway machinery, the wires and wire supports, the padlocked sheds, the Coke cans and crisp packets, the mysterious numbers painted on the trackside walls . . . it all seemed real enough, but what if it wasn't? What if there was something wrong with me? What if I was seeing things that weren't there? How would I know? How could I tell the difference? For all I knew, everything was an illusion – me, the hospital, Ryan, Casing, Kamal . . .

The rails started humming.

I looked up and saw the lights of an approaching train. I got to my feet and watched it pull into the platform. It rattled and slowed . . . rattled and slowed . . . rattled and slowed . . . and finally ground to a halt. I glanced inside, looking for unwelcome faces, then I opened the door and got on the train and immediately went looking for a toilet.

The train sighed – *pishhh* – then settled on its metal sound and lumbered slowly out of the station. Inside the rattling toilet cubicle, I let out a long wheezing fart and emptied my bladder. The toilet bowl was stuffed full of creamy-white paper. I stood there peeing for a long time, steadying myself with a hand against the wall, and when I was done I felt weightless and empty and hungry. My urine smelled bad. I smelled bad. Sour and sulphurous, like the smell of someone else.

I washed my hands and looked at myself in the mirror above the sink. The glass was cracked and dull, and my reflection was smeared and unfamiliar. I said hello to myself.

'Hello, Robert.'

It was good and bad to be alone again.

I rubbed a finger of hot water into my gums and over my teeth, then leaned over and retched into the sink. Nothing came up but some thin spitty stuff that stuck to my lips in shiny strings. I wiped it off with the back of my hand and rinsed my mouth from the tap. The water tasted metallic. I belched, then my stomach heaved and I threw up.

I wanted to cry then. I was so scared, so sick, so confused . . . so everything. It was too much, all of it, too much to think about . . . I didn't want to *think* about anything. I just wanted to cry, uncontrollably, like a lost child sobbing for its mother . . . but I couldn't.

I can't.

I've never been able to cry. Whenever I feel like crying, something happens to me – a door closes, the lights go off, I disappear.

I took the bottle of water from my rucksack and rinsed out my mouth again and again – rinse and spit, rinse and spit, rinse and spit – until all I could taste was the clean tang of water. I looked at myself in the mirror again. What I saw was just a face – pale, tired, confused – but still just a face. I sniffed, spat a final gob into the sink, then I began to undress.

It didn't feel good, standing naked in that stinking little rattle-box . . . naked and cold and sick. It seemed dirty

59

and wrong, and it made me feel as if I didn't know myself any more.

I gazed down at my belly.

It didn't look too bad – a crooked black gash, a reddened slash. Pink. Some white. Bruise-brown and dirt-yellow. A slight swelling. It was healing fast . . . *I* was healing fast.

Most of my early childhood is hazy. The memories are there, but they don't mean anything to me. Unknown people and unknown places. Faces, voices. Houses, Homes. Hard wooden chairs, squeaky floors, the smell of disinfectant. None of it means anything.

But I do remember things.

I remember a voice, from a long time ago. A woman's voice.

'Oh, he's a fast healer, that one,' I remember her saying. 'He's a fast healer, all right . . .'

I don't remember who she was, or what she was to me.

But she was right. I *am* a fast healer. Cuts, scrapes, bruises . . . I've always healed quickly. Quickly and cleanly.

I dressed in the clothes I'd got from Sainsbury's – underwear, trousers, shirt, jacket, shoes – then I transferred the contents of Ryan's jacket to my new jacket and stuffed the old clothes into the rucksack.

A final look in the mirror, then I flushed the toilet and left.

As the train rattled and hummed through the darkness, I gazed through the window and tried to think about things – what was I doing? where was I going? what the hell was going on? – but I just couldn't do it. It was all too big. Too confusing. Too much to think about. And I was so tired. I just wanted to close my eyes and drift away . . . just for a moment . . .

I closed my eyes.

I didn't know where I was when I woke up. The train had stopped at a station and now it was just sitting there – humming and murmuring, hissing and moaning, not going anywhere. I looked out at the platform. There weren't many people around. No station staff. No uniforms. No men in suits. I looked around for a station sign, but I couldn't see one.

The train groaned for a moment, something hissed . . . and then it went quiet again.

I sat there for a minute or two, listening to the ticking silence, then I got up, walked down the aisle and got off the train.

As I left the station and started walking, I still didn't know where I was. I think it was probably Romford or Ilford, somewhere like that. One of those *ford* places. Somewhere near London, but not *in* London. Not that it mattered. The way I saw it, if I didn't know where I was, neither would anyone else.

The streets outside the station were busy with traffic. Cars, taxis, buses, vans, lorries, motorcycles, bikes. People were moving, going places. Going home, going out, going somewhere.

No one cared about me.

Why should they?

I kept my head down and kept walking. Down wide pavements of grey-white concrete, past closed shops and noisy pubs and greasy little kebab places. Past bus stops and nightclubs, taxi ranks, wine bars . . .

I kept moving, kept going.

Away from the town centre, into the outskirts. Past black-glassed office blocks and leisure centres, past beggars and skateboard kids and girls dressed up for the night . . .

I walked.

The pain in my stomach dulled to an ache.

The rain kept falling.

I kept walking.

Into the night.

I walked for a long long time.

Until, eventually, after walking forever, I finally reached Paradise.

6

The Paradise Hotel was seven floors of dull grey concrete on the outskirts of a dull grey town. I didn't know how I'd got there, and I didn't know if it was a good idea to stay there or not, but I was bone-tired and wet, and my stomach was hurting, and I just couldn't walk any further. But, most of all, I needed to be on my own. I needed to start thinking about things. I needed to do something.

Without giving it too much thought, I opened the hotel doors and went inside.

It was a fairly big place, and fairly smart. Smoked-glass doors, a dark-carpeted lobby, pillars and panels, plants in brass pots. There was a bar at the far end of the lobby and a restaurant off to one side. Both were quite busy. Men in suits, women in suits, everyone drinking and having a good time.

I felt out of place.

I'd never been in a hotel before. I didn't know what to do. I didn't know the procedure. So, for the next five minutes or so, I just stood in the doorway – glancing at my non-existent watch now and then, as if I was waiting for someone – and I watched what was happening. How it worked. Where people went. What they said.

Then, when I'd worked it all out, I smoothed back my hair, straightened myself up and crossed the lobby towards the reception desk.

The young woman behind the desk was sleek and well dressed. She had a thin face, a false smile and slick blonde hair. As she watched me crossing the lobby, I wondered what I looked like to her. You're just an ordinary young man, I told myself. You're wearing an ordinary jacket and an ordinary shirt, and you're carrying an ordinary brief-case and an ordinary rucksack. You're ordinary, that's all you are. That's what she sees.

'Good evening, sir,' she said. 'How can I help you?'

'I'd like a room, please.'

It was easier than I thought – the procedure.

She asked me questions, I answered them.

'How many nights?'

'One.'

'Single or double?'

'Single.'

'Smoking or non-smoking?'

'Non.'

'Newspaper in the morning?'

'Yes, please.'

'Which one?'

'Any one.'

The only tricky part was when she asked me for a credit card. I had credit cards. I had Ryan's and Kamal's credit cards. But I didn't want to use them. Credit cards are trace-able. I didn't want to be traced.

'There's a problem with my card,' I told the receptionist, giving her what I hoped was a weary smile. 'It's been playing up all day. I think there's a faulty computer or something. Is it OK if I pay in cash?'

She hesitated for a moment, then smiled and nodded. 'Cash? Of course, cash is fine. We'll need some identification, though – credit card, driving licence, passport . . . something like that. And full payment in advance, of course.'

'Of course.'

I was thinking hard now, thinking fast, trying to work out what to do. What could I use for ID? And what would the receptionist do with it? If I gave her a credit card, would she swipe it? And if she did, would Ryan find out? What if I used Ryan's ID card? No, that was no good, it had his photograph on it. Kamal's driving licence? No, that had a photo on it too. And, besides, who in their right mind would believe that I was called Kamal Ramachandran? What else could I use? My medical card, Ryan's business card . . . ?

'It doesn't matter if your credit card's faulty,' the receptionist said. 'We're only going to make a photocopy.'

I smiled at her. I still wasn't sure what to do, but I knew she'd start getting suspicious if I didn't do something soon. So, still smiling, I took Ryan's wallet out of my pocket, selected his Amex card, glanced briefly at the signature on the back, then passed it over.

The receptionist barely looked at the card. She just smiled at me, made a quick photocopy, then gave it back.

The rest was easy. She pressed buttons on her keyboard, gave me a form to fill out and sign – Ryan's signature was just a scrawl – then she took my cash, and that was it.

Room 624. Sixth floor.

Through the doors, down the corridor, the lift's on your left.

Thank you, Mr Ryan.

Thank *you*.

It was a small room – single bed, cupboards, TV and VCR, bathroom. I locked the door behind me and dropped my bags on the bed. I went over to the window, pulled back the edge of the curtain and looked outside. I was at the back of the hotel. All I could see was a plain brick wall and the rear of the kitchens down below. I turned on the TV, clicked through the channels, then turned it off. I went into the bathroom, looked around, took a glass tumbler from a shelf over the sink, then came back out again. I sat down on the bed and put the tumbler on the bedside cabinet. There was a telephone on the cabinet. I stared at it for a while, imagining how simple it would be to just pick up the phone and press a few buttons . . .

Hello?

Bridget? It's me, Robert –

Robert! Where are you? What's going on . . . ?

No. It wouldn't be simple at all.

I leaned across the bed and opened the cabinet drawer. Inside was a pad of writing paper, a hotel pen and a Bible. I took out the Bible and flipped through the pages, then put it back in the drawer.

I knew I was just playing for time, putting off what had to be done. And I knew I couldn't put it off any longer.

It was time to think about it now.

Right now.

I emptied my pockets and tipped the contents of the rucksack and the briefcase on to the bed. Then I just sat there and stared at them, making myself see the bare truth of those things: X-rays, photographs, a videotape, scalpels, needles, syringes, papers, medical records, an automatic pistol, wallets, cash, clothes, vodka, chocolate bars, chicken, painkillers . . .

It was an unthinkable collage.

And I knew what I had to do.

I picked up the glass tumbler and half filled it with vodka. The smell of it made me gag. I hate vodka. I hate alcohol. I hate the taste of it, the smell of it, how it makes you feel. I *hate* it.

But it was necessary.

I topped up the glass with Coke.

Took two paracetamol.

I drank, shuddered, and drank again.

It was necessary.

I started examining the items on the bed.

The X-rays. Blurred images of bones and organs on a plastic film. X-rays. *Normal*, Casing had said. *Normal*. I held the X-rays up to the light and studied them, but they didn't tell me anything. I didn't know what I was looking at. I didn't know what I was looking *for*. What does *normal* look like? I put the X-rays to one side and turned to the pile of papers.

The papers. Photocopies of my appointment card and admittance record, my name and address, a few personal details on a handwritten sheet. Blank pages. Papers. Nothing about

Ryan, nothing by Ryan. Nothing to tell me what had happened. I collected all the papers together and placed them on top of the X-rays.

The medical records. Cramped handwriting on small white cards. I glanced through them, looking for anything unusual, but there was hardly anything there. In fact, apart from the details of my stomach problem, there was nothing there at all. No broken bones, no diseases, no ailments.

Was that normal?

I tried to remember if I'd ever been ill. I knew I'd had colds. Snuffles, sneezes, a cough. Colds and chills. But, no, I couldn't remember anything serious. Nothing that needed medical attention.

Nothing?

Ever?

Chickenpox, measles, mumps . . . ?

No.

Nothing. Not as far as I could recall.

Only bad dreams.

I didn't know what to think about that.

I took another drink.

Refilled the glass. Three parts vodka, one part Coke.

The photographs. Black-and-white stills taken from the endoscopy video. Unclear images of unclear things. Strange things. Strange shapes. Cones, flecks, weird black chambers. Wiggles of white, curves, ridges, trails. Patterns. I didn't know what I was looking at. There was no sense of dimension or direction. No reference points.

Not yet.

I stacked the photographs and placed them beside the videotape.

Another drink.

The pistol. It was matt-black, slightly oily, with a moulded grip, chunky little sights and seven vertical grooves gouged into the rear of the barrel. On the side, it said MADE IN AUSTRIA, and below that, GLOCK. It was a gun. A 9mm automatic pistol. I thumbed a little catch and the magazine slid out. I counted sixteen bullets. I replaced the magazine – *snick* – and hefted the gun in the palm of my hand.

It felt solid and primed. Powerful.

It felt like death.

I placed the pistol on the left-hand side of the bed.

Putting things in order. That's what I was doing. I was picking things up, one by one, examining them, studying them, seeing what they told me. Then I was arranging them in separate piles on the bed. On the right, the stuff that told me nothing, the stuff I could get rid off. On the left, the stuff I needed to keep. And in the middle, right in front of me, the stuff I needed to look at.

Order. Keep things in order.

I liked to keep things in order.

Chocolate bars, water, paracetamol – left. Map – left. Ryan's wallet and penknife – left. Old clothes – right. Kamal's wallet – left. Car keys – right. Cash – left. Photographs – middle. Video – middle . . .

Left and right.

69

Right and left.

Middle, middle, middle.

There was a carrier bag in the waste bin. I gathered all the stuff from the right-hand pile and packed it into the carrier bag, then I placed the carrier bag in the corner of the room. The pistol, the map, everything else from the left-hand pile, I put into the rucksack. Then I changed my mind about the pistol, removed it from the rucksack and placed it on the bedside cabinet.

What was left? Videotape, photographs, syringes, needles, scalpels.

It was almost time.

I put the endoscopy video in the VCR and sat on the bed with the remote in my hand. I drank more vodka and Coke. The alcohol was getting to me now, making me sick and numb and stupid. It was doing what it had to do.

I stared at the blank television screen. Grey-green. My thumb hovered over the PLAY button.

Whatever you see, I said to myself, whatever's there . . . there's a thousand ways it won't be you.

I thought . . . don't think.

I drank some more . . . and pressed PLAY.

The screen turned white, flickered, then cleared. On the screen, the endoscope was moving inside me like an electric eye. I was seeing things that I didn't understand. Black things, grey things, blurred and formless. Then suddenly everything came into focus and I was seeing definable shapes. A tube, smooth as metal, smooth as plastic. Dulled silver-white, shining dark in the light of the eye. The walls of the tube were lined with tiny asymmetrical grids, like . . . like nothing I'd ever seen before. Intricate patterns of dots and lines, circles and waves. Fine hairs, like slender worms, moving to the flow of something invisible . . .

PAUSE.

It was too much to look at. Beautiful, terrifying, unfathomable. Sickening. The paused picture shimmered on the screen. It could have been anything: organic, manufactured, living . . . metal, plastic, carbon, flesh.

It was me.

It said so at the bottom of the screen: 281105SMITH-R1042ANDREWS.

It was me.

I rested my hand on my chest, feeling where my heart should be. How did it feel? It didn't feel wrong. But how do you know how you're supposed to feel?

PLAY.

The picture started up with a jerk and the electric eye moved on, crawling down through a thin gauzy membrane and out into the roof of some kind of chamber. For a second or two the camera light dimmed, and then – my God! – I was inside the body of a wondrous cavern. I was inside it, and it was inside me. The light of the eye turned slowly and I watched, breathless, as the inner structure was revealed. A sizeless space, shaped like a broad-shouldered bottle, with irregular walls of blackened leather. A cavern, rising and swirling with fantastic alien machineries:

filaments, struts, crystals, ties, pillars, pipes, valves, ribbons, sheaths, valleys, tunnels, veins, countless glimmering particles . . .

Words don't mean anything. These things were beyond description. They moved without movement. They were solid liquids and liquid solids. They were with and without form and colour. They were unknowable.

PAUSE.

With the picture paused, the after-images danced around inside my mind. Particles, spheres, discs, rods, cones, cylinders, strings, stars. Crystalline compounds with radiating shards. Elements in a structure. A structure of elements. A sub-atomic dome, a dark cathedral, a perfect abomination.
   Inside me.
   In me.
   It was me.

I rewound the tape and played it back.
   I rewound it again and played it back again.
   And again.
   And again.
   And again.

How could it be?
   There was no conceivable explanation.
   It had to be a mistake. A joke. A hoax. A trick. An absurd misunderstanding.
   It *had* to be.

Because if it wasn't . . . if it wasn't . . .

I had to face it. If it *wasn't* a mistake, if those things I'd seen . . . those alien things inside me . . . if those things were real . . .

What did that mean?

What did that make me?

It made me sick.

I drank more vodka and forced myself to consider the only question: if I'm not normal, if I'm not human . . . then what am I? What? What else *is* there? Robot? Cyborg? Alien? Android? No. Impossible. No. No. *NO*. I couldn't even believe the *sound* of those words. This was the real world. This was reality. This was Essex, England. This wasn't a story. It wasn't a *fantasy*, for God's sake.

I couldn't be a *machine*.

That was impossible.

Absolutely impossible.

And even if it *wasn't* impossible . . . even if there *were* such things – machines of unimaginable complexity, humanoid machines, machines that looked and functioned *exactly* the same as a human being – well, even then . . . it still wasn't possible for *me* to be something like that, was it?

I'd know, wouldn't I?

I'd *know* . . .

Wouldn't I?

Would I?

How would I know?

If I *was* some kind of a machine, a machine that looked and functioned exactly the same as a human being, then how was I to know that I *wasn't* a human being? If I looked the same as everyone else, walked the same as everyone else, talked the same as everyone else . . . how was I to know that I *wasn't* the same as everyone else?

What would tell me?

What did I have to tell me?

How would I know?

How can you wonder what you are?

Twinkle twinkle, little star . . .

I was drunk now. Drunk enough to do what I had to do.

The floor tilted slightly as I got off the bed, but I was steady enough to function. I went into the bathroom, fetched some towels and a handheld mirror, then went back and sat down on the bed. I placed the towels beside me. I took two more painkillers, another long drink . . . waited for the sickness to pass. Then I unbuttoned my shirt and gazed down at my stitched-up belly.

It looked like a sunset, an ugly sunset – a bruised yellow sun on a white-skinned sky. My skin. A map of sick colours – puce, black, dull red-brown. There were faded stains around the stitches, the remains of leaked fluids. Like blood, but darker. Like dried runnels of blackberry juice.

I wet my finger and cautiously rubbed at the stains. My fingertip reddened. I looked at it. Sniffed it. Licked it. It didn't taste like blackberry juice. It tasted sour and metallic, like something alien.

It could have been anything.

I looked down at the fresh scar on my belly. It was

74

slightly raised, like a wormy ridge, criss-crossed with dried dark stitches. I touched it. It was tender, sore, but not particularly painful. It was already healing.

The tip of my finger tingled.

I turned my attention to the pile of surgical paraphernalia laid out on the bed – syringes, needles, scalpels.

I picked up a scalpel.

I couldn't breathe.

I leaned back slightly and spread the towels around my body.

I positioned the mirror on the flat of my belly, just below the wound.

And now I was ready.

Holding the scalpel firmly, I took a tentative pick at the hook of a stitch. The thread snipped. There was a little pain, but not much. The alcohol had numbed me. I picked again. The scalpel blade sliced through another stitch – easy – then another, and another, and another. I kept going until all the stitches were cut.

I wanted to rest now, but I knew that I had to keep going. If I stopped now, I'd never do it.

I put the scalpel down, gripped the cut end of one of the stitches and pulled. It was stuck. I pulled a little harder, feeling the pain now, and out it came. Pop. A reddened stitch-hole remained. Quickly, but carefully, I pulled out the rest of the stitches. One, two, three, four, five, six . . .

When I was done, the wound was loose, but still fixed. Held together by a wafer-thin ridge of flesh.

Or something like flesh.

I lay my hands flat on either side of the wound and gently pulled at the skin. Gently, slowly, firmly . . . my hands moved . . . the wound stretched . . . and stretched . . . until the join began to give. A crack appeared, and a dribble of thin brown liquid oozed out. I pulled harder, wincing at the pain. The ridge of flesh was splitting open, but it was still joined to something below. I pulled harder. It hurt. I was sweating, hot and cold, groaning, gritting my teeth. God, it *hurt*. The pain was dull and distant, but deep. I kept pulling, flat hands tugging the skin, and the mouth of the wound began to open. Not much, about half a centimetre. Like a tiny pink abyss. I looked in the mirror, angling it, trying to see what the flesh was joined to. After searching for a few moments, I saw something. Just below the skin . . . some kind of seal. A flexible hinge.

I picked up the scalpel again.

Emptied my head.

And then I was plunging the scalpel into the wound and slicing down into the hinge. Oh God, it hurts so much so much so much . . . keep going, keep cutting, keep slicing . . . nice and clean and quick and strong . . . and the blade keeps cutting through the pain . . . and the liquids stream, red and black and white . . . and I can hear that stone-cold whistle in my head saying stop stop stop stop stop STOP.

I stopped cutting.

The wound lay open.

My stomach was red. My skin, my fingers, my hand. A red skeleton hand.

I breathed.

Listened.

Breathed.

My hand was shaking.

The wound lay open and bleeding.

I could feel something, but I didn't know what it was. A numb, dull, black feeling. A reaction to the pain, perhaps. I don't know. I don't think I cared. I wasn't there any more.

There was blood on the sheets. Blood on the towels.

It didn't matter.

I had to do this now. I had to finish it.

I picked up the mirror and held it over the gash in my belly. What did I see? I saw a darkness . . . like oil and water on a hard surface. Movement. It was unclear. I took a quick breath, placed a hand on the edge of the wound and pulled it to one side. A sudden jagged pain ripped through me like a knife, and just for a moment I was gone – shut down in nothingness – and then suddenly I was back again. The wound was gaping open now, like a black and bloody teardrop. Red-rimmed like a lipsticked mouth. And I could see right down inside myself. I could see blood and an oily brown blackness. A thick and inky liquid that moved as if magnetized. I reached in and touched it. The liquid shimmered like mercury. I felt inside the lips of the wound. It stung. But I was a long way beyond the pain now. I felt around some more, and I felt something hard. Rigid. Thick-skinned. Hollow. It moved stiffly to the touch, as if heavily sprung. I remembered Casing's voice: *This . . . I can't get through it. It has – look – patterning. Like bone structure. Outlines. It could be some kind of shield. That might explain the X-rays.*

I positioned the mirror to get a better look. I saw something brown . . . brown and hard, like plastic. But it was the brown of something alive. Something internal. An inner shell. Bone, shell, metal, fibre. Patterned, etched, embossed, formed, engineered, designed, evolved . . .

Christ . . .

A silver shred flickered through an unseen pore, then dissolved and lost itself in a trail of black.

Something quite perfect.

I looked inside myself.

For a long long time.

What can I say?

It was all there, inside me.

It *is* there.

It is.

I am.

It.

Eventually, with drunken fingers and a shattered mind, I took the needle and surgical thread and started sewing myself back together again. Flesh slipped in the sweat of my fingers. The needle trembled as I guided it through the bleeding holes and knotted the thread. The pain of it was pure and sharp.

When I'd finished, my stomach was butchered and ugly. Badly stitched, swollen and bruised, stained with nightmarish colours – yellowy-black, brown, red, inky-blue, puckered pink. But at least the wound was closed. Whatever was inside me was back inside me.

Hidden away.

Finally, while my mind was still reeling, there was just one more thing to do. Just to make sure. I took the blood-stained scalpel in my right hand, clenched the fist of my left hand, held the arm out in front of me, then pressed the blade into the fleshy part and slowly drew it down. A thick red slice opened up and my heart screamed dully. I lifted my arm to my face and studied the cut. Beneath the flow of blood, a luminous shiver of pale white liquid was enmeshed with a shine of black, like milk and oil. I wiped away the blood with a towel and looked closer. I saw something metallic pulsing in the liquid. I saw red things, silver things, a flash of tiny stars. I saw the shadows of silver bones.

I kept looking. Mesmerized.

After a while – ten, fifteen minutes – the blood darkened and began to solidify. Visibly, the flesh was starting to dry. A scab was already forming.

Twenty minutes.

The wound was closed.

With a sense of some futility, I ripped the sleeve off Ryan's shirt and wrapped it tightly round my arm.

It was nearly two thirty in the morning. I was lying on a bloodstained bed on the sixth floor of the Paradise Hotel, and I didn't know what was happening to me. I was bleeding. I was drunk. I was exhausted.

I wanted to go to sleep, but I knew that I couldn't.

I was too scared.

Scared of what was inside me.

Scared of myself.

7

The rest of that night is a timeless blur. I don't know what I did. I don't know if I slept or not. I can't remember. I don't think I did. I think I might have dozed off once or twice, but all I can really remember is sitting on the bed all night, thinking myself into a sleepless void.

Nothing made sense.

I kept going over and over everything that had happened – trying to understand it, trying to make sense of it, trying to make it into something real – but no matter how much I thought about it, no matter how many questions I asked myself, I couldn't find any answers.

How did it happen?

How *could* it happen?

How could I be something else?

Why should I be something else?

What else *is* there?

Who's Ryan?

What is he?

What does he want?

Where did he come from?

What does it all mean?

The questions didn't get me anywhere. All they did was

swirl around inside my head like shapeless things in a whirlwind, roaring and spinning, twisting and turning, until eventually I didn't even know what I was thinking about.

Everything was too much, too vague, too impossible.

I couldn't do it any more.

I had to think about something else, something that meant something.

I had to think about what I was going to *do*.

It was six thirty in the morning now. I rubbed the tiredness from my eyes and gazed around the hotel room. A slow grey light was seeping in through the curtains, giving everything a flat and empty look, like a picture in an old magazine. The room was a mess. There was blood and stuff all over the place – on the bed, on the towels, on the floor. There were piles of papers and photographs, empty food wrappers, clothes, wallets, syringes, scalpels. The air smelled bad – a stale mixture of alcohol, blood, weariness and fear.

What are you going to do?

I knew I couldn't stay here, not with all this mess I'd made. The room looked like a slaughterhouse. As soon as the cleaners saw it, there'd be questions, and I didn't want questions. So I knew I had to move on. But where? Where could I go? The only place I wanted to go was back home to Bridget and Pete, but that was out of the question. Ryan would be watching them. He'd have people watching the house, watching Pete's office. He'd have taps on Bridget's and Pete's phones. Wherever they went, whatever they did, whoever they spoke to – Ryan would know.

So . . . where could I go?

I didn't have any family.

I didn't have any friends.

I had no sanctuaries.

There was nowhere to go.

As I sat there, trying to think about it, I could feel the sounds of the hotel getting inside my head. The silence of the room, the random noises from the corridor outside . . . empty and unknown, belonging to no one, echoing dully with unwanted noise.

I couldn't think.

My head was throbbing.

My legs were heavy.

My throat was dry.

I went into the bathroom, drank from the tap, then opened my shirt and examined my belly in the mirror. The stitches were crusty and black, the stitch-holes ringed with a strange coppery colour. The wound was closed, almost healed, and the bruising had faded to a faint yellowy-blue. I ran my hand over the wound.

There was no pain. None at all.

I untied the bandage on my arm. All that remained of the cut was a knobbly ridge of hardened skin. I flexed my wrist. The ridge cracked open a little and a drop of clear liquid oozed out. I wiped it clean and retied the bandage.

This wasn't just fast healing. I knew that now. This wasn't just cuts and bruises . . . this was something else.

This was something that simply shouldn't be.

*

I looked in the mirror again. Look, I told myself, it's just a body. A face. Nothing untoward. A thing of skin and bone. Lips, teeth, eyes, a soft scrape of beard. And beneath the skin . . . ?

My reflection shimmered, and just for a moment I saw what I could be. I saw struts and cages and bowls of bone, or something like bone. I saw red-and-white strips of ribbony bands, sockets, holes, hinges. I saw levers and wires and multi-coloured canals, bellows and pumps, tubes and pipes, weird white sacs, veined vessels, jellies and liquids, metallic cords . . .

Christ.

I saw the spine of a giant snake, the dead-domed visage of a titanium-white skull.

Look at yourself.

The mirror shimmered again and the images died. I got undressed, turned on the shower and tried to wash the memories away.

Half an hour later I was back on the bed again, back to thinking about what I was going to do, when suddenly I heard a thump outside the door. It wasn't much, just a faint little *thump*, but it was enough to set my shredded nerves jangling. I reached for the pistol and pointed it at the door. I could hear muffled footsteps, moving quietly along the corridor. I thumbed the safety catch on the pistol. I listened hard. The footsteps were still there, but they were moving away from my door now, and when I heard another faint thump, and then another, I put down the pistol and relaxed.

Newspaper in the morning, Mr Ryan?
Yes, please.
Nothing to worry about, it was just the newspaper.

Why had I asked for a newspaper in the morning? Because that's what an ordinary young man would have done, and that's all I was – an ordinary young man.

Ordinary jacket, ordinary shirt, ordinary newspaper in the morning.

The first thing I saw when I opened the door and picked up the paper was a photograph of someone who looked like me. Similar face, similar eyes, similar mouth. Then I looked closer . . . and I realized it *was* me. I couldn't believe it. But I had to. It was right there – front page of the *Daily Express*, bottom left-hand corner. A photograph of me. It was a school photograph. I'd only had it taken about six months ago. In the original photograph I didn't look too bad, but the graininess of the picture in the newspaper made me look shadowy and gaunt, like something from the underworld.

'Shit,' I whispered, folding the newspaper and going back into my room. I shut the door and locked it behind me, then opened the paper again.

The photograph was still there.

The caption beneath it said:

ROBERT SMITH: FRENZIED ATTACK

I stared at the words for a while – ROBERT SMITH: FREN-ZIED ATTACK – then, with a terrible sinking feeling inside me, I forced myself to read the story.

SURGEON SLAIN

A police investigation was under way last night after a knife attack in an Essex hospital left a leading surgeon dead.

Professor Ian Casing, 58, a father of three, died from multiple stab wounds following a frenzied attack by a 16-year-old patient, Robert Smith (above). After what police described as a 'horrendous' killing, Smith made his escape from Stoneham General Hospital in a white Ford Fiesta which was later found abandoned at Heystone railway station.

Detective Superintendent Mark Dennet appealed to members of the public who may have information about Smith's current whereabouts to come forward.

I sat down on the bed and read through the story again, just to make sure I wasn't mistaken, but I knew I was wasting my time. The words were still there – *Professor Ian Casing . . . multiple stab wounds . . . Robert Smith . . . horrendous killing . . .*

I stared at nothing, trying to think . . .

How?

Why?

But I knew I didn't have time to think. I wasn't an ordinary young man any more, I was a murderer. I was on the front page of the *Daily Express*. People had seen me – the hotel receptionist, people in the street, people on the train – they'd call the police. The police would call Ryan . . . he might be here any minute.

I emptied my head and got moving.

Shoes on, jacket on, pistol in pocket. I ran round the

room, grabbing a few clothes and throwing them in the rucksack, then I stopped for a moment and took a quick look round at the rest of the stuff – the papers, the photographs, the video, the scalpels – wondering if I should take any of it or not.

I stuffed the videotape into the rucksack, leaving everything else, and went across to the door. I paused for a moment, listening at the door, then I slowly opened it. The hallway was empty. I put my hand in my pistol pocket, moved out into the hallway, and paused again.

Which way should I go?

The lifts were to the left; the stairs were to the right.

Come on, *think*.

Which way?

Left or right?

I turned right and headed for the stairs.

Just as I got to the stairway door, I heard footsteps down below. Hurried steps, coming up the stairs. I let go of the door and stepped back, scanning the hallway for another way out. I glanced down at the lifts, then back at the stairs again.

The lifts were too risky.

Maybe I could go *up* the stairs . . . ?

Then I saw the door. It was just past the stairway. A glass-panelled door with a sign on it: NO ADMITTANCE – STAFF ONLY. I didn't stop to think about it, I just hurried over, glanced quickly through the glass panel, then pushed open the door and stepped through into a cold and gloomy corridor. As the door swung shut, I heard the distant *ting* of the lift arriving behind me. I turned round, crouched down behind the door, and peered back through the glass panel. At the end of the hallway, two figures were emerging from the lift. One of them was a sharp-eyed woman in a cream-coloured raincoat. The other one was Ryan. Black coat, hard face, cold silver eyes. As he turned and said something to the woman – who I guessed was Hayes – a third figure entered the hallway from the stairs. A dark-haired man in a suit. He passed directly in front of me, headed down the hallway and stopped outside room 624.

I squatted down, out of sight, then turned round and started crawling away from the door. After I'd gone about ten metres or so, I got to my feet and started running – down the corridor, through another door, then along another short corridor to another door and a zigzag flight of stairs.

As I hurried down the stairs – my footsteps echoing around the cold stone walls – I felt an empty sickness growing inside me. It wasn't a physical sickness, it was just the sudden realization that what was happening was happening. I was running. I was being chased. I was being hunted. It was *happening*. And it wasn't anything like a scene from a film or a book, or something from a dream. It wasn't exciting. It wasn't fun. It wasn't a game.

It was just shit.

At the bottom of the stairs was another door, this one marked PRIVATE. It was a drab-looking thing, barely painted, with a tarnished brass handle and a flap of frayed rubber fixed to the bottom edge. I shoved it open and found myself in a greasy little room with a bank of grey lockers around the walls. I guessed it was a staffroom.

There was a table, chairs, a hot-water urn, a sink. Across the room was another door. As I headed towards it, I reached up and snatched an old trilby hat from the top of one of the lockers. I put it on. It was a good fit. A pathetic disguise, but a good fit.

I was halfway through the door when a distant shout broke the silence: 'Angela!'

A man's voice. It came from the corridor outside. I heard footsteps approaching, then the shouting voice again: 'Angela! Where are you?'

I hurried through the door, along another dim corridor, through another door, along another corridor . . . doors, corridors . . . doors, corridors . . . I just kept going. The further I went, the gloomier it got. Cheap linoleum flooring, stained and curled. Clammy-looking walls, dripping pipes, peeling paintwork . . .

'Who are you?'

The voice came from behind me. I stopped suddenly and turned round. A dark-eyed girl in a green uniform-dress was standing in a doorway, staring at me. She looked nervous and offended, rubbing a thumb into the palm of her hand. The name badge on her dress said ANGELA.

'What are you doing here?' she said.

'I'm sorry,' I muttered. 'I'm lost. I'm a guest . . . I . . . uhh . . . got lost.'

'This is staff only,' she said. 'You shouldn't be here.'

'I know, I'm sorry. I'm lost.'

She closed the door behind her and stepped to one side, revealing a sign on the door that said LADIES. She was very short, this Angela, just over five feet tall. She had a plain face and small features. Her dark-brown hair was fastened with a plastic hairband. I didn't like the way she was looking at me. She was looking at me as if she was trying to place my face, and it was making us both uneasy.

'Where did you get that hat?' she asked me.

'What?'

She was looking at the trilby on my head. 'That's Walter's hat.'

'Who's Walter?'

'That's his hat. Why are you wearing his hat?'

'I'm not . . . this is mine. I've had it for ages . . .'

She stepped back a little more, glancing nervously over her shoulder. 'You shouldn't be here,' she repeated. 'This is staff only.'

'Yeah, I know.' I smiled at her. 'Do you think you could show me the way out?'

'Back there,' she said, gesturing with her head, 'the same way you came.'

I smiled again. 'Is there another way? Out on to the street? I was on my way out, you see. I have to meet someone.'

'What do you mean?'

It was a good question.

'Well . . . I'm late. I got lost. I have to meet someone.' I shrugged. 'I just thought there might be another way out. You know, a back exit.'

I was doing my best, but it didn't seem to be working. Angela kept edging away from me.

'You have to go,' she said.

I pointed down the corridor. 'Can I get out down there? Is there a back door?'

She didn't answer, she just stared at me, chewing on her

lip, and I could see that she was losing it. Her eyes were blinking too fast. Her lips were quivering. Any second now, I thought, she's going to start screaming. And I knew I couldn't let that happen. I could feel my fingers tightening on the pistol in my pocket. I didn't like how it felt. I didn't like what I was thinking.

But then, somewhere in the distance, a door slammed shut, breaking the silence, and Angela suddenly said, 'Just down there, at the end of the corridor. There's a door on the right.'

And without another word she scuttled away.

I watched her go, wondering if this was how it was going to be from now on – running all the time, lying to people, scaring people, not caring, just doing what had to be done.

I didn't like it.

The door on the right at the end of the corridor was a fire door. I pushed down on the bar and stepped out into an alleyway lined with wheelie bins and piles of flattened cardboard boxes. Nothing happened. No gunshots, no blinding lights, no shouts to surrender. It was cold and wet. The sky was yellowy-grey. The air smelled of traffic fumes.

I hitched the rucksack over my shoulder, pulled down my hat and headed for the street.

8

A thin grey drizzle of rain was falling when I came out of the hotel alleyway on to the street. The roads were busy, packed with rush-hour traffic, and the narrow pavements were crowded with people on their way to work. I glanced down the street to my left. The hotel entrance was about twenty metres away. Two uniformed policemen were guarding the doors, and standing next to them was a man in a bulky black coat. The man in the coat was talking to someone on a hand-held radio. Police vehicles were parked on double-yellow lines in front of the hotel – two patrol cars, a Transit van, a Range Rover.

I stepped back into the alleyway, wiped some sweat from my brow, then cautiously leaned out and took another look.

The hotel doors were opening now. A familiar-looking head popped out and said something to the man in the coat. The man in the coat listened, then nodded, and the head popped back in again.

Ryan.

The man in the coat said something to one of the police officers, then he moved down the steps and started scanning the street. I waited until he was looking away from me, then I stepped out of the alleyway and turned right, walking as confidently as I could. No faltering, no running, no looking back. I was just another body in the street. Same as all the rest. Going to school, going to work . . . just another human being.

A short distance ahead of me, a single-decker bus was juddering to a halt at a bus stop. As the doors swooshed open and a ragged queue of people started shuffling forward, I joined the back of the queue and started shuffling along with them – just another passenger, going to school, going to work. Same as all the rest. We smelled of sweat and damp clothing. We slid our feet, taking tiny little steps, inching towards the bus doors. We were impatient and tired, cold and wet.

Rubbing wearily at the side of my face, I risked a quick glance at the hotel.

There were more men milling around the entrance now. More men, more searching eyes. More cars pulling up. As I watched, some of the men started running towards the alleyway.

Passers-by were beginning to stop and stare.

I heard a shout, the blip of a siren, street murmurings.

'What's going on?' someone in the bus queue said.

I kept my head down and kept shuffling. The queue was getting shorter. I was nearly there now.

Another shout rang out from the hotel: 'Round the back!'

I stepped on to the bus.

The man in front of me dropped some coins into the bus driver's tray.

'Stratford,' he said.

The driver pressed buttons.

The man took his ticket.

And now it was my turn. I had no idea where I was going. I didn't even know where I was. The driver was looking at me.

'Stratford,' I told him, dropping some coins into the tray.

He pressed buttons.

I took my ticket.

The doors closed, the bus lurched and we were away.

I moved along the aisle and sat down.

The bus was on the same side of the road as the hotel, so I knew we'd have to pass it, and I knew it seemed stupid. But I was hoping that Ryan and his men wouldn't expect me to be stupid. I was hoping they'd expect me to move *away* from the hotel, not towards it.

That's what I was hoping.

Even so, as the bus approached the hotel, I started hiding my face, turning away from the window . . . but then I realized that all the other passengers were staring curiously *through* the window, trying to see what was going on at the hotel, which made me look out of place. And I didn't want to look out of place. Out of place was out of place. Out of place was bad. So, pulling down the brim of my hat, I joined in with everyone else and stared through the window at the hotel.

The entrance was crowded now. Uniformed police, hotel staff, Ryan's men, Hayes . . . and there, standing alone in the midst of all the frenzy, was Ryan himself. Silver-eyed and alert. Motionless. Like a Buddhist assassin. Without moving his eyes, he barked an order to a man beside him, and immediately the man lifted a radio to his ear and gave out a message.

Power.

Ryan had to have power. Who else but a powerful man could place a false story in the newspapers? And he had to be clever too. He knew he couldn't tell the rest of the world about a sixteen-year-old kid who wasn't human, so he'd turned the kid into a murderer instead. And everyone hates a murderer. So now Ryan had the rest of the world on his side.

The bus moved on, past the hotel, and when I was sure that I hadn't been seen, and I was fairly sure that no one was following me, I settled back into the seat and tried to relax.

But I soon realized I couldn't.

The man sitting in front of me was reading a news-paper. It was the *Sun*, and he was looking at the sports pages, so I couldn't tell if my picture was on the front page or not, but as I cautiously gazed around the bus, I realized that most of the other passengers were reading newspapers too. And even if Ryan's story about me was only in the *Daily Express*, which I somehow doubted, there was still a good chance that someone on the bus was reading a newspaper with a photograph of me on the front.

I tugged down the brim of my hat, pulled my collar up and slouched down low in the seat. I was nothing . . . nothing worth looking at . . . just another tired passenger, going to school, going to work . . . slumped in the seat, leaning against the window, head in hand . . . tired and cold . . . same as all the rest.

It was the best I could do.

I felt empty.

Used up and dirty.

My clothes were damp with sweat and rain. My eyes hurt. The back of my neck was throbbing. My hands felt itchy, as if they were covered with some kind of invisible residue.

The bus moved on.

Things and places passed by. Shops, offices, cars, people. Normal people doing normal things – walking, talking, frowning, smiling. They all seemed distant to me now. Different. Disconnected. Unrelated. They weren't the same as me any more. I wasn't the same as them. I was here, they were there. And the world out there had become something else. It was an alien territory now, a place where I didn't belong. The only world left to me was the world that turned behind my eyes . . . and I wasn't even sure I could trust that.

I wasn't sure of anything.

What was I?

What could I be?

Where did I come from?

Was I born? Was I created?

Was I flesh and blood?

Or not?

And, if not, so what?

If I couldn't tell the difference, what difference did it make? What's the difference between complicated meat and complicated metal? What is a life? What makes a life?

History? Time? Memories? Senses? How do you see things? What do you see? How do you hear things? How do you feel? How do you do anything? How do you breathe? How do you grow? How do you think?

I wondered if I was going mad.

I knew it was possible.

This whole thing, everything that was happening to me . . . it could all be some kind of delusion. I could be imagining it all. Maybe I *had* killed Casing in a frenzied attack and this was the only way I could cope with it – by making it unreal, by making it something else . . . by making *myself* something else. I didn't know if that was possible or not, but I'd seen enough therapists over the years to know that I couldn't dismiss it.

It wasn't *im*possible.

But then, I thought, if I *am* going mad, if all of this *is* some kind of delusion, I shouldn't be aware of it, should I? Because being aware of it means it's not a delusion. And I *am* aware of it. So it can't be a delusion. So I'm probably not going mad after all.

But I wished that I was.

The bus stopped at a junction. A siren started wailing on the street behind us, and everyone on the bus looked out of the window as a police car screamed past in a blaze of flashing lights, and then – before I had time to think about it – it was gone again.

I breathed out quietly.

I put my hand inside my coat and gently felt my stomach.

Whatever it was that I'd seen last night . . . whatever it was, it was there. No illusion. No delusion. I saw it. It was there.

You have to accept it.

Accept it and what?

Nothing. Just accept it.

I glanced across at the man who'd been in front of me in the queue. The man going to Stratford. I studied him – lank hair, cheap jacket, sickly pale skin. What does *he* know about himself? I asked myself. Does he care how he works? Does he care what's inside his body? Does he *know* what's inside his body? No. He has no idea what makes him move, what makes him breathe, what makes him *him*. He doesn't keep his body alive – it uses him to keep *itself* alive.

About twenty minutes later the bus pulled into a bus depot and the lank-haired man started getting up out of his seat, so I guessed we were at Stratford. I got up and followed the man off the bus. He paused for a moment to light a cigarette, then he put his hands in his pockets and sloped away across the concourse.

He might not know what's inside his body, I thought to myself, but at least he knows where he's going.

I didn't have a clue where I was going. I was just standing there, looking around, seeing what there was to look at. I saw a futuristic-looking bus depot with a weird white roof. White Teflon pillars with upturned Teflon umbrellas on top. I saw a train station across the road. A broad paved area, buildings, lots of shiny black glass. And opposite me, on the other side of the road, I saw the entrance to a covered shopping centre. Colours, plastic, people.

I thought about it for a moment . . .

Bus depot.

Train station.

Shopping centre.

. . . then I headed off towards the station.

I bought a Travelcard from a ticket machine, took the Central Line to Liverpool Street, then changed to the Circle Line and got off at King's Cross. A maze of tunnels and escalators led me up to the mainline station, and I headed across the concourse towards the ticket office. I paused at the doors, took off my hat, then went inside.

The ticket office clerk was a fat black lady.

'Yes?' she said.

'Single to Edinburgh, please.'

Her fingers skipped over the buttons of her keyboard.

'When are you travelling?' she asked me.

'What?'

'When are you travelling?'

'Now, the next train.'

'£93.10,' she said.

I give her Ryan's Visa card. She swiped it through her machine and I hoped I'd guessed right. I knew they'd have a trace on Ryan's card, but I was guessing they wouldn't stop it. Because if they stopped it, I'd run, and they didn't want me to run. They just wanted to know where I was. So they'd let Ryan's card go through and then they'd get down here as quickly as they could. They'd surround the station. They'd search the trains. They'd question the ticket clerk – what did he look like, where was he going? – and she'd tell them what I looked like and where I was going. But she'd be wrong.

And I was right.

The credit card went through without any trouble. The ticket clerk passed me a receipt. I signed it – *David Ryan* – and passed it back. She didn't even look at the signature on the back of the card, just slipped me a train ticket and a copy of the receipt, then yawned and looked over her shoulder at a clock on the wall.

I left the ticket office, went back down to the Underground station and jumped on a Piccadilly Line train. As the doors closed and the train headed off into the darkness, I allowed myself a little smile. By the time Ryan and his people had got to King's Cross, surrounded the station, questioned the ticket clerk, searched the Edinburgh train and finally realized that I wasn't there, I'd not only be some*where* else but – with a little bit of luck – I'd be some*one* else too.

I sat back in the seat and closed my eyes.

For the first time in what felt like ages, I knew where I was going.

9

Until all this happened, I'd never really thought about my mother that much. I'd never tried to find her, or find out who she was. I'd never felt the need to find out why she didn't want me. What was the point? She didn't want me. She'd left me in a pram outside a maternity hospital. As far as I was concerned, that's all there was to it. I didn't have a mother. She just didn't exist.

But now . . .

Well, now it was different.

Now I *had* to think about it, because now there was a possibility that none of it was true. It was all a lie. I *wasn't* abandoned at birth. I *wasn't* an orphan. My mother's non-existence had nothing to do with her not wanting me: she simply didn't exist. I had no mother. Never did. I was just a thing – a birthless and ageless thing – and things don't have mothers.

I was still trying to think about it as I got off the Underground train at Finsbury Park, but I couldn't quite get hold of anything. My thoughts were floating, drifting . . . strangely unreal. It was as if I was stuck in a continuous awakening from a dream. Everything around me seemed detached and remote – the rainy streets, the dark skies, the taxi places and convenience stores. I was there, within it – moving, being, taking up space – but I had no natural connection to it. I had no belonging.

I started walking down Seven Sisters Road. It was raining hard now, soaking me to the skin. When I dipped my head, drops of rain dripped from my hat and I caught the drops on my tongue. They tasted cold and bitter.

I walked on, lost inside myself.

Looking for my self.

I knew I *had* a self, a past, a history, but it all seemed so vague – half-remembered images, broken pictures of places, people, feelings, days – and I didn't know if it really belonged to me or not. I didn't know what I could trust any more.

What could I trust?

All the Homes I'd ever lived in, all the foster parents, the carers, the social workers, the therapists . . . could I trust them? Maybe they'd never been what they seemed. Maybe they'd never been there to look after me – they'd been there to watch me instead. To observe me. To study me. Maybe they'd all been in on it from the start . . . whatever *it* was.

Maybe even Bridget was in on it.

It was painful to think about, but I knew it wasn't impossible – that she'd been part of it, that she'd known all along, that there'd been nothing wrong with her sister on Monday . . .

I didn't *want* to believe it.

But I just didn't know.

I didn't know what to believe any more.

*

I'd nearly reached Manor House now. The park was on my left and the junction with Green Lanes was just up ahead. There was a fried chicken place across the road. I wasn't hungry, but I hadn't eaten for a while and I knew I ought to get something inside me. Food. Fuel. Energy.

I needed food.

My body needed food . . .

It didn't make sense.

I breathed, I ate, I drank, I consumed. I excreted. I slept. I dreamed. I hurt. I was affected by drugs – alcohol, anaesthetic. I had bad feelings. Good feelings. I had desires. I got tired. I thought of things – good things, bad things, useless things. I didn't want to die. I laughed. I smiled. I hummed, I whistled, I yawned. I followed the functional rules of an organism. But I seemed to be made from non-organic materials . . .

It just didn't make sense.

It didn't matter.

I crossed the road, bought two pieces of chicken, fries and a coffee, then took it all back over the road, went into the park and sat down on a bench.

The chicken was undercooked. Hot on the outside and cold in the middle. The fries were hard and black round the edge, and the coffee was weak. But it was all right. It was food and drink. It was fuel. It was energy.

I shovelled it down and thought about where I was going.

It's hard to make friends when you're moving around all the time, and I'd spent all my life moving around. Different

Homes, different schools . . . a couple of years here, a couple of years there. I'd never spent more than a couple of years anywhere. So I'd learned a long time ago that it just wasn't worth getting attached to anyone, because as soon as you did, they were gone. And I'd always liked being on my own anyway. I'd never enjoyed all the stuff that goes with friendship – all the rules, all the games, all the ups and downs. And, besides, even if I had been bothered about making friends, it wouldn't have made much difference, because most people didn't seem to like me much anyway. I don't think they *dis*liked me. I mean, they didn't hate me or anything. I think they just found me unsettling . . .

I read something once that one of my social workers had written about me. We were in her office, discussing my monthly report, and when she got up and left the room for a minute I leaned over her desk and sneaked a look at my file. *Robert has always been a rather solitary boy,* she'd written. *Despite the disrupted nature of his schooling, he has a keen – if slightly strange – intelligence, and often displays a maturity beyond his years. Socially, however, he shows little interest in his surroundings, and at times can be worryingly undemonstrative and somewhat cold. Previous carers have found this discomforting, and unless Robert's problems are addressed, his prospects of finding a long-term placement remain poor.*

So maybe that's why people found me unsettling, because I was *undemonstrative and somewhat cold.* Or maybe they'd always sensed something unhuman about me. Or, then again, maybe they'd just never liked me that much.

I guess I'll never know.

Not that it matters.

All that matters – and all I'm trying to say – is that just because I didn't have any friends, that didn't mean I didn't *know* lots of people. Because I did. I'd been to dozens of schools and dozens of Homes, and over the years I'd met thousands of people.

And one of them was a kid called John Blake.

And it was Blake who'd taken me to see Eddi Ray.

And that's who I was going to see now.

I'd met John Blake a few years earlier when I was living at a Home on the outskirts of Chelmsford. He was a couple of years older than me, a real hard-head. One of those kids who live for the bad stuff – robbing, fighting, taking drugs. He didn't care what he did, and he didn't care what it did to him. He just did it. None of the other kids liked him much, and I didn't like him either, but for some weird reason he kind of latched on to me for a while. I don't know why, but he was always trying to get me to go places and do stuff with him. *Come on, Rob, let's go for a drink. Let's have some fun. Come on, I know where we can get some gear . . .*

That kind of thing.

I usually turned him down – *No thanks, John. I'm all right. Yeah, I'll see you later* – but when he asked me one day if I wanted to go to London with him, I surprised us both by saying yes.

I still don't know why I did it. Maybe I was just bored. Bored with saying no all the time, bored with never going anywhere. Bored with being boring. Or maybe it was something more than that. Maybe it was something to do with now . . .

Is that possible?

Could I have known things back then without being aware of it? Could I have known that John Blake was going to take me somewhere that might prove useful in the future?

I don't know.

Probably not.

But he *did* take me somewhere useful.

Eventually.

He spent most of that day in London getting wrecked – drinking with his hard-head friends, popping pills in tower blocks and squats, shoplifting in Oxford Street. He tried to get me to join in – *come on, Rob, have a drink, have a smoke, enjoy yourself* – but I was fine as I was. Just hanging around, watching. Just being there. It wasn't much fun and I wished I hadn't agreed to come, but it didn't really bother me. As far as I was concerned, it was just another time and another place.

It was some time in the late afternoon when John suddenly decided to visit Eddi Ray.

'Hey, Rob,' he said, 'tell you what . . . let's go see Eddi. You'll like her, man. She's cool.' He was talking like that by then – like he was full of shit. Which he was. 'She's my brother's ex,' he explained. 'Left him when he got banged up. Took over most of his business too.' He laughed. 'He's going to kill her when he gets out.'

And that was about all there was to it.

He took me to see Eddi Ray.

We went to her flat in Finsbury Park.

We hung around for an hour or so, and then she threw us out.

It wasn't much of a night to remember.

But I remembered it. Partly because Eddi Ray *was* really cool, and partly because she was just the kind of person I needed right now. But mostly I remembered it because no one knew that I knew her, apart from John Blake, and he'd died from an overdose about six months ago. So *no one* knew that I knew Eddi Ray. No one at all. And if no one knew, then Ryan wouldn't know.

I got up off the bench, dropped the chicken remains in a litter bin and started walking.

10

Eddi Ray's flat was on the seventh floor of a high-rise
tower block in a sprawling estate called Gillespie Heights.
There were about half a dozen other tower blocks on the
estate and they all looked pretty much the same – cold
and grey and scary. Some of the ground-floor flats had
bars on the windows, others had reinforced doors. There
were bicycles chained to balconies. Broken saplings. Broken
needles scattered on the ground.

As I cut across a patch of grass and followed the path-
ways into the estate, I kept my eyes open and my hand
on the pistol in my pocket.

After a while, Eddi's tower block came into sight. It
was straight ahead of me, standing tall and dark against
the North London sky. In front of the tower block, a bunch
of Asian kids were karate-kicking each other around a
ruined playground, and a skinny Alsatian mongrel was
squatting to crap by the swingless swings.

There was no one else around.

No one was watching me.

No silver eyes.

No men in suits or coats.

It was around midday now. The air felt tired and washed out.

I went inside the tower block and took the lift to the seventh floor.

The hallway was empty when I stepped out of the lift. It smelled of soup, cigarettes, marijuana, petrol and piss. Thick heavy bass booms were thumping out from a flat down below – *doomp doomp d-doomp, doomp doomp d-doomp, doomp doomp d-doomp*. The air was stale and the hallway was grimly lit – yellowy-white, scratched and cold. The walls seemed to lean inwards. At the end of the hallway, a bleak window showed a rectangle of rainy-day sky.

I walked towards it.

Doomp doomp d-doomp . . .

The beat went on.

Eddi's flat was 722. The door was fitted with black steel mesh. As I stood there staring at it, I suddenly realized that I hadn't given this much thought. What if she didn't let me in? What if she wasn't at home? What if she didn't even *live* here any more?

It was too late to start worrying now.

I took off my hat and rang the bell.

After about thirty seconds, a voice called out from behind the door, 'Who is it?'

A female voice. Sweet but hard.

I stared at the peephole in the door. 'My name's Robert Smith,' I told the invisible eye. 'I came here about a year ago with John Blake.'

'Who?'

I hesitated, wondering what she meant. Who's John Blake? Or who's Robert Smith?

'I'm Robert,' I said. 'I was here with John Blake –'

'He's dead.'

'Yeah, I know.'

'What's your name?'

'Robert Smith.'

'What do you want?'

I hesitated again. What *did* I want?

'I'm in trouble,' I told her. 'I need your help.'

Silence. I could feel her watching me through the peephole, thinking about me, deciding what to do.

'Does anyone know you're here?' she said.

'What?'

'Did you tell anyone else you were coming here?'

'No.'

'Just a minute.'

I heard bolts thunking, chains rattling, locks unlocking . . . then the door finally opened and there she was – Eddi Ray. Black vest, ripped jeans. Peroxide hair, short and spiky. A sculpted face. Pale skin glinting with studs and rings.

She was a lot prettier than I remembered.

Pretty and hard.

She looked over my shoulder, checking that I was alone, then she stepped back and ushered me inside.

It was a fairly big flat. A large front room, two bedrooms, a hallway, a kitchen, a bathroom. There were locks on all the doors, and the windows were masked with heavy black curtains. The only light in the front room came from the flickering glow of countless computer monitors and TV screens. CNN played silently on a widescreen TV in the corner. CCTV images stuttered on a black-and-white portable – images of the hallway outside, the lobby, the estate. The room was filled with equipment – laptops, PCs, printers, scanners, phones, copiers, cameras, work desks, tools, piles of papers. The air hummed with electric heat.

'You're wet,' Eddi said to me.

'It's raining.'

She nodded, smiling at me. Her smile didn't look right – too false, too kind. I couldn't work it out.

'Sit down,' she said, gesturing at a leather settee. 'You want a drink or something?'

I shook my head. 'I'm all right, thanks.'

I put my rucksack on the floor and sat down. Eddi remained standing. I didn't know how old she was, but I guessed she was around nineteen or twenty. She was slim and short, strong, well balanced. Her feet were bare, her toenails painted black. She had very blue eyes. She was still smiling at me . . .

And that bothered me. She shouldn't have been smiling at me. She should have been wary, wondering what I wanted, wondering what I was doing here.

'It's a shame about John,' she said.

I shrugged.

She lit a cigarette. 'You know Curt's dead too, don't you?'

'Who?'

'Curtis, John's brother. My ex.'

'Really?'

She nodded. 'Never got out of prison. Got popped inside.' She drew on her cigarette and smiled again. 'So,' she said, blowing out smoke, 'what can I do for you, Robert? How can I help?'

Whatever I was, I'd lived my life by certain rules.

Never believe anything.

Never back down.

Never get used to anything.

Never trust anyone who offers to help.

Over the years, I'd expanded that last one into never trusting anyone at *all*, but the basic principle was still the same: charity stinks.

Selfless charity doesn't exist. Everyone wants something. No one does anything for free. There's always a catch.

It sounds pretty dirty, I know. But that's how it is.

So, when Eddi offered to help me – all smiles and kind looks and caring blue eyes – I knew that something was wrong. I could feel it, sense it. I could see it in her eyes. She knew something. She was treating me like a friend, but I wasn't a friend. I was just some kid who'd come round to her flat one night with her ex-boyfriend's brother. It was over a year ago. I'd only stayed for an hour, barely said a word. She shouldn't have even remembered me. But here she was, treating me like a long-lost friend. And that wasn't right.

'Could I use your bathroom, please?' I asked her.

'Of course,' she said. 'It's just down the hall on the left.'

I could feel her watching me as I got up and crossed the room. I was trying to stay calm, trying to act as normally as possible. But I was also trying to look round her flat without letting her know that I was looking. I didn't know what I was looking for – something out of place, something that might tell me something . . .

Whatever it was, I didn't see it.

I went down the hallway and into the bathroom. I peed. Flushed the toilet. Washed my hands. Then I looked in the mirror. And as my face looked back at me – bedraggled and damp – I suddenly realized that I *had* seen something in the front room. I knew it. I'd seen something. I still didn't know what it was, but I knew I'd seen something.

I closed my eyes and pictured myself leaving the room. What had I seen? Settee, carpet, computers, table . . .

Table.

That was it. There was a table by the door. I could see it now. A little wooden table, a telephone table or something. And on the table . . . on the table there was a newspaper. An *Evening Standard*. Folded in half. Front page. I closed my eyes tighter and focused on something at the foot of the front page . . . the bottom edge of a photograph . . . a familiar grainy photograph.

'Shit,' I said, opening my eyes.

My photograph was on the front page of the *Evening Standard*. Ryan's false story about me – *Robert Smith, frenzied attack, horrendous killing* . . .

Eddi had seen it.

'Shit.'

When I went back into the front room, Eddi was sitting on the settee, smoking a cigarette. I paused in the doorway and looked down at the table. The newspaper had gone. I looked over at Eddi again.

She smiled at me. 'All right?'

I looked round the room, then put my hand in my pocket. 'Where is it?' I asked her.

'What?'

'The newspaper. Where is it?'

'What newspaper? What are you talking about?'

I looked down at the table again, then back at Eddi. 'The *Evening Standard*,' I said. 'It was here when I went to the bathroom.'

'I'm sorry,' she said, still smiling. 'I really don't know –'

She stopped speaking as I pulled the pistol from my pocket and aimed it at her head. She stopped smiling too. Her mouth dropped open and she just sat there, staring in surprise at the pistol.

I was surprised to see it too. I wasn't quite sure how it'd got there. One second it'd been in my pocket, the next thing I knew I was looking down its barrel into Eddi's shocked eyes.

'What are you *doing*?' she said.

'Where is it?' I asked her again.

'What *is* this? What's going on?'

'The newspaper, Eddi. Where's the newspaper?'

'What newspaper?'

Something was happening inside me now. Something was taking over. And I didn't want it to be there. I wanted Eddi to give me the paper before I lost control.

'Please,' I said to her, 'just give it to me.'

She tried smiling again, but her fear and surprise wouldn't let her. Her lips were too tight to smile. 'Come on, Robert,' she said, trying to sound cheerful. 'This is stupid. I don't know what –'

The pistol kicked in my hand. I heard a dull *thwack*, a gasp of breath, then the room was still and silent. *Doomp doomp d-doomp*. Eddi was frozen white, breathing hard, staring wide-eyed at me. I'd pulled the trigger, fired a shot into the leather settee. I could feel the shock in my bones.

'The newspaper,' I said quietly.

Without taking her eyes off me, Eddi reached under a settee cushion and pulled out the newspaper.

'Bring it here,' I told her.

'Look,' she said. 'I don't want –'

'Bring it to me.'

She got up slowly and brought the paper over to me. I took it from her outstretched hand.

'Sit down,' I told her.

She backed across the room and sat down rigidly on the settee. I stared at her for a moment, then unfolded the newspaper and placed it on the table. I kept the pistol levelled at Eddi, glanced at her again, then turned my eyes to the front page.

They'd used the same photograph as the *Daily Express*, the one that made me look shadowy and gaunt.

The caption beneath the photo said:

ROBERT SMITH: £50,000 REWARD

I stared at the words for a while – ROBERT SMITH: £50,000 REWARD – and then, with the same sinking feeling I'd felt in the hotel, I forced myself to read the story.

REWARD IN HUNT FOR KILLER

Essex police are still seeking a 16-year-old youth in connection with the brutal murder of Professor Ian Casing on Monday.

Robert Smith (pictured above) is described as slim, 5ft 11in tall, with medium-length black hair and dark brown eyes.

Detective Superintendent Mark Dennet, leading the investigation, believes that Smith may have fled to London. 'We have unconfirmed sightings in the Stratford and King's Cross areas,' said DS Dennet. 'Smith may be armed, and we would advise the public not to approach him but contact the police immediately if they know where he is.'

A reward of £50,000 is being offered for information leading to an arrest and conviction.

There was a phone number at the end of the article. A London number. I took Ryan's wallet out of my pocket, found his business card and checked the number against the one in the newspaper.

They weren't the same.

I looked over at Eddi. She was just sitting there, staring at me. Her eyes were still shocked and her face was rigid with fear, but she didn't look out of control. She wasn't terrified.

'You've seen this?' I said, showing her the newspaper.

She nodded.

'Have you told anyone?'

She shook her head.

'You'd better not be lying.'

'I'm not lying,' she said. 'How could I have told anyone? You've only just got here.'

'Why did you hide the paper?'

'Why do you think? It says you *killed* someone –'

'I didn't.'

She shrugged.

'It's a set up,' I told her. 'I haven't killed anyone.'

'You've got a gun,' she said. 'You took a shot at me, for Christ's sake. What am I supposed to think?'

I was coming back to myself now. I was beginning to feel like Robert Smith again.

'It's not what it seems,' I said.

'No?'

'No.'

'What is it, then?'

I didn't say anything. What could I say? How could I explain anything? I didn't *know* anything. And even if I did, it wouldn't have made any difference. She'd never have believed me.

'What are you going to do?' she asked me.

'What?'

'What are you going to do?'

'I don't know,' I said. 'What are *you* going to do?'

She smiled warily. 'Look, Robert,' she said. 'I was frightened, OK? I saw the thing in the newspaper about you, and I remembered who you were, that's all. I wasn't going to do anything about it. What *could* I do? I didn't know where you were until you turned up here. And then I didn't know what to do. It was just a bit of a shock, you know? I mean, what would you do if I came round to your place and you'd just seen a story in the newspaper saying that

I was a murderer?' She lit another cigarette. 'I panicked, that's all. I didn't know what to do.'

'I didn't kill anyone,' I told her again.

'OK,' she said, 'if you say so. But I don't really care what you've done. I'm not going to grass you up, am I?'

'Why not? £50,000 is a lot of money.'

She laughed. 'You think I want anything to do with the police? Come on, Robert . . . you know what I do.' She looked at me. 'I mean, that's why you're here, isn't it?'

She was right. I *was* there because of what she did. Because what Eddi did was fake ID. That's how she made her living – producing, providing and selling fake ID. That's what all the equipment was for – the scanners and the cameras and all the rest of it. Fake ID. Passports, driving licences, birth certificates, medical cards. Anything and everything. If you had the right money, Eddi Ray could give you a brand-new life.

The trouble was, I didn't have the right money.

And now there was this £50,000 reward to think about too.

Eddi was smart. She had to be in her business. And I was pretty sure she could work out a way to get hold of the reward money without the police finding out what she did. But I needed her. I needed a new identity. Name, appearance, documents. I needed a brand-new life. Without it, I wasn't going to last much longer.

We were staring at each other now. Eddi was thinking, I was thinking. We were both trying to work it all out.

'I don't want any trouble,' I said.

'What trouble?' she said breezily. 'There's no trouble. Everything's fine.'

'No, it's not.' I tapped the newspaper with the pistol. 'If these people find me, they'll kill me.'

She laughed. 'Don't be stupid –'

'They'll kill me, and then they'll kill you.'

She shook her head. 'The police don't *kill* people –'

'It's not the police.'

'What do you mean? It says in the paper –'

'They'll kill you, Eddi. Believe me. If they find out I've been here, they won't let you live.'

She started to say something else, but the look in my eyes made her change her mind. She was remembering the gunshot now. Remembering what I could be. She lowered her eyes and looked away.

'I need to be someone else,' I told her.

She looked up at me. 'What?'

'I need to be someone else. I need some ID. Passport, driving licence, bank account, credit card –'

'How much?' she said.

'How much what?'

'Money. How much money have you got?'

'Not much,' I admitted. 'A couple of hundred in cash, a Switch card, some credit cards . . .'

Eddi frowned at me. 'That's it? That's all you've got?' She shook her head. 'I can't do much for that.'

I pointed the pistol at her. 'I think you can.'

We spent the rest of the day making me into someone else. It took a long time, but Eddi was very thorough. Even though she was working at gunpoint, she took pride in her work, and she did a good job.

First of all, she took me into the bathroom to cut my hair. It was quite awkward, because I wouldn't let her stand behind me with a pair of scissors in her hand, just in case she decided to stick them in my neck, and if she was standing behind me, I couldn't cover her with the pistol. So I sat in a chair and made her stand in front of me, which meant she had to lean right over me to get to the back of my head, and that meant I got a face full of her breasts. Which was kind of unsettling. And she knew it. So she leaned in more than she needed to.

So I was sitting there holding the gun to her belly, and she was pressing herself into my face, and it was making me feel stuff . . . physical stuff. It was getting to me. Exciting me. And I wondered how that could be. I mean, if I wasn't human . . . how did it *work*? How did a certain touch make a certain part of me do certain things? And that got me thinking about other stuff too – about me, and girls, and what I'd done. Because I *had* done things. I had *had* sex. Not very often, and probably not very well, but – as far as I knew – there hadn't been anything unusual about it. Everything had worked.

And I was starting to think about that, wondering what it meant, and I was trying *not* to think about what was happening to me now . . .

Then Eddi said, 'Keep *still*, for Christ's sake. Stop wriggling around.'

. . . and I forced myself to think of nothing.

After she'd trimmed my hair, she asked me if I wanted it dyed.

'I don't know,' I said. 'What do you think?'

'It's up to you,' she shrugged. 'You're the one with the gun.'

'You think I *want* to do this?' I asked her. 'If I had the money, I'd pay you. But I don't. So I don't have any choice.'

'You could trust me.'

I smiled at her.

She shrugged again, but this time there was a hint of a smile on her face. 'Do you want your hair dyed or not?'

'Will it make me look different?'

She nodded. 'Quite a bit. I can give you some glasses too. They'll look like prescription glasses, but they're clear.'

'OK,' I said.

'You want it dyed?'

'Yeah.'

'What colour?'

We settled on blond.

This time, as Eddi was leaning over me, massaging all kinds of crap into my hair, I tried to ignore her body. Her fingers, her hands, her breasts, her belly . . . I tried to just think of them as things. Shapes, textures, forms, matter.

But it didn't work.

A certain part of me still did certain things.

By early evening, Eddi had started work on my new identity. I already had a new look – short blond hair and designer glasses – and a new passport photograph – smartly dressed and clean-shaven – and now Eddi was finding me a new name. She was sitting at her desk, surrounded by blank passports and blank driving licences and all kinds of other stuff: official stamps, computer printouts, credit cards, birth certificates. She was sifting her way through it all, checking this and checking that, tapping at a keyboard every now and then, glancing at the screen, making notes, chain-smoking cigarettes. Meanwhile, I was just sitting there, watching her, occasionally running my fingers through my soft blond hair.

I felt all right.

For now.

I felt strangely comfortable.

'How long have you been doing this?' I asked Eddi.

'What?'

'Fake ID . . . how long have you been doing it?'

'A while,' she said.

'How did you get started? I mean, how did you learn how to do it?'

'Curtis.'

'What – he taught you?'

She nodded. 'It used to be his business. He taught me everything I know. How it all works, how to make money, how to stay out of jail.'

'So how come *he* ended up in jail?'

'I grassed him up.'

I stared at her. She was bent over the table in concentration, looking through a lens at one of my new passport photographs.

'Why?' I asked her.

'What?'

'He was your boyfriend. Why did you grass him up?'

'I wanted his business.'

I watched her in silence for a while, wondering if she was really that ruthless, or if there was something she wasn't telling me. Curtis had been her boyfriend. They could have had relationship problems, personal problems, problems she didn't want to tell me about. And, besides, why should she tell me anything anyway? I had a gun on her. I was forcing her to work for nothing. Why should she even *talk* to me?

I carried on watching her. She was leafing through a pile of birth certificates now, looking at the names and birth dates.

'Do I get a choice?' I asked her.

'What?'

'A choice of name.'

'No,' she said, without looking up from her desk.

From the tone of her voice, I guessed she wanted me to shut up and let her concentrate. So I shut up and let her concentrate.

After a while, though, she said, 'How old are you?'

'Sorry?'

She looked over at me. 'I need to find you a birth certificate. It has to be someone who's dead, someone who'd be about the same age as you. What are you – eighteen, nineteen?'

'Sixteen,' I told her.

She raised her eyebrows. 'You could easily pass for nineteen.'

I smiled at her. 'I've always looked older than I am.'

She picked out one of the birth certificates and studied it. 'This'll have to do – 30 March 1987.' She looked over at me again. 'You'll have to be eighteen. It's the best I can do.'

'OK.'

She glanced back at the birth certificate. 'Robin Ames.'

'What?'

'That's your name – Robin Ames.'

'Robin?'

She grinned. 'You can still call yourself Rob.'

'I've *never* called myself Rob.'

'Well, you'd better start getting used to it . . . Rob.'

It was OK. The rest of the evening, the rest of the night
. . . it was fine. Eddi worked away – printing and copying,
cutting and pasting, sticking and stamping – and I watched
her doing her stuff. We talked a bit. I asked her questions.
She answered them. Sometimes we just sat in silence.

The hours passed by.

It was still an awkward situation, what with the gun
and everything, but we both did our best to ignore it. It
wasn't always easy, though. Especially when one of us had
to use the bathroom. The first time Eddi had to go, I went
into the bathroom first and checked it out. It seemed safe
enough. The window was too small to climb through, and
we were on the seventh floor anyway. And I couldn't find
anything she could use as a weapon. No razor blades, no
pointy objects.

'All right,' I said to her, stepping out. 'I'll wait for you
here.'

She shook her head. 'How many times do I have to tell
you? I'm not going to *do* anything.'

I didn't answer.

'I suppose you want me to leave the door open?' she
said.

'No,' I muttered, 'that's all right.'

'You're too kind,' she said sarcastically, shutting the door in my face.

An hour or so later, when I had to use the bathroom, I didn't know what to do. I thought about it for a long time. Eventually, I gave Eddi a choice.

'Look,' I told her, 'this is really embarrassing, but I need to use the bathroom, and I can't just leave you alone.'

'Yes, you can.'

'I can't.'

'What do you think I'm going to do? Run away? Call the police?'

I shook my head. 'I'm sorry. I can't do it.'

'Why not?'

'I just can't. You'll either have to stand by the bathroom door or I'll have to tie you up.'

'You *what*? I'm not going to stand by the door watching you take a *piss*.'

'I'm really sorry . . .'

She glared at me for a moment, then her face suddenly softened into a smile. 'You know what'd be a whole lot easier?'

'What?'

'Lock me in the bedroom. Easier for me, easier for you.' She grinned. 'And a lot less pervy for both of us.'

I blushed then.

She led me down the hall to her bedroom and waited in the doorway while I looked it over. I removed a baseball bat from beside the bed, a phone from the bedside table, and then I had to embarrass myself again by searching through all her cupboards and drawers. Clothes, underwear, women's things . . .

'Enjoying yourself?' Eddi said from the doorway.

I looked at her – sleek and slim, smiley and hot – and I wished that things were different. The same, but different. I wished I was here, just being here, and Eddi was just being like this because she wanted to be like this . . .

But, deep down, I knew that if things *were* different, I'd never have come here in the first place. And, even if I had, Eddi wouldn't have let me in. She wouldn't even have remembered me if she hadn't seen my picture in the newspaper.

I locked her in the bedroom and used the bathroom.

It was almost midnight by the time Eddi had finished my new ID. She called me over to her desk and showed me everything she'd done. I had a passport and a driving licence (complete with three points). I had credit cards (Visa and Mastercard). I had a birth certificate. I had gas bills and water bills and letters from my bank. I had a National Insurance number. I even had an unpaid parking ticket.

'The passport's fine,' Eddi explained. 'I've entered it into their files. But the driving licence won't stand up to much. I can't access the DVLA's database. The address on everything should be OK. It won't check out against the electoral roll, but that's not a problem. If anyone asks, just tell them you haven't lived there very long.' She showed me the credit cards. 'The PIN's four zeros, the credit limit's £2,000 on each. If you're taking out cash, they've both got a daily limit of £500. But once you've used them, max them out fast. They won't last forever – OK?'

'Right.'

She put everything into a carrier bag and passed it to me. 'That's it. If I'd had more time, I could have got you a chequebook. But you can use all this to open a genuine bank account if you want. You'll need to get yourself a proper address . . .' She yawned, and her voice trailed off.

'That's great,' I told her. 'Thanks.'

She nodded. 'You know how much I could have charged for all this?'

'A lot, I expect.'

'Enough to pay for my holiday twice over.'

Holiday?

'What holiday?' I said.

Eddi looked at me, suddenly hesitant. 'You're letting me go, right?'

'Go where?'

'Spain. I'm flying out tomorrow. Andalusia.' She looked genuinely concerned. 'You're not going to stop me going, are you?'

I didn't know the answer to that. I hadn't really thought about what I was going to do next. I'd got what I'd come for – my new ID – but what good would it be if Eddi started shouting her mouth off as soon as I left? If Ryan found out that I had a new name – and he was bound to find out if Eddi went to the police – then there was no point in having a new name.

'Robert?' Eddi said.

I looked at her. 'It's all right. I'll be gone by to-morrow . . .'

'So I can go?'

'Yeah.' I smiled at her. 'Don't forget your passport.'

*

I still didn't know what I was going to do. I had no idea. I was just playing for time. Waiting to see what happened.

Looking back on it now, it might have been better if I'd done something else. Not waited. Not played for time. Maybe I should have just got up and walked out the door . . .

But I didn't.

'You can stay the night if you want,' said Eddi.

That's how it started – *You can stay the night if you want*.

'No,' I told her. 'I'd better go . . .'

'Where? Where are you going to go?'

'I'll find somewhere.'

'You haven't got any money.'

'I've got credit cards –'

'Christ, Robert,' she sighed, 'why don't you just *relax*? When are you going to realize that I'm not going to *do* anything? I'm *not* going to tell anyone where you are. I'm *not* going to call the police. I'm not going to tell anyone *anything*. OK?'

I looked at her. She was lying on the settee with a glass of wine in one hand and a joint in the other. It was her third glass of wine, second joint. She was pretty whacked out.

It was one o'clock in the morning now. Sweet-smelling smoke was drifting in the air and the muffled music was still booming down below. *Doomp doomp d-doomp, doomp doomp d-doomp, doomp doomp d-doomp* . . .

Eddi smiled at me, a lopsided grin. 'Look,' she said softly, 'you can't sit there all night with a gun in your hand. It's ridiculous. Just put it down, for God's sake. Come *on*, Robert. Put the gun down, have some wine, get some sleep.'

It was tempting. And I was tempted. I didn't want to leave. It was cold outside. And I didn't want to sit here all night with a gun in my hand. I didn't want any wine either, but when Eddi rolled off the settee and started pouring me a glass, I didn't do anything to stop her.

I knew I shouldn't have any wine. Apart from not liking it, I had to stay focused. I had to stay sharp. It was no good just sitting there, staring at Eddi's backside as she knelt down on the floor and poured me a glass of wine . . . it wasn't doing me any good. The shape of her body, the texture, the form, the matter . . .

Certain things, uncertain things.

'I can't help it,' I heard myself mutter. 'I'm only human.'

Eddi looked puzzled as she brought the wine over, but she was too far gone to be over-puzzled.

'D'you say something?' she said, passing me the wine.

'Just talking to myself,' I told her.

When she sat down next to me, she misbalanced slightly and leaned into me. Her hand pushed against my thigh. She giggled.

'Sorry,' she said.

'It's all right.'

'I would have done it for you,' she said quietly, still leaning into me.

'Done what?'

'All the ID stuff. I would have done it for you anyway. For nothing.' She smiled at me. 'I mean, I'm not saying I wouldn't have taken your money if you'd had any . . . but you didn't need this.' She touched the pistol in my hand. My fingers tightened on the grip. She looked at me, still smiling, her lips moist with wine. 'You look good,' she said. 'Your hair . . .'

She touched my hair.

Stroked it.

I felt very human.

'Drink your wine,' she whispered.

Something inside me tried to stop me, but I ignored it. The wine was strong and sweet, and I drank deeply, enjoying the sensation as it soaked down into my belly, then rose up into my heart like a warm balloon.

Eddi took the empty glass from my hand and placed it on the floor. She looked at me, her eyes shining blue, then she reached over and gently removed the pistol from my other hand. She carefully placed that on the floor too.

Then she smiled again.

And kissed me slowly.

And took me off to bed.

11

nunuuuuuuuunuuuuunnnununnunsaasaaa
tah I I I juh juh juhs nee thhahh ah hta ta ta mburra
borrofyourfl at at at fuwhile   fcka ah ah couplewees eeks
na hn na no jus borrow it   I just need to nkborrow
it. cantellyou. no. no. no. pa you pay you. fi thousand th
tht yes. five thousand. two weeks   so I live there.
yes yes

A voice.

No I cant tellyou. yes yesYes   Issre re really important

Whiteness. Sweet wine.

Memories of a voice.

Lie down, Robert. Take off your clothes . . .

Sheets. White fog. The taste of lipstick and wine. What is
this? My head hurts. I'm tired. I'm lying on my back with
my eyes closed. A white sheet covers my body. Beneath
the sheet I'm naked.

Words . . .

Here, let me help you . . . Christ, what's that?
  Uh . . . ?
What happened to you? Your stomach, your arm . . .
you're covered in scars.
  Scars . . .

I can't remember.
  I can't move.
  White fog . . .
  Sex fog.
  Sounds.

Doomp doomp d-doomp.

Swimming in white.
  Black white black . . .
  Whiteness whirling around and around, sucking me
down into terrible places . . .
  Everything's black.
  White black white.
  It's all the same.
  What is this?
  Where am I?

Doomp doomp d-doomp.

I'm drunk . . . but I'm not drunk. I'm something else.
Somewhere else.

Voices. A whispered voice. In the front room. I can hear a voice.

When can you let me know? I need to know.

Telephone. Eddi. She's talking on the phone.

Wake up.

It's impossible.

Kill the dream.

Something inside me . . .

Move.

Something electric shifting inside me.

Get up.

Move.

Get up!

And then I was moving. Getting up, getting out of bed, feeling the cold night air on my naked skin. Feeling everything. I was awake now. I was moving. Across the bedroom, opening the door, into the front room.

Eddi was standing by the settee, talking on the phone. She

was half-dressed in ripped jeans and a white lace bra. The pistol was on the table beside her. When she saw me, she stopped talking, put down the phone and picked up the pistol.

'Stay where you are,' she said, raising the gun.

Her eyes were steady.

I didn't stay where I was. I walked towards her, naked and knowing. I knew what had happened now. She'd drugged me. Drugged the wine. And now she was trying to sell me out. I carried on walking towards her. I knew she wouldn't shoot me.

She pulled the trigger – *BANG!* The gun jerked in her hand and something punched me in the arm. Something hot and hard. I staggered slightly, but it didn't seem to hurt that much. I just carried on walking.

Eddi stared at me. I could see the cold light of my face in her eyes. She was trying to level the gun again now, but she was too late. I was too close. Right in front of her. My arm shot out and I grabbed the pistol, forcing her hand down to the side. She grunted, hissed, fought like a snake.

'Shit . . . bastard, fuck off . . .'

She wouldn't let go of the gun.

I grabbed her wrist in both hands, gripped it tight. Twisted it, squeezed it, yanked it . . .

She wouldn't let go.

Suddenly, she doubled over and bit my hand, sinking her teeth to the bone. As the pain ripped through me, I wrenched the pistol out of her hand, whipped up my arm and cracked the barrel against her head. She grunted, then sighed, and I felt her go weak. And then she just slumped to the floor.

Breathing hard, I stepped back and looked down at her. She was lying face up against the wall, her right arm twisted awkwardly under her body. There was an ugly gash on the side of her head, but it didn't look too deep. And I could see she was still breathing. I crouched down beside her and gently pulled her arm out from under her body. Then I stood up and gazed down at her again.

Despite everything, I still thought she was beautiful. White bra, ripped jeans, blonde hair, pale skin . . . beautiful and pure and quiet.

I stood there for a long time, just looking at her.

Then I went into the bedroom and got dressed.

When I came back, I sat down in an armchair and examined the bullet wound in my arm. It was starting to hurt now, but it didn't look too bad – a shallow groove in the flesh, a red-raw slice. The bullet had only clipped me. I held my arm up to my eyes and gazed at the injured flesh. Beneath a film of blood, I could see the severed ends of tiny silver filaments – dull on the outside, shiny in the middle. Like freshly cut cables. They seemed to be growing, renewing themselves. My hand, too, was healing itself. The ripped skin where Eddi had bitten me was already flaking off. Fresh white skin was forming underneath.

Rebuilding the machine.

I sat back in the armchair and waited for Eddi to wake up.

By the time she'd come round and come to her senses, it was just gone three o'clock in the morning. The thumping music had finally stopped and the flat was cold and silent.

I'd fetched a glass of water for Eddi, and now she was sitting on the settee, cradling the glass in her hands . . . just sitting there looking at me. I was gazing back at her. The pistol was resting in my lap.

'What?' she said eventually. 'What do you want me to say?'

'I don't know.'

'I'm not going to apologize, if that's what you want.'

I shook my head. 'I just want to get this sorted out.'

She reached up and touched the cut on her head, wincing slightly.

'How does it feel?' I asked her.

'Horrible.' She glanced at me. 'How does it look?'

'You can hardly see it.'

She lit a cigarette. 'How's your arm?'

'It's all right.' I smiled. 'Just a flesh wound.'

She didn't smile back. 'What about all the rest of it?' she said. 'All those scars on your body. Christ . . .' She shook her head at the memory. 'What the hell happened to you?'

'It's a long story.'

'Is that why you're here? I mean, whatever happened . . . is that what this is all about? The story in the paper and everything?'

'You should have asked me that before you drugged me.'

'I didn't know –'

'You knew about it when you were on the phone. You'd seen all the scars by then. But you were still trying to get the reward money, weren't you?'

'No, I wasn't –'

135

'Yes, you were. I *heard* you . . . I heard you talking on the phone. I know what you were trying to do. You were trying to borrow someone's flat so you could sell me out without the police coming round here.'

'I wasn't trying to borrow anyone's *flat*,' she insisted. 'You've got it all wrong. I was just –'

She stopped suddenly as the phone started ringing. We both turned our heads and stared at it. After about ten rings, the answerphone message kicked in – *Hi, this is Eddi, leave a message*. The phoned beeped and a man started talking. 'Hey, Ed,' the voice said, 'it's Lawrence. I think we got cut off earlier on. Look . . . I've been thinking about what you were saying. You know, about borrowing the flat? Well, the thing is . . . it's just a bit difficult right now. I know you said it's really important, but I'm going to have to say no. I'm really sorry, Ed . . . hope you don't mind. Call me back if you want to talk about it. See you later.'

I looked at Eddi. 'You were saying?'

She didn't look at me, just stared at the floor.

'What were you going to do?' I asked her. 'Stick me in a bin bag and drag me across London to this Lawrence's flat?'

She shrugged. 'I hadn't worked that bit out yet.'

'And what did you think I'd do when you turned me over to the police? Did you think I wouldn't tell them anything about you?'

'Like I said, I hadn't really thought about it . . .'

'Yeah, well . . . you would have been wasting your time anyway. The only reward you would have got was a bullet in the back of your head.' I looked at her again. 'I told you before, Eddi, these people, the ones that are after me

. . . once they've got me, they'll kill you. There's no reward. No £50,000. It's all a lie.'

She sat there smoking her cigarette for a while, just smoking quietly, staring at the floor. Then she took a final drag, put it out in an ashtray and slowly looked up at me. 'How did you wake up?' she asked me. 'There was enough stuff in your wine to knock you out for at least three or four hours. How the hell did you wake up?'

I shook my head. 'You wouldn't believe me if I told you.'

'Try me.'

'Why? Why should I tell you anything? You drugged me. You lied to me. You *shot* me, for Christ's sake –'

'You shot me first.'

'I didn't *shoot* you . . . I shot *at* you.'

'Oh, right,' she sneered, 'and shooting *at* someone is all right, is it?'

I shook my head, exasperated.

Eddi stared at me. 'Why don't you just tell me the truth, Robert?'

'What truth?'

'The truth you've been hiding ever since you got here. I know you want to tell someone about it, I can see it all over your face. It's driving you mad, isn't it? You have to tell *someone*. And right now, I'm all you've got.'

I didn't say anything for a while. I just sat there in the dead-of-night silence, thinking about things. There was a lot to think about. A lot of hard choices to make. A lot of unknowns to consider. But, in the end, it all boiled down to one simple question: what do I do with Eddi?

As I thought about it, I remembered talking to Kamal in his car. I remembered asking him what he would do if he was me.

If I were you? he'd said.

What would you do?

I think you have two choices. Either you trust me or you kill me. If I were you, I would trust me.

Why?

Because you don't want to kill me.

I don't want to trust you either.

It's the better option.

Is it?

I think so.

You would.

I do.

'Have you got a car?' I asked Eddi.

'What?'

'A car . . . have you got a car?'

'Yeah . . . I've got a car. Why do you want –'

'Do you really want to know the truth about me?'

'Yeah, but –'

'Yes or no.'

'Yes,' she sighed. 'I want to know the truth.'

'Right,' I said. 'Get yourself dressed. We're going for a drive.'

12

It was still dark as we drove out of London and headed up the A12 into Essex. The roads were quiet, the air was icy, the sky was starless and black. A pale white moon shone brightly in the distance, and as we raced along through the morning darkness, I watched it moving around us. It seemed wary, like a circling dog. One minute it was off to our right, then it would disappear for a while, and then suddenly I'd see it looming up on the horizon in front of us. If I'd been able to see the man in the moon, I probably would have thought he was following us. But I've never been able to see him. I've never been able to see anything up there – no faces, no moon dogs, no lovers' broken hearts . . .

I just can't see it.

I looked across at Eddi. She hadn't spoken to me since we'd left the flat, and she didn't look back at me now. She was just sitting there, driving in silence, her face cold and blank. I guessed she was still upset with me for not telling her where we were going. Or why. All I'd told her was that if she wanted to know the truth about me, she'd have to come with me and get it from someone else.

'Why?' she'd said.

'Because if you get the truth from me, you won't believe it. But if you get it from someone else . . . well, you probably still won't believe it, but at least you won't think I'm crazy.'

'Why should I think you're crazy?'

'You'll find out when we get there.'

She didn't like the idea of driving off to an unknown place to meet an unknown person in the early hours of the morning, but she'd still gone along with it. I didn't know why. Maybe she was just curious. Or maybe she thought there was something in it for her. Or maybe she was just scared of what I might do if she refused. Whatever the reason, I didn't really care. If she *had* refused, I would have had to think of something else, and I didn't want to think of anything else. The truth was . . .

Well, that was it: the truth.

That's what this was all about – finding out the truth. Not for Eddi's sake, but for mine. I didn't really care if Eddi thought I was crazy or not, but *I* needed to know. I needed to prove to myself that I wasn't going mad, that I wasn't imagining all this, and the only way I could do that was by getting someone else to tell me. Someone who knew the truth.

The real truth.

I looked across at Eddi. She was wearing a little black hoodie over a loose white shirt, a fresh pair of ripped jeans, and a black felt beret, pulled down low to cover the cut on her head. Her lips were shiny with bright red lipstick.

'What?' she said suddenly.

'Sorry?'

'What are you looking at me like that for?'

'Like what?'

'Like you're *thinking* about me.'

'I'm not thinking about you.'

'No? What *are* you thinking about, then?'

'Nothing. I was just . . .'

'Just what? Just looking?' She glanced across at me, half-smiled, then turned her attention back to the road. I could feel her grinning at my embarrassment as I looked away, and I wasn't sure if she was making fun of me or just *having* some fun with me. Laughing *at* me or laughing *with* me. And as I gazed out through the windscreen, looking for the moon, I wondered why I cared either way.

What did it matter whether she liked me or not?

What difference did it make?

Why was I even thinking about it?

The moon had gone now. I couldn't see it anywhere. The road was still quiet and the air was still icy, but in the distance a hazy band of yellowy-grey light was creeping over the horizon, revealing the murky shapes of dawn-lit clouds. The day was beginning to stir.

I glanced at my reflection in the side-view mirror. With my neat blond hair and my designer glasses, I hardly recognized myself. It was like looking at someone else. It felt strange.

'Are we still going the right way?' Eddi asked me.

'Yeah,' I said. 'Just keep going. I'll tell you when to turn off.'

'How much further is it?'

'I don't know . . . where are we?'

'Somewhere near Chelmsford.' She looked across at me, struck by a sudden thought. 'Hey, this is where you live, isn't it? Don't you live in some kind of kids' Home round here?'

'Not any more,' I told her. 'I left there a while ago.'

'Where are you now, then? Another Home?'

'Foster parents.'

'Yeah?'

I nodded, thinking about Bridget and Pete. Wondering what they were doing . . . where they were . . . what they were . . . what they knew . . .

'What are they like?' asked Eddi.

'They're OK,' I shrugged. 'Pretty good, actually . . .'

'How long have you been with them?'

'About a year.'

'Is that normal? I mean, how long do you usually stay with foster parents?'

'It depends . . . some kids stay with the same ones forever, other times it's just for a month or so. It can be anything really – days, weeks, years.'

'What about you? What's normal for you?'

'I've never stayed with anyone for this long before. The longest placement I had before Bridget and Pete was four months.'

Eddi looked at me. 'Why's that?'

'I don't know . . .' I smiled at her. 'I find it hard to get on with people.'

'But you get on all right with Bridget and Pete?'

'Yeah, I suppose . . . I mean, they're not fantastic or anything, but they're better than most. Especially Bridget.'

'Is she nice?'

'Yeah . . . she's a bit hippyish . . . you know, all Mother Earthy and organic and stuff. And she was always asking me too many questions about feelings and things, which I never knew how to answer . . . but at least she made me smile now and then.'

Eddi glanced at me as I went quiet. I could see lots of questions in her eyes – why aren't you with Bridget and Pete now? where are they? do they know where you are? do they know what's happening? don't you want to get in touch with them? – but she didn't say anything. And I was glad she didn't. Bridget and Pete were part of the other me now, the me that used to be me, and I didn't want to think about that.

'It's not far now,' I told Eddi. 'We should be there in about twenty minutes.'

She nodded. 'How long is this going to take?'

'Why?'

'I'm going on holiday – remember? I'm flying out to Spain today.'

'What time's your flight?'

'Seven o'clock tonight. I have to be at Stansted by six at the very latest. And I still haven't packed or anything –'

'It won't take long,' I said. 'You'll be back in London by lunchtime.'

She looked at me. 'Are you sure?'

'Yeah.'

'And you're definitely letting me go, aren't you?'

'Why shouldn't I let you go? You're not going to tell anyone about me, are you?' I looked at her. 'Because, if you do, I'll tell them all about you – OK?'

'OK,' she agreed.

I could tell by the look in her eyes that she didn't have much faith in me. I didn't blame her. I didn't have much faith in myself either.

13

We got to Stoneham around seven o'clock. The sun was up now, the early-morning sky streaked with bands of orangey-grey light, but as we drove across town towards the hospital, the clouds rapidly darkened and the rain began falling again, shrouding the streets with a haze of yellowy-black gloom. I gazed through the window, remembering another rainy day . . . another life, another me . . .

It all felt weirdly schizophrenic: familiar and unfamiliar, real and unreal, ordered and disordered. Safe and unsafe. It felt as if I was coming home, but I didn't live here any more. I felt sick and excited, fluttery inside. Like I was hungry, but not hungry. Too hungry to eat.

Like a frightened child.

'Robert?'

I looked at Eddi. 'What?'

'Which way?'

I peered through the windscreen. We'd stopped at a junction. 'Turn right,' I said, 'then follow the signs to the hospital.'

'The hospital?'

'Yeah.'

'We're going to the hospital?'

'Yeah.'

She started to say something else, but then someone behind us beeped their horn and she turned her attention to them. An angry look in the mirror, a few choice words, then she put the car into gear and got going.

Five minutes later we pulled into the hospital car park and Eddi slotted the car into an empty space right next to the ticket machine. While she got out and fed some coins into the machine, I checked the pistol in my pocket, glanced at myself in the wing mirror, then picked up my rucksack from the back of the car and stepped out into the rain.

I was beginning to feel vulnerable now.

I was beginning to think that perhaps this wasn't such a good idea after all. Coming back here . . . back to where it all started. This was stupid.

I looked around, scanning the car park for watching eyes, but the only person watching me was Eddi.

'What are you doing?' she said, leaning into the car and sticking the parking ticket on the windscreen. 'Who are you looking for?'

'No one,' I told her. 'I'm just looking.'

She stared at me for a moment, then shut the car door and locked it. 'Right,' she said. 'Are you going to tell me what we're doing here now?'

'I want you to meet someone.'

'Who?'

'His name's Kamal. Kamal Ramachandran.'

'Rama *what*?'

'Ramachandran. He's an anaesthetist. He works here.'

'An anaesthetist?' She frowned at me. 'You brought me all the way out here to meet an *anaesthetist*?'

'Yeah.'

'Why?'

'I'll let him tell you that.' I started walking. 'Come on, it's this way.'

As I led Eddi along the driveway towards the main hospital building, I couldn't stop looking around all the time, looking out for the things I didn't want to see – silver eyes, hard faces, wrong faces, men in suits, men in coats. Ryan's people. They could be anywhere. They could be anyone – people in cars, sick people in wheelchairs, people hanging around smoking cigarettes. In an alleyway at the back of an annexe building, away from public view, a group of whistling men in dull green overalls were loading large sacks and plastic bins labelled MEDICAL WASTE into the back of a white Transit van. They could be Ryan's people. I just didn't know.

'Are you all right?' Eddi asked me.

'Yeah.'

'Is there someone here you don't want to see?'

'Possibly . . .'

'Are they looking for you?'

'Probably.'

'How many of them?'

'I don't know.'

'What do they look like?'

'I don't know.'

She looked at me.

'Suits,' I said. 'Men in suits . . . I don't know who they are. I don't know what they look like.'

She smiled at me. 'But you think they're wearing suits.'

We carried on walking.

When we got to the hospital entrance, I started feeling sick and empty inside. My stomach was hurting. My skin felt raw and tingly. I stopped outside the doors. Eddi looked at me.

'Aren't we going in?' she said.

'No, this'll do.'

The area around the entrance was dotted with cigarette smokers – hunched over in the rain, puffing and coughing away. The air stank of smoke and the ground was littered with flattened cigarette ends. It wasn't very nice. But I just couldn't face going inside. All those corridors and waiting rooms, all those hospital trolleys and operating theatres . . . they brought back too many bad memories.

I glanced up at a CCTV camera over the door. Then I looked back over at the car park. It was a long way away.

'Does this Ramalamadingdong guy know we're here?' asked Eddi.

'It's Ramachandran,' I said.

'Whatever – does he know we're waiting for him out here?'

I didn't answer. A nurse had just come out of the hospital, walking briskly, looking at her watch.

'Excuse me,' I said to her. 'Do you know –'

'I'm off duty,' she said without stopping. 'Ask at reception.'

I watched her scurry off into the rain.

Eddi glared at me. 'He *doesn't* know we're here, does he?'

Again, I didn't say anything. She stared at me for a

moment, shaking her head, then she turned away and lit a cigarette.

While she smoked, I just kept my eyes on the doors and waited.

After a while, another nurse came out. This one looked friendlier than the last one. More approachable. Less hurried. I let her move away from the doors, then I walked up beside her.

'Excuse me,' I said. 'I'm sorry to bother you . . .'

She didn't stop walking, but she didn't tell me to go away either. She just kind of smiled at me, waiting for me to go on. I glanced over my shoulder as Eddi walked up behind me, then I turned back to the nurse and smiled back at her.

'I'm looking for someone who works here,' I said. 'Kamal Ramachandran. He's an anaesthetist. I'm not sure what –'

'Kamal?' she said, suddenly stopping. 'Kamal Ramachandran?'

Her face had changed now. She looked awkward, disconcerted. Her eyes were uncertain, her smile had gone.

'Do you know him?' I asked her.

She glanced at Eddi, then turned back to me. 'Was he a friend of yours?'

'No, not really. I had an operation here a while ago, and Kamal was . . .'

Was?

Was he a friend of yours?

I looked at the nurse. 'What do you mean – *was*?'

She touched my arm. 'I'm sorry,' she said gently. 'Kamal passed away on Monday night.'

'What?'

'His car went off the road —'

'He's *dead*?'

She gave my arm a slight squeeze. 'I'm so sorry,' she said. 'I didn't know him that well —'

'Was he on his own?'

'What?'

'You said his car went off the road.'

'That's right.'

'Were any other cars involved?'

She looked slightly puzzled. 'No . . . I don't think so. It was late at night, the roads were icy. He took a corner too fast —'

'And this was on Monday?'

She nodded again. 'Are you all right?'

No, I wasn't all right.

Kamal was dead.

Nothing was all right.

I don't know what happened to me then. Just for a moment, something went dark inside my head. A crack of blackness. Then everything was whirling, spinning, like a terrible black wind . . .

And then, without any warning, it just stopped. Everything suddenly cleared, my eyes opened and I could see all around me. I could see the nurse walking away from me and Eddi just standing there, looking at me. And over at the hospital doors, I could see a man in a dark suit, talking on a mobile, his eyes fixed on me. He could have been a doctor, or a hospital manager or something . . . but I knew that he wasn't. Doctors and hospital managers don't look like that. They don't have hunters' eyes. They don't have killing faces.

The man in the suit had both.

He knew I was on to him now. He'd seen me looking at him, seen the look on my face. He knew. And, just for a second, he paused – thinking about it, making decisions – then he put his phone in his pocket and started moving towards me. Not running, but walking fast.

'Shit,' I said.

Eddi looked at me. 'What's the matter? What's going on?'

Without taking my eyes off the man in the suit, and keeping my lips as still as I could, I whispered to Eddi, 'Don't look round. Pretend you don't know me.'

'What?' she frowned.

The man in the suit was about ten metres away from us now. He looked a bit like Ryan – cold and dark and hard – but he was younger than Ryan. And his eyes weren't silver, they were green.

'Just pretend you've never met me before,' I hissed at Eddi. 'Please . . . I'll explain everything later. Trust me.'

Eddi glanced over her shoulder at the man in the suit, then looked back at me again. I wasn't sure if she understood what I was saying or not, but there wasn't time to say anything else. The man in the suit was only a few metres away now.

I yanked the pistol from my pocket and grabbed Eddi round the neck.

'Hey!' she cried. 'What are you –?'

I pulled her in front of me, so she was between me and the man in the suit, and I put the gun to her head. She gasped, stiffened. The man in the suit stopped. He was about six paces away from me.

'All right, Robert,' he said. 'Take it easy. Don't do anything –'

'Shut up.'

Eddi started struggling, twisting and squirming. I tightened my arm round her neck and she went still.

The man in the suit edged forward, keeping his eyes fixed firmly on me.

'I'll shoot her,' I warned him.

He stopped moving.

'Get rid of the gun,' I told him.

'What gun?'

'Get rid of it.'

He looked at me for a moment, then reached inside his jacket.

'Slowly,' I told him.

He opened his jacket, letting me see the gun in his shoulder holster. He looked at me. I nodded at him. He slowly removed the pistol and held it out to me by the barrel.

'Throw it,' I told him. 'Over there.'

As he lobbed the pistol on to the lawn at the edge of the driveway, I whispered to Eddi, 'OK?'

She didn't say anything, but I felt a slight nod of her head. I looked over at the man in the suit again. He'd stepped away from the edge of the driveway and was holding out his hands, palms up, trying to calm everything down.

'Listen, Robert –' he started to say.

I told him to shut up, then I glanced quickly around. Most of the people around the hospital had scattered to a safe distance now, but I could see them all watching us – the cigarette smokers, ambulance men, faces in the hospital windows. Some of them were talking on mobile phones. Calling the police.

I had to go.

I had to go *now*.

I looked over at the car park, but I knew it was too far away. I'd never make it all the way back there. Then I heard the sound of a car coming up behind me. I looked over my shoulder and saw a pale-blue Corsa creeping along the driveway towards me. The old woman in the driver's seat was staring at me, a worried look on her face. She was slowing down, not sure what to do.

I wasn't sure what to do either, but before I had time to think about it, I dragged Eddi into the middle of the driveway and stepped in front of the Corsa, blocking its way. The old woman stopped the car. I pointed the gun at her.

'Get out!' I shouted.

She didn't move, just sat there staring at me.

'*Out!*' I yelled, waving the gun at her.

She started to panic then, fumbling with her safety belt, scrabbling at the door handle . . .

'*Robert!*' Eddi hissed.

I looked over at the man in the suit and saw him inching towards his gun. 'Hey!' I barked at him. He stopped, raised his hands and backed away. I turned back to the car. The old woman had finally got out now. She was shuffling backwards across the lawn, breathing heavily, her ancient face ashen with fear.

And just for a moment, I thought to myself: *You really are the monster now.*

I didn't like it.

But I knew it had to be done.

I pointed the pistol at the man in the suit. 'Get in the car.'

He looked at me, shaking his head. 'This is stupid. You'll never get –'

'Shut up. Just get in the car. Now!'

He thought about it for a moment, then started moving over to the Corsa.

I watched him, wondering if I was doing the right thing. I didn't *want* to take him with us, but I knew I couldn't leave him here. If I left him here, he'd be on the phone to Ryan as soon as we'd gone. Then Ryan would know what I looked like, what I was wearing, who I was with, what kind of car I was in . . .

The man in the suit had reached the Corsa now.

'Driver's seat,' I told him. 'Leave the door open.'

He got into the driver's seat.

'Open the rear door.'

He leaned over, unlocked the rear door and pushed it open. I moved towards it, dragging Eddi with me, keeping the gun to her head.

She was really playing the part now – lips quivering, eyes wide open, scared to death. I bundled her into the back of the car, threw my bag in, got in after her and slammed the door shut.

'Get going,' I told the man in the suit. 'Turn the car round and get us out of here.'

He glanced at me in the rear-view mirror. 'Let the girl go, Robert,' he started to say. 'You don't need –'

'Just shut up and drive.'

*

As he turned the car round and drove back along the hospital driveway, I found myself thinking of Kamal. I remembered sitting in his white Fiesta, driving along this driveway, not knowing where to go or what to do . . .

Nothing had changed. The hospital grounds, the rolling lawns, the bushes and shrubs . . . all of it veiled behind a silver-black mist of rain. The gun in my lap. The sound of the engine, the sound of the rain on the roof of the car.

It was all the same.

Except Kamal wasn't here any more.

He was dead.

And I was a thousand years older.

'Which way?' the man in the suit asked me.

I looked at the clock on the dashboard. It was eight fifteen in the morning.

Different time.

Different people.

Kamal was dead.

They'd killed him.

'Which way, Robert?'

The man in the suit was looking at me in the rear-view mirror. I looked back at him, wondering if he'd killed Kamal. His eyes looked perfectly capable.

'Turn left,' I told him.

He turned left out of the hospital gates, and for the next ten minutes I just concentrated on telling him where to go.

Right at the roundabout.

Left at the junction.

Straight on.

Left again.

Right, left, right . . .

At one point I heard the sound of police sirens in the distance, but they were a long way off and they were moving away from us. The man in the suit heard them too, but he didn't say anything. I guessed he was thinking, trying to work out what to do.

Just like me.

I looked out of the window. We were approaching a junction at the end of a long straight road. There was a woodland park to our left, houses to the right. I didn't know exactly where we were, but I knew enough to know where to go.

'Turn left at the junction,' I said.

The man in the suit slowed the car, checked for traffic, then pulled out to the left. We were moving away from Stoneham now. Heading into the countryside.

I wanted to look at Eddi, to let her know that everything was going to be all right. But I couldn't. I just had to sit there, cradling the pistol in my hand, trying to work out what to do.

I wondered briefly if it was all worth it. All this running around, all this hiding, all this lying . . . what was the point? Why not just give up? I asked myself. Give up. Give in. Just give the pistol to the man in the suit and tell him to do what he wants.

Why not?

I looked up and saw the man in the suit watching me in the rear-view mirror. His face was anonymous. Nothing. Forgettable. Just a face.

'What's your name?' I asked him.

'My name?'

'Yeah, your name.'

'Paul Morris,' he said.

'Morris? You're Morris?'

He nodded.

I said, 'You were there when it happened, weren't you?'

'Sorry?'

'You were there, at the hospital on Monday. With Ryan and Hayes.'

He didn't answer me, but he didn't have to. I knew he'd been there. I remembered Hayes talking to Professor Casing. *Tell Ryan that Morris is with Peter Young*, she'd said. *Tell him it's under control.*

I stared at Morris's eyes in the mirror. He'd been with Pete. He'd talked to him. And I knew now that I had to talk to Morris. On his own. I had to ask him some questions.

I looked out of the window again.

'Turn right,' I told him.

He turned right and we headed off down a narrow country lane. The rain was still falling, silver and black, and the clouds were getting darker all the time. In the stormy half-light, the country lane was quiet and empty. Farmland stretched out on either side of us – barren fields, ragged hedges, miles of nothingness – and up ahead, in the distance, the dark skies glowed dully in the light of a hidden sun.

'Pull in over there,' I told Morris.

He slowed the car and pulled up beside a rickety wooden gate at the side of the lane. On the other side of the gate, a muddy track led across to a derelict barn – rusty girders, walls of corrugated iron, gaping holes in the roof. I couldn't see any other buildings. No farmhouses, no animal sheds, no lights, no nothing. It was just a derelict barn, alone in a derelict yard.

It wasn't ideal, but it would have to do.

'Open the gate,' I told Morris.

I wound down the window and kept the gun on him as he got out of the car and walked over to the gate. The air smelled cold and shitty.

'Are you all right?' I whispered to Eddi.

'What the hell are you *doing*?' she hissed back. 'Who's that guy? What does he want? What *is* all this?'

'I'll tell you later. I promise. Just keep doing what you're doing, and everything will be all right.'

Morris had opened the gate now. I leaned out of the window and told him to get back in the car. As he got back in, I told him to drive over to the barn. He drove.

The rain was getting heavier now. The wheels of the car slipped and slid in the mud.

'Stop here,' I said.

Morris stopped the car beside the barn.

'Turn off the engine.'

He turned off the engine.

'Give me the keys.'

He passed me the car keys.

'And your phone.'

He reached into his pocket and passed me his mobile. I check it was switched off, then put it in my pocket and turned to Eddi.

'Have you got a phone?' I asked her.

She nodded her head.

'Give it to me.'

She took a mobile out of her pocket and handed it over. I put it in my pocket and glanced at Morris.

'Stay there,' I told him.

I opened the door, stepped out into the rain, then leaned back into the car.

'Get out,' I told Eddi.

She stared at me.

'Please,' I said. 'Just get out of the car. I'm not going to hurt you.'

She looked at Morris, her eyes pleading for help, but he didn't want to know. He didn't care about her. He *looked* like he did – the caring face, the caring eyes – but it was all just a show. All he cared about was me.

'It's all right, Miss,' he said calmly to Eddi. 'Just do as he says. You'll be all right.'

I stepped away from the door, giving her room to get out. She clambered cautiously from the car. I stepped further back. She was shivering – cold and wet – and she looked tired and scared. I nodded my head at the barn behind her.

'Wait in there,' I said.

She looked over her shoulder, then turned back.

'Why?' she muttered. 'Why do you want me to go in there? What are you going to do?'

I glanced inside the car at Morris. He was watching us, listening to us.

'I'm not going to do anything,' I told Eddi. 'I promise. I just want you to go inside the barn and stay there. Nothing's going to happen.' I looked at her, not sure if she was still just playing along or if she was genuinely frightened. 'Listen,' I said, 'I'm sorry. This is just . . . it's not . . .' I shook my head. It was too hard. I didn't know what I was trying to say. 'I'm sorry. Please, just get in the barn and stay there.'

She gazed at me for a moment or two, then turned round and walked over to the barn. It didn't have a door, just a hole in the wall. I waited until she'd disappeared through the hole, then I turned back to the car. Morris was staring at me through the rain.

Staring at the beast.

I opened the car door and got in the back.

14

Morris didn't react when I leaned forward and pressed the gun to the back of his head. He didn't move, didn't flinch, didn't even blink. He just sat there, perfectly still, watching me silently in the rear-view mirror. His eyes were cool and steady.

'What happened to Kamal?' I asked him.

He smiled at me. 'Who?'

I rapped the gun barrel against his head. Not too hard, but hard enough to hurt him.

'Shit!' he said, jerking forward. 'What the fu–?'

'Shut up.'

He glared at me. His eyes weren't cool and steady any more.

'Sit up straight,' I told him.

He rubbed the back of his head, glared at me again, then slowly sat up straight.

I rested the pistol against his neck. 'What happened to Kamal?'

'He died.'

'I know that. How did it happen?'

'Road accident.'

'Don't lie to me.'

'I'm not. It was an accident.' Morris looked at me. 'He was driving too fast, simple as that.'

'I don't believe you.'

He shrugged.

'I think you killed him,' I said.

'You can think what you like.'

'You killed him because he knew too much. You don't want anyone to know the truth about me, do you?'

Morris said nothing, just stared at me.

'What have you done with Bridget and Pete?' I asked him.

He shrugged again. 'We haven't done anything with them. As far as I know, they're still at home, waiting for you to get in touch. They're worried about you, Robert. We all are.'

'Yeah, right. You're so worried about me that you killed Kamal –'

'We didn't kill anyone –'

'What about Casing?'

'What about him?'

'Has he been killed too? Stabbed to death in a frenzied attack . . . ?'

Morris shook his head, like he was listening to a raving madman, and I knew I was wasting my time. He was never going to tell me anything. And I didn't have time to waste.

But still . . .

He was here.

Morris.

He was right here in front of me. And he *knew*. He had to know something about me. And I wanted to know.

I had to know. I had to know what was happening to me. I had to know what I was, what I wasn't, what I was . . .

I had to know.

'Tell me why I shouldn't kill you,' I said.

Morris frowned at me. 'What?'

'You heard.'

His mouth moved, looking for an answer, but nothing came out.

'I don't have anything to lose,' I explained to him. 'I'm either human or I'm not. If I am, then I'm already wanted for Casing's murder, so another one isn't going to make any difference. And if I'm not . . . well, if I'm not human, it doesn't really matter, does it? A machine can't be guilty of murder.'

Morris just stared at me.

'Do you see what I'm saying?' I said.

He nodded slowly.

'So,' I continued, 'what's it going to be? Are you going to tell me what I want to know, or do I have to kill you?'

We stared at each other in silence for a while. Morris's eyes were blank. Empty and emotionless . . . almost unhuman . . . and I wondered for a moment what I looked like to him. Did he know what I was? Did he see me as something else? And then it suddenly occurred to me that maybe he *didn't* see me as something else, because maybe I *wasn't* something else to him. I was the *same* as him. He was the same as me. We were *both* something else – unhuman, unreal. And if Morris was the same as me, then the others had to be the same too – Ryan, Hayes, Cooper . . . all of them. Maybe Bridget and Pete were the same. Maybe there were hundreds of us, thousands . . . maybe *everyone* was the same as me.

I looked at Morris in the mirror, trying to see myself in his eyes.

'All right, Robert,' he said quietly. 'What do you want to know?'

He sounded genuine, pained and resigned, and for a moment I was convinced he was telling the truth. He really *was* going to tell me what I wanted to know. But then his eyes flicked suddenly to the right, as if he'd just seen something outside, and even as I turned to see what he was looking at, I realized I'd been tricked.

But it was already too late.

The instant I took my eyes off him, Morris released the seat handle and thrust out his legs, shoving himself backwards with all his weight. His seat slammed into my chest, emptying my lungs and throwing me across the car, and as I thudded against the back of the rear seats, the pistol flew out of my hand. I was too shocked to move for a moment. I couldn't breathe. I just sat there, slumped in the seat, dazed and breathless, vaguely aware that Morris was already clambering over the seat, his killing eyes fixed on me. I saw him draw back his arm, and I tried to get out of the way, but I was too slow. He smashed his fist into my head, then almost immediately rammed his arm against my neck, shoving me up against the back seat. He had me pinned down now. My head was whirling, filled with blackness, and his arm was crushing the life out of me. I struggled, trying to kick him, but he just leaned in harder and hit me again, cracking his left hand into my jaw. It didn't hurt – none of it seemed to hurt.

I was insensible, painless. Switched off. Numb. I was just a thing. But I couldn't function any more. There was too much blackness inside my head, the air was too thick. I couldn't do anything.

With his body jammed between the two front seats and his right arm rammed up against my neck, Morris started scrabbling around with his other hand, looking for the pistol. I knew where it was. It was on the floor, under my right foot. I could feel it through the sole of my shoe – the hard steel, the trigger guard, the barrel. I forced myself to move my foot, trying to slide the pistol out of Morris's reach, but he'd seen it now. I could feel him grabbing hold of the barrel, wrenching the gun from under my foot. I tried to stop him, kicking his hand away with my left foot, but it didn't have much effect. He was too big, too strong. He just shouldered my leg to one side and grabbed hold of the pistol again. I was too weak to do anything about it. I could feel the gun slipping out from under my foot . . .

Then the car door opened.

It's hard to remember exactly what happened next. My head was still reeling, and Morris still had me jammed up against the seat, so I could barely see anything at all. I *heard* the door beside us opening, and I *felt* the sudden rush of cold rainy air, and I knew that *some*one was there, but I couldn't see who it was. All I could see was a shape in the rain, standing beside the open door.

Everything froze for a fraction of a second – the figure just stood there, Morris stopped moving – and then suddenly they both made a lunge for the pistol. I still couldn't see what was happening, but I felt the figure stooping down and diving into the car, and I felt another hand making a grab for the pistol, and then Morris was chopping at the hand, smashing it into the floor, and I heard the figure crying out in pain. Then almost immediately I felt another lunge, and Morris suddenly jerked and gasped – 'Shit, you *bitch*!' – and I felt his hand whipping back . . . and I knew then that the figure was Eddi. She'd just bitten Morris's hand. And now she had the pistol. But as she started to get up off the floor, Morris suddenly let go of my neck and clubbed his fist into the back of her head. She grunted, and I felt her crash back down to the floor. Morris raised his arm again, aiming to finish her off, but he'd forgotten about me. I wasn't pinned down any more. I could move. I sprang forward and hammered my head into Morris's skull. The impact rocked through my head, spinning me round in a sickening swirl of blackness, but it didn't matter. Through the blackness I could see Morris slumped against the back of the front seat, his head hanging down, his eyes closed. I'd hit him hard enough to momentarily knock him out, and that was enough to let Eddi get hold of the pistol again and struggle up off the floor.

The next few seconds are the hardest to recall. I was still dazed, my head was still spinning, and whenever I think about it, everything seems to start whirling again. But this is how I remember it.

Eddi had just about got to her feet again and was leaning into the car, kind of half-in and half-out of it, steadying herself against the back of the seat. Her face was very pale, her eyes unfocused. The gun was in her left hand. She was aiming it at Morris, but I don't think she was going to shoot him. She was just covering him, waiting for him to wake up. But when he *did* wake up, opening his eyes quite suddenly, Eddi had briefly turned away from him to look at me, and before I could warn her, he'd reached out and grabbed her left hand, fighting to get hold of the pistol. She reacted quickly, tightening her grip on the pistol and clutching at his wrist with her other hand, and then he got both hands on the gun, and they were both pulling and twisting, fighting over the pistol, and then . . . I don't know. I just don't know how it happened. One moment they were struggling, both of them grunting and gasping, and then – *BANG!* – the gun went off, loud as hell, and a shower of wet stuff sprayed into my face.

I didn't realize what had happened for a moment. Everything was silent and still. The wet stuff on my face was warm, then suddenly cold. Nothing was happening. I closed my eyes, wiped my face, then opened my eyes again. Morris had fallen between the two front seats. One of his legs was twisted up under him, the other one was sticking out between the gap in the seats. From the neck down, he still looked like Morris – dark suit, white shirt, shiny black shoes – but he wasn't Morris any more. He was just a thing: a thing with half its head blown off.

I sat there for a while, just watching stuff ooze from Morris's head. I didn't want to keep looking at it, but I couldn't seem to stop. His blood was thick and slow-moving, like tar. Black, crimson, pink. There were bits of bone in it. Flecks of white. There were globs of grey stuff on the seat, like lumps of thick grey snot.

They were human things.

No metal, no silver, no plastic.

Morris had definitely been human.

But now he was nothing.

I looked at Eddi. She was just sitting there staring at Morris too. Her face was shocked white, her eyes glazed with horror. She still had the gun in her hand.

'Jesus . . .' she whispered. 'Shit.'

Her voice was shaking.

I leaned forward and touched her arm, but she didn't seem to notice.

'Eddi,' I said quietly.

She carried on staring at Morris.

'It's all right, Eddi,' I said, gently squeezing her arm. 'It wasn't your fault. It was an accident. It's all right . . .'

She suddenly went even paler. Her eyes closed, her throat gulped, then she leaned out of the car and threw up.

It took us a while to get Morris's body into the barn. Neither of us was thinking straight, so instead of just driving the Corsa over to the barn, we wasted ten minutes getting the body out of the car, then another fifteen minutes dragging it across the mud-soaked yard. By the time we'd finished, we were both exhausted and covered in all kinds of crap – blood, mud, cow shit, rain . . .

But at least Eddi wasn't in a trance any more. She was pale and breathless, and her hands were shaking, but she wasn't in a trance.

'Are you all right?' I asked her as we walked back to the car.

'All right?' she said, lighting a cigarette. 'I just *killed* someone, for Christ's sake.'

'It was an accident –'

'Yeah, right. I *accidentally* shot his head off, and now we've just *accidentally* dumped his body in the barn.'

'You know what I mean.'

She sighed. 'Yeah, I know . . .'

'If you hadn't shot him . . .'

She looked at me. 'What? What would have happened if I hadn't shot him, Robert? What was he going to do?'

'I don't know . . .'

'And what were you going to do with *him*? Why did you make me go in the barn?' She stopped beside the car. 'Who was he anyway? What was he doing at the hospital?'

I stopped beside her. 'There isn't time to explain now, we have to get going –'

'No,' she said firmly. 'I'm not going anywhere until you tell me what this is all about.' She stared at me. 'I just *killed* a man for you. The least you can do is tell me who he was.'

I looked back at her. Her face was streaked with blood and rain. Her hair was soaking wet. She was angry. Afraid. Confused. She was inappropriately beautiful.

'We have to go,' I said calmly. 'If we stay here any longer, someone's going to see us. We need to get in the car and leave here right now.' I put my hand on her shoulder. 'As soon as we're safe, I'll explain everything. I promise.'

She carried on staring at me in silence for a while, the rain dripping pink on her face, then eventually she took a deep breath, slowly let it out, and nodded. 'All right,' she said. 'But you'd *better* tell me –'

'I will.'

'Everything?'

'Everything.'

She took a final drag on her cigarette, dropped it in the mud, then opened the car door and got in the driver's seat. I didn't move for a second. I just stood there, gazing down at the still-smoking cigarette, wondering why I wasn't picking it up. It was evidence. DNA. Evidence that Eddi had been here.

'Are you coming or what?' Eddi called out to me.

I looked at her, smiled, then walked round and got in the passenger seat.

15

We just drove for a while, neither of us knowing or caring where we were going, just as long as it was away from the barn. The barn was north, so we headed south.

'It's probably best if we get off these country lanes,' I suggested.

'I know. That's what I'm doing.'

I shut up then and let Eddi get on with it. As she drove, I searched through the glove compartment. Most of the contents were useless – a bag of boiled sweets, a tube of lipstick, some kind of nasal spray – but I managed to find a road map and a box of tissues. There was a bottle of water in the side compartment of the door. I uncapped the bottle and passed it to Eddi. She took a long drink, then gave it back. I wet some of the tissues and passed them over.

'What am I supposed to do with these?' she said.

'We need to clean ourselves up.'

She pulled down the sun visor and studied her blood-stained face in the mirror. 'Oh, God . . . why didn't you *tell* me?'

'I just did.'

We spent the next five minutes wiping our faces and

scrubbing at our clothes, trying to clean off the worst of the mess. It wasn't easy, and for Eddi it was doubly difficult because she had to concentrate on driving at the same time. I thought about offering to help her, but I didn't think she'd want me to. It wasn't a very pleasant task, and neither of us wanted to talk about it, so we worked in silence – scrubbing, rubbing, scouring Morris's blood from our skin.

It felt like madness.

Obsession, compulsion.

Denial.

It was as if we both thought that by cleansing ourselves of Morris's blood we were cleansing ourselves of his death. No blood, no death, no memories, no guilt. But it didn't work. You can't wipe away death with a box of damp tissues.

After a while I realized we were back on the A12 again, heading towards London. I didn't know if Eddi knew where she was going, or if she was still just driving, putting as much distance between us and Stoneham as possible. I glanced across at her, trying to decide if I should ask her or not.

'Where's the nearest railway station?' she said.

'What?'

'The nearest railway station . . . look on the map.'

'Why?'

'We need to get rid of this car. The police will be looking for it. We need to ditch it and get another one.'

'How are we going to get another car?'

'Well, we're not going to *buy* one, are we?' She looked

at me, shaking her head at my naivety. 'We're going to steal one, OK? And the best place to steal a car is from the car park of a railway station. Lots of cars, not many people.'

'Right,' I said.

She looked at me. 'So?'

'What?'

She sighed. 'You've got the map. Find me a station.'

I looked at the map and started searching for a railway station, but I knew I was wasting my time. I didn't know where we were. I knew we were on the A12, somewhere between Stoneham and London, but it was a long stretch of road, and there were lots of railways stations . . . we could be anywhere. I looked out of the window, trying to work out where we were, but there were no road signs. I looked back at the map again.

I was starting to feel really stupid now, and I didn't understand why. Why didn't I just ask Eddi where we were? Why did I feel awkward about it? Why did I feel embarrassed?

'It's all right,' Eddi said, suddenly changing lanes. 'You can stop looking now.'

I glanced up from the map and saw that we were heading for a turn-off up ahead. A sign at the side of the road said SHENFIELD, and next to it was a sign for the railway station.

I closed the map and put it away.

I drank some water.

I looked out of the window.

I knew I had to concentrate now. I had to stop thinking about what I was feeling and start thinking about what I was going to do. At some point soon, Eddi was going to ask me to explain everything, and I had to decide what to tell her.

Did I tell her the truth?

Could I tell her the truth?

Or did I have to lie?

That's what I had to think about now.

Truth or lies.

By the time we'd driven into Shenfield and found the railway station, I still hadn't made up my mind. I didn't *want* to lie to her, and I'd been fine with the idea of Kamal telling her the truth, but that was then . . .

And this was now.

And, for some reason, everything felt different now.

As we entered the station car park, Eddi started looking around at the rows of parked cars.

'What kind of car are we looking for?' I asked her.

'Something old, but not too old. Nothing too flashy. Just a nice easy steal. An old Escort would be good. Or a Hyundai . . . they're easy . . .'

'How do you know all this stuff?' I said.

'I'm a crook,' she said simply. 'I steal things. Now shut up and keep looking.'

We eventually found what we were looking for at the far end of the car park. It was a grey Honda Civic, about ten years old. No alarm, no steering lock. Out of sight of the CCTV cameras.

'Perfect,' said Eddi.

She parked the Corsa in the nearest free space, then told me to get an overnight parking ticket from the machine.

'Why?' I said. 'What's the point?'

'If we leave the Corsa without a ticket, someone's going to notice it. And we don't want anyone to notice it – OK?'

I looked around the inside of the car. There was a lot of blood on the seats. Blood, mud . . . other stuff.

I looked at Eddi. 'Shouldn't we try cleaning up before we go?'

'You can try if you want,' she said, opening the car door, 'but don't expect me to wait for you.'

She got out of the car, shut the door, and I watched her heading over to the Civic. I waited for a moment, not sure what I was waiting for, then I got out of the car and went looking for a ticket machine. It was a big car park, and it took me a while to find a machine. Then I had to get a ticket, take it back to the Corsa, stick it on the windscreen, get my rucksack . . .

All in all, it must have taken me the best part of five minutes.

But even so, I was still surprised when I walked up to the Civic and saw Eddi sitting in the driver's seat.

'That was quick,' I said. 'How did you –?'

'Get in,' she said without looking at me.

I walked round to the passenger side and got in. Eddi was reaching in under the steering wheel now, pulling out wires from the dashboard. She had a little penknife in her hand. She worked quickly – selecting wires, stripping them, twisting them together – and in less than a minute she had the engine going. She sat up, revved the car a couple of times, took a quick look round, then calmly drove out of the car park.

*

175

As we rejoined the A12 and started heading south again, Eddi asked me for her mobile phone. I took it out of my pocket and passed it over. She pressed a button, glanced at the display, then placed the phone on a shelf on the dashboard. She lit a cigarette.

'So,' she said to me, 'do you think we're safe now?'

'I don't know . . . I suppose so. They don't know where we are, or where we're going. They don't know what car we're in. They don't know where Morris is. I suppose we're as safe as we can be for now.'

'You'd better start talking, then.'

I looked at her.

'You promised,' she said. 'Remember? You told me you'd explain everything as soon as we were safe.' She looked at me. 'What the hell's going on, Robert? What have you dragged me into?'

I started with the truth. I didn't know if I was going to end with it or not, but it was the easiest way to begin, because it meant that I didn't have to think about anything. You don't *have* to think about anything when you're telling the truth, all you have to do is tell it.

So that's what I did.

I told Eddi about my suspected ulcer, my hospital appointment, my endoscopy. I told her about taking the bus to the hospital on my own, about getting to the hospital, showing my appointment card . . . walking down the endless corridors, following the signs . . . putting on a hospital gown, sitting in the waiting room . . . lying on the trolley in the small white room, watching the doctor as he inserted the needle into the back of my hand . . .

I told her everything I could remember.

She didn't say anything. She just carried on driving, listening intently, hanging on my every word.

When I got to the bit about waking up in the basement theatre, I had to stop for a moment. I couldn't speak. I was remembering how it was – waking up on the trolley . . . paralysed, petrified, not knowing anything. Hearing strange voices. Seeing strange things. Impossible things . . .

No one would ever believe it.

'Robert?' Eddi said.

I looked at her. She was quiet – quiet eyes, quiet face, quiet everything.

'What happened?' she asked me. 'The doctor gave you a shot . . . then what happened?'

'I don't know . . . the doctor told me it was only a mild anaesthetic and it probably wouldn't knock me out . . .'

'But it did?'

I nodded. 'As soon as he stuck the needle in my hand, that was it. I was out like a light. I don't remember anything until . . .'

'Until what?'

'When I woke up . . .' I paused, clearing my throat. 'When I woke up, I wasn't in the same place any more. I was still lying on a trolley, but I was in a different room. I had a tube down my throat. There were wires taped to my hands and my chest. I was breathing some kind of gas . . .' I paused again, remembering the taste in the back of my throat . . . plastic, chemicals, whiteness. I cleared my throat again and carried on. 'There were different people in the room too. There was a surgeon, an anaesthetist –'

'Kamal?'

'Yeah . . . and there were others too. People who don't belong in a hospital.'

'What kind of people?'

'People like Morris.' I looked at Eddi. 'He was there. I didn't see him, but I heard the others talking to him. There was a guy called Ryan. A woman called Hayes. And there was a big guy called Cooper guarding the door. Cooper and Ryan had guns.'

Eddi frowned. 'I don't get it. Who were they? What were they doing there?'

This was it now – truth or lie? I looked through the windscreen at the long grey road stretching out ahead of us. Did I tell her the truth or did I tell her a lie? Truth or lie? Truth or lie? Truth or –

'Robert,' she said impatiently, 'what were they *doing*?'

'They were looking inside me,' I heard myself say.

'*What?*'

'The surgeon – Professor Casing – he'd cut me open. Just here . . .' I drew my finger down my belly, showing her where Casing had cut me. 'I was lying there with a big slice in my belly, and Ryan was digging around inside me.'

'Inside your *body*?' Eddi whispered.

'Yeah.'

'Christ.' She glanced across at my belly. 'The scar . . . that's how you got the scar . . .' She looked up and stared at me. 'They cut you *open*?'

I nodded. 'I thought at first that something had gone wrong with the endoscopy . . . you know, I thought maybe they'd found something and they'd had to do an emergency operation. But they were talking about all this secret stuff, about keeping it quiet and not letting anyone know . . . and then I saw Ryan leaning over me, and I could see the gun in his belt, and the big guy guarding the door.' I shook my head. 'I didn't know what was going on.'

'God, Robert . . . it must have been terrible. What did you do?'

I didn't say anything for a moment. I needed time to gather my thoughts, to calm my lying heart. To remind myself that I wasn't human. That I had no heart. So what did I care if I lied or not?

I gazed out of the window again. The traffic ahead of us was backing up to get through some roadworks. Cars were switching lanes, trying to find the fastest way through. Eddi didn't bother with any of that, she just slowed the Civic, moved into the inside lane and stayed there. I wound down the window to get some fresh air, but all I got was a blast of exhaust fumes. I wound it back up again and got back to the truth.

I told Eddi about taking Ryan's gun and knocking him out . . . about forcing Casing to stitch me together again. I told her about my escape from the hospital, my time with Kamal, my room at the Paradise Hotel. I told her how I'd gone into that room and lay down on the bed . . . how I'd doped myself up with vodka and pills . . . how I'd decided there was only one thing to do.

When I told her how I'd sliced open the wound in my belly, she nearly ran into the car in front of us.

'Shit!' she gasped, hitting the brakes and screeching to a halt. The car stalled, but she didn't try starting it again. She just stared at me. 'You did *what*?'

'I cut myself open . . . I had to. I had to find out why they'd been poking around inside me.'

'Why didn't you just *ask* them?'

'They had guns . . . I didn't know who they were. All I wanted to do was get out of there. There wasn't time to ask anyone anything.'

'Yeah, but cutting yourself open . . . I mean, for Christ's sake, Robert. How could you *do* that? Didn't it hurt?'

Just then a car horn beeped behind us. Eddi started the car and got moving again. We inched up to the car in front of us, then stopped. Eddi looked at me, waiting for me to say something.

'I was drunk,' I told her. 'I just did it. I could feel something inside me, inside my body. I had to find out what it was.'

'And did you?'

'Sort of . . .'

'What do you mean?'

I paused again, taking a deep breath, trying to imagine what I could have found inside my body. 'There was something under my skin,' I told her. 'Not just *under* the skin, but deep down inside, buried beneath all the muscles and stuff. I could feel it when I put my hand inside the wound. It felt like a . . . I don't know. Like a flat piece of metal, or hard plastic.'

Eddi shivered.

'I couldn't get it out at first,' I told her. 'It was fixed to something inside me. I had to dig inside and cut it out with a scalpel.'

'Shit,' Eddi murmured. 'What was it?'

The queue of traffic wasn't moving any more, but I

don't think Eddi was even aware of it. She was almost spellbound now. Just sitting there, staring at me, like a wide-eyed kid listening to a bedtime story.

'What *was* it, Robert?' she asked me again. 'This thing you cut out of your body . . . what was it?'

'I'm not sure,' I told her. 'I think it was some kind of microprocessor . . . you know, like a computer chip. I don't know . . . it was about the size of a matchbox . . . but flat. Like a credit card.'

'A *microprocessor*?'

'I don't know . . . I mean, I don't know anything about computers and stuff, but it was that kind of thing. You know . . . kind of thin and plasticky and black. Shiny and hard . . . a bit greenish too.' I closed my eyes, imagining this imaginary object. 'It looked like it had loads of stuff inside it, complicated stuff . . .'

'What kind of complicated stuff?'

'Connections . . . little blocks, dots, lines . . .'

'Like a circuit board?'

'Yeah.'

'Shit,' Eddi said, shaking her head. 'And this was *inside* you?'

I nodded.

'*Fixed* inside you?'

I nodded again. 'It had some kind of miniature connection sockets all around the edge, little gold things . . . and there were wires, tiny silver filaments . . .' I closed my eyes again, remembering the things I'd seen. Black things, grey things, blurred and formless. Filaments, dulled silver-white, shining dark in the light of the eye. Intricate patterns of dots and lines, circles and waves.

Fine hairs, like slender worms, moving to the flow of something invisible . . .

'Where is it?' Eddi said.

'Sorry?'

'This thing . . . where is it? I want to see it.'

I looked at her. 'I left it behind.'

'You what?'

'I left it at the hotel.'

She stared at me. 'Why, for Christ's sake?'

I told her about the newspaper then. 'I panicked,' I told her. 'As soon as I saw the story about me, I realized I had to get out of the hotel before Ryan showed up. I didn't have time to think. I was desperate. I just grabbed a few clothes and ran. By the time I realized I'd left this thing behind, it was too late. The police were all over the hotel by then – the police, Ryan's people . . . they were everywhere. I saw one of them going into my room just after I'd left.'

'So whatever this thing is – and whoever these people are – they'll have it back now.'

I nodded.

Eddi glanced at me, then turned back to the road. We were moving again now. We'd got through the roadworks and the traffic was beginning to get back to normal – speeding cars, lorries, vans . . . everyone in a hurry to get where they were going.

I stared through the windscreen.

I was tired of talking. Tired of lying. Tired of everything. I hadn't slept for a long time. I didn't know where we were going. I didn't know what I was doing. I didn't know why I was lying. I didn't know what to think. I didn't know what to do. I didn't know what I was.

I didn't know anything.

I was just a thing – tired and unknowing.

The heater was on, filling the car with a dusty heat, and as the silence hummed and the world passed by, I closed my eyes, emptied my head, and started to drift off to sleep.

I didn't get very far, though.

Just as I was falling into that twilight state between consciousness and unconsciousness, Eddi began asking me questions.

'These people,' she said, 'the ones at the hospital, the ones with the guns . . . you've no idea who they were?'

'No.'

'How did they address each other?'

'What do you mean?'

'First names, last names . . . what did they call each other?'

I thought about it, trying to remember. 'Hayes called Ryan *Sir* a few times. But apart from that I think it was mostly just last names – Ryan, Hayes, Morris . . .'

'And they were all in plain clothes? No uniforms?'

'I didn't see any uniforms.'

'And Ryan was in charge?'

'Yeah, definitely.' I suddenly remembered the stuff I'd got from his wallet – his ID card, the business cards. I took out the wallet, removed the ID card and one of the business cards and passed them over to Eddi. 'They're Ryan's,' I told her. She looked at them, resting the two cards against the steering wheel so she could see them without taking her eyes off the road for too long. She studied them in detail, staring hard, examining every word and every number. 'What do you think?' I asked her.

She tapped the business card with her finger. 'That's not a regular London phone number. The first three digits are wrong. They should refer to a specific area, but they don't.'

'What does that mean?'

'I'm not sure . . .'

'What about his ID card?'

She shook her head. 'It's not police-issue. It could be from one of the Security Services, but I know most of them, and I've never seen one like this before. It's not MI5 or MI6. It's not Special Branch.' She shook her head again and passed the cards back to me. 'Was there anything else in his wallet?'

'Some cash, a couple of credit cards –'

'What kind of cards?'

I looked in his wallet. 'American Express and Visa.'

She nodded. 'I'll check them out when we get back.'

'Back where?' I said.

'To my place.'

'We're going back to your place?'

After a moment's pause, she said, 'Look, Robert, I don't understand any of this. I don't know what it means . . . to you, to me, to *either* of us. I just don't get it. Right now, all I know is that we're both in a lot of trouble.' She looked across at me. 'I don't know who these people are, or what they want with you, but I've just killed one of them. And they're not going to like that.'

'They'll probably think it was me that killed him.'

'Maybe . . . but they're still going to be looking for me. My car's at the hospital, my prints are all over the Corsa . . . I probably left a ton of DNA at the barn. They'll find out who I am. It might take them a while, but they'll get

184

there eventually – and I want to be long gone by then.'

'So why are we going back to your flat?'

'I need to pick up some stuff.'

'Right . . .'

She looked at me. 'What?'

'Nothing . . .'

'What's the matter?'

'Nothing.'

'Don't worry,' she said, smiling at me. 'I'm not going to abandon you.'

'I'm not *worried* . . .'

'No?'

'Why should I be worried?'

'No reason.' She grinned. 'No reason at all. I just wanted to let you know, that's all. Wherever I go, you're coming with me.'

'Thanks,' I said, 'but you don't have to look after me.'

'I'm not looking after you, I'm looking after *me*.' Her smile had gone now. 'You know too much about me,' she said, 'and I know too much about you. The only way we're going to get through this is by trusting each other, and the only way we can trust each other is by staying together.' She shrugged. 'So, that's how it's going to be for a while – whether we like it or not. All right?'

'Yeah, I suppose . . .'

'You *suppose*?'

I looked at her, trying to hide my feelings. I didn't really know what those feelings were – although I knew they had something to do with *not* wanting to be on my own any more – and I wasn't sure why I was feeling them, or even if they were genuine or not. But, whatever they were,

I didn't want Eddi to see them. She glanced back at me for a moment, a slightly puzzled look in her eyes, then she looked away again and started asking me more questions. She had a lot of questions . . .

Was the newspaper story completely false?
Was Casing still alive when you last saw him?
Do you think Casing knew Ryan?
What do you think they were doing?
Do you think they were taking this thing out of you, or do you think they were putting it in?
How big was it again?
How heavy?
What did it feel like?
Did it make any noise?
Did you see anything else inside you?
Has anything like this ever happened before?
How did you feel?
How do you feel now?

. . . and by the time we got back to Finsbury Park, I felt totally shattered.

16

Just before we got to Gillespie Heights, Eddi turned right into a grim little back street and pulled up at the side of the road. The street was grey and empty – parked cars, low-rise flats, cracked pavements, black railings. A dead-looking place.

Eddi picked up her mobile phone, hit a speed-dial button and put the phone to her ear. 'Bean?' she said. 'It's me. Is everything OK?' She paused, listening. 'All right, listen. Get round to the garages and wait for me. I'll be there in a minute. I'm in a grey Civic. Got that?' She listened again, then closed the connection and put the phone in her pocket.

'Who was that?' I asked her.

'Bean.'

'Who's Bean?'

'Who's been what?'

She smiled at me, then put the car into gear and got going.

Bean, it turned out, was a skinny little twelve-year-old black kid. Dressed in a zipped-up hoodie, an over-sized basketball shirt and the baggiest pants I'd ever seen, he was waiting for us at a row of lock-up garages at the back of Eddi's tower block. When Eddi drove up and stopped the car, he looked round, jerked his neck, then ambled over towards us.

Eddi grinned at me as I watched him.

'It's all right,' she told me, 'he knows what he's doing.'

'What *is* he doing?'

She smiled at me again, then opened the car door and got out, leaving the engine running. Bean walked up to her and they started talking. I watched them for a moment, then I reached over to the back seat, picked up my bag and stepped out of the car to join them.

'This is John,' Eddi told Bean as I walked up beside them. 'You haven't seen him – OK?'

Bean nodded, barely even looking at me. 'You got keys for that?' he asked Eddi, nodding at the Civic.

She shook her head. 'It's wired. I want you to get rid of it, but not round here – all right?'

'How much you want for it?'

'Nothing, just make sure it doesn't come back to me. And don't do anything till I've gone. I've got another job for you.' Eddi glanced over at the Civic, then turned back to Bean. 'I'll be about an hour or two. Put the Civic somewhere safe till then. I'll call you when I'm ready.'

Bean nodded.

'I'll be in my flat,' Eddi told him. 'Keep your eyes open. If you see anyone you don't know, call me.'

'The police looking for you?' Bean said.

'Something like that.'

They smiled at each other for a moment, then Bean nodded his head again and started loping off towards the Civic.

Eddi looked at me. 'All right?'

I shrugged, watching Bean. 'Do you trust him?'

'I pay him.'

I looked at her.

She smiled at me. 'I don't trust anyone.'

'Not even me?'

'Especially not you.'

As soon as we were back in her flat, Eddi asked me for Ryan's wallet.

'I used one of his credit cards,' I told her, handing over the wallet.

'When?'

'I don't know . . . what day is it now?'

'Wednesday.'

'And when did I get here?'

'Yesterday,' she sighed. 'Tuesday.'

'Right . . . it was Tuesday then. I bought a train ticket to Edinburgh with Ryan's Visa card.'

'Where did you buy it from?'

'King's Cross.'

She looked at me. 'Why the hell did you buy a train ticket to Edinburgh? And why did you use Ryan's Visa?'

'I thought they'd be tracking it. I thought they'd think I was going to Edinburgh.'

'But you weren't.'

'No, I was coming here.'

Eddi grinned. 'You're not as dumb as you look.'

'Thank you.'

She took Ryan's wallet over to a desk, booted up one of her computers and started tapping away at the keyboard.

I sat down in the armchair and watched her. She took the credit cards out of the wallet, studied them for a moment, then slotted one into a little gadget beside the computer. The gadget beeped. She tapped the keyboard again and stared at the screen . . .

I looked up at a clock on the wall. It was one thirty.

One thirty, Wednesday afternoon.

Wednesday, Tuesday, Monday.

Monday morning, eight o'clock . . . I'd said goodbye to Bridget, left the house and walked down the street to the bus stop. The sky was grey, the wind was cold . . . everything was perfectly normal.

It seemed like a lifetime ago.

I looked over at Eddi again. She was still tapping away, still staring hard at the computer screen.

'Are you sure this is a good idea?' I asked her.

'What?'

'Being here . . . I mean, what if they've already found your car at the hospital –'

'It's registered in a false name. False address.'

'What about the rest of it?'

'The rest of what?'

'The Corsa, the barn . . . you said yourself there'd be fingerprints and DNA all over the place. They could be checking it all right now . . .'

Eddi stopped tapping and looked at me. 'I'm good at what I do, Robert. I make my living out of false ID. Do you think I'm going to use my real name for anything?' She shook her head. 'This flat's in a false name. The phone's in a false name. Everything I *own* is in a false name.'

'Yeah, but your DNA and fingerprints –'

'A DNA check takes weeks, and all they'll get from their fingerprint database is a 22-year-old woman called Sheila Davies who was arrested two years ago on suspicion of fraud. Arrested but not charged, by the way. And Miss Davies's last known address is a non-existent flat above a chip shop in Ilford.' Eddi smiled at me. 'So don't worry, we're all right here for a while – OK?'

I nodded wearily.

Eddi started tapping again. 'Why don't you get some sleep?' she suggested. 'You look exhausted. I'll wake you up when I'm ready to go.'

'Go where?' I muttered. 'Where are we going?'

'Somewhere safe.' She glanced over at me. 'Don't worry, I'll still be here when you wake up. I'm not going to do anything.'

'That's what you said last night,' I muttered, 'just before you drugged me. You told me you weren't going to do anything, and then . . .'

And then you kissed me, I wanted to say. *You kissed me and took me into your bedroom. And I thought everything was going to be OK. But it wasn't.*

I looked at her.

She'd lowered her eyes and was staring at the desk. 'I'm sorry about last night,' she said sadly. 'I'm just . . . I don't know. I can't help it. It's what I do. It's just . . .' She sighed heavily and looked up at me. 'I'm sorry, Robert.'

'Yeah, well,' I said, 'I'm sorry I dragged you into all this.'

She nodded. 'It's not your fault.'

I had to look away from her then. Her eyes were too much for me. Everything was too much.

'Why are you doing this?' I asked her.

'Doing what?'

'Helping me . . . staying with me . . .'

'I told you before,' she said. 'The only way I'm going to get through this is by sticking with you –'

'You don't need me,' I said, shaking my head. 'You could just say goodbye and leave me to it. It's me they're after, not you. Once they've got me, they're not going to bother looking for you. And even if they *are* looking for you, there's nothing I can tell them that they're not going to find out anyway.' I looked at her. 'You'd be a lot better off on your own.'

'You think so?'

I shrugged.

She stared at me. 'What if it's the other way round?'

'What do you mean?'

'What if we split up and they find me first? What am *I* going to tell them about *you*?'

'Nothing,' I said, slightly puzzled. 'You won't know anything –'

'Exactly. I won't know where you are, I won't know where you're going, I won't know anything about you.'

I frowned at her. 'So?'

'So I won't have anything they want, will I? And if I don't have anything they want, I won't have anything to bargain with.' She shook her head. 'I'm sorry, Robert, but you're all I've got at the moment. I need you as much as you need me.'

I didn't know what to say to that. I didn't know if it made any sense or not, and even if it did, I didn't know if I believed it . . . or if I *wanted* to believe it. I didn't know what I wanted. I just didn't know . . .

'Get some sleep,' Eddi said quietly. 'I'll wake you up in a couple of hours.'

I didn't want to go to sleep.

But I was too tired to care any more.

Too tired to think.

Too tired to talk.

Too tired to play games.

Too tired . . .

17

For the first time in days, I woke up without any fog in my head. There were no voices, no surgeons, no people with guns. There was no whiteness, no strangeness, no nakedness. There was just me – sitting in an armchair, fully clothed. Just me and an empty room.

I rubbed my eyes and looked around. The curtains were closed and the computers and TV screens were all switched off. The room was dim and silent. I could just make out the shapes of some bags on the floor – a holdall, a rucksack, a handful of bulging carrier bags. I squinted through the dimness for a while, trying to work out what was in the bags, then a muffled sound suddenly cut through the silence, and I turned and stared at the hallway door. The sound had come from somewhere behind it. A faint spluttering noise. I listened hard. After a few moments, I heard it again. It was louder this time. Loud enough to recognize. It was the sound of someone sobbing.

I got up out of the armchair, crossed the room and went down the hallway to the bathroom. The door was open. I stood in the doorway and looked down at Eddi. She was sitting cross-legged on the floor, holding her head in her hands, rocking to and fro, crying herself to death. Her hair was damp. She was wearing a dressing gown. Her body was shaking and heaving, and I could see the tears streaming down her face.

'Hey,' I said softly, moving towards her.

At the sound of my voice, she looked up suddenly, and just for a second her face was paralysed with fear. She looked as if she'd been caught doing something terrible.

'It's all right,' I said, keeping my distance, 'it's only me.' I smiled at her. 'I was just making sure you were OK . . .'

'Yeah, yeah . . .' she muttered, quickly grabbing a tissue and frantically wiping her face. 'Yeah, I'm all right.' She sniffed hard and wiped a string of snot from her nose. 'Shit,' she said, sniffing again. 'Jesus *Christ* . . .'

I passed her a towel.

She buried her face in it for a moment, and I saw her take a few deep breaths, then she started wiping her face again. After a while, she breathed out hard, then dropped the towel to the floor and looked up at me.

'Sorry about that,' she said. 'Did I wake you up?'

'I was already awake. Are you all right?'

'Yeah . . .' She shook her head. 'Shit.'

She started to get to her feet. She looked a bit wobbly, so I held out my hand and helped her up. Her hand was as cold as ice.

'Thanks,' she said, rubbing her eyes. She grinned sheepishly at me, then looked in the mirror. 'Christ, what a mess.' She turned on the taps and started washing her face.

'I'll wait for you in the front room,' I told her, and started to leave.

'It was Morris,' she said quietly.

I stopped and turned round.

She looked at me, drying her face with a fresh towel. 'I just started seeing him . . . you know, his face and everything. I couldn't get it out of my head. All that blood . . . the way he was just lying there, all twisted up . . . I don't know. I suppose it just hit me. The reality of it all. And then I just started crying like a baby, and I couldn't stop.' She sighed again, a big shaky breath. 'God . . . I totally lost it.'

I nodded at her, not sure what to say.

She smiled at me. 'You weren't supposed to see me like that.'

'It's all right,' I said. 'I won't tell anyone.'

Still smiling, she reached up and briefly placed her hand on my cheek. It didn't mean anything, I knew that. It was just a kind gesture, a friendly touch, an unspoken thank you. I *knew* that.

But it still ripped me apart.

'You need to get rid of those clothes,' she said.

'What?'

She smiled. 'Not now . . . I mean after you've had a shower.' She nodded at a laundry bag on the floor. It was filled with her bloodstained clothing. 'We need to get rid of everything that might have Morris's blood on it,' she told me. 'So when you've showered, put all your clothes in the bag with mine. And I mean all of them. I'll get rid of the bag before we go.'

'These are the only clothes I've got,' I said.

'I'll find you something to wear.' She turned away from me to hang up the towel. 'I won't be a minute. I just need to dry my hair and get dressed.'

I didn't move. I just stood there like an idiot, remembering the feel of her hand on my face.

'Robert?' she said.

'Oh, right . . . yeah. Sorry.'

I backed out of the bathroom and left her to it.

While Eddi was in her bedroom, drying her hair and getting dressed, I took a quick shower and changed into the clothes she'd left out for me. Dark shirt, pants, socks, a plain black suit. I wondered where she'd got them from – a boyfriend, Lawrence, Curtis?

I decided not to ask.

When I came out of the bathroom, Eddi was waiting for me in the front room. She'd slicked back her hair and removed most of the studs and rings from her face, and she'd put on a little black jacket and skirt. She looked cool and neat and businesslike. I passed her the laundry bag full of dirty clothes and she put it with the other bags on the floor.

'Is there anything else you need to get rid of before we go?' she asked me.

'Like what?'

'Knives, weapons . . . anything that won't get through airport security.'

'Airport security?'

'I'll explain later.' She nodded at my rucksack. 'If you've got anything dodgy in there, get rid of it now. Put it in one of these carrier bags.'

I opened my rucksack and started going through it, but there was hardly anything in there any more – I'd left most of it at the Paradise Hotel. All I could find to leave behind was Ryan's penknife and the videotape of my endoscopy.

The videotape . . .

My mind flashed back to a wondrous cavern, rising and swirling with fantastic alien machineries. Filaments, struts, crystals, ties, pillars, pipes, valves, ribbons, sheaths, valleys, tunnels, veins, countless glimmering particles . . . a sub-atomic dome, a dark cathedral, a perfect abomination . . .

Inside me.

In me.

It was me.

Whatever you see, I'd told myself then, *whatever's there . . . there's a thousand ways it won't be you.*

I put the videotape back in the rucksack, then went over and dropped the penknife in one of the carrier bags. There were three of them, all jam-packed with papers and disks and files . . .

'What is all this stuff?' I asked Eddi.

'My life,' she said simply. 'My business . . . everything. Hard drives, client lists, contacts, names, places, numbers. Everything. Once I've got rid of it, the flat's clean. They can take it apart, computers and everything, but they won't find anything useful.' She looked down at the bags. 'Not much of a life, is it? Three carrier bags full of crap.'

'I'm sorry,' I said. 'I didn't realize . . .'

'It's all right,' she muttered. 'It was probably time for a change anyway.' She gazed around the flat for a moment, taking one last look at what she was leaving behind, then she turned back to me and smiled. 'Right,' she said. 'Are you ready?'

'I suppose so . . .'

'OK, let's get out of here.'

On the way to the lift, Eddi called Bean and told him to meet us on the ground floor. As we waited for the lift to arrive, she took Ryan's wallet from her pocket and gave it back to me.

'I couldn't find anything on his credit cards,' she told me. 'I searched everything, every illegal database there is, but he wasn't on any of them. I also ran searches on his ID card and his telephone number . . . but they all came up blank.' She looked at me. 'I don't understand it, Robert. I've got access to almost everything here. Ryan's details should show up somewhere, but I can't find anything at all.' She shook her head. 'It's as if he doesn't exist.'

'Maybe he doesn't,' I suggested. 'Maybe I just imagined him.' I looked at her. 'Maybe I'm making the whole thing up.'

'I've already thought of that,' she said. 'But then where did you get the credit cards from? And the ID card? The wallet, the business cards, the pistol? And what about Morris? He *existed*, didn't he? He was after you. And I know he wasn't police.'

The lift doors opened. We picked up our bags and stepped inside. Eddi hit the button for the ground floor. The doors closed and the lift started moving.

'How do you know that Morris wasn't a policeman?' I asked her.

'The police don't carry pistols in shoulder holsters, for a start. And the police wouldn't have been waiting for you at the hospital. And, even if they were, they wouldn't have left a man on his own.' She rubbed her eyes. 'Dennet's a policeman, though.'

'Who?'

'Detective Superintendent Mark Dennet, the one they quoted in the newspaper story. I checked him out. He's CID, based in Stoneham.'

'What does that mean?'

'I don't know.'

'But he's definitely real? I mean, Dennet definitely exists?'

'Yeah.'

'And so did Morris.'

'Yeah.'

'So you don't think I'm making it all up, then?'

'No,' she replied, 'not all of it.'

Before I had a chance to ask her what she meant, the lift clunked to a halt and the doors slid open.

Bean was standing there waiting for us.

'Everything all right?' Eddi asked him.

'Yeah.'

'Anyone around?'

'No.'

'Good.' She gave him the laundry bag and the three carrier bags. 'These are for the incinerator,' she told him. 'Do it before you get rid of the Civic. And make sure there's nothing left.'

He nodded.

Eddi turned to me. 'Give him the pistol.'

'What?'

'The pistol . . . give it to him.'

I knew I had to get rid of it, but I felt strangely reluctant to part with it now. I'd got used to it. Its reassuring weight in my pocket . . . its solidity, its power. I'd got used to knowing it was there if I needed it.

I took the pistol out of my pocket and passed it to Bean.

'Clean it and get rid of it,' Eddi told him.

He nodded.

Eddi unzipped her holdall and dug around inside. She pulled out a handful of £50 notes and passed them to Bean. He slipped them in his pocket without counting them.

'I'm not going to be around for a while,' Eddi told him. 'You don't need to watch the flat any more, but let me know if anyone comes round. Use email, not the phone. I'll make sure you're all right.'

'You coming back?' he asked her.

She smiled at him. 'Yeah . . . I'm coming back.'

He nodded again, then turned round and walked off with the carrier bags. Eddi watched him until he'd left the tower block, then she picked up her holdall and slung her rucksack over her shoulder.

'Come on,' she said to me, heading for the doors.

I followed her out of the tower block and around the back to the lock-up garages. The Civic had gone. There was no one around. Just a row of garages, a couple of wheelie bins and a skip full of bricks and plasterboard. Eddi went over to one of the garages, unlocked the door and opened it up. There was a car inside, a white BMW 525.

'Is that yours?' I asked her.

She nodded. 'Unregistered, untraceable, almost unused.'

'Have you got any more cars hidden away?'

'Nope,' she said. 'This is my last one.'

We threw our bags in the back, got in the front, and

Eddi started the car. She put it into reverse, adjusted the mirror, then paused for a moment and looked at me. I thought she was going to say something . . . something meaningful, or something wise, or maybe something I didn't want to hear . . . but she didn't. She just stared at me in silence for a while, then she looked over her shoulder and started reversing the BMW out of the garage.

It was late afternoon now and the rush-hour traffic was beginning to build up. It took us almost two hours to get out of London, and then we got stuck in more roadworks again, and by the time we got through them and were finally moving again it was just gone six o'clock. I hadn't really been paying much attention to where we were going, but as Eddi put her foot down and we joined a stream of motorway traffic, I looked out of the window and saw a sign that said: MI THE NORTH.

'We're not going to Stansted, then?' I said to Eddi.

'What makes you think that?'

'Well, we're going the wrong way for a start. And you said your flight left at seven, so you had to be at Stansted by six at the latest. It's gone six now. But you don't seem too worried.'

'I cancelled the flight,' she said. 'I've booked us on another one. Seven o'clock tomorrow morning from Leeds Bradford International.'

'Where are we going?'

'Where do you think?'

'Spain?'

'Correct. And do you know why we're going from Leeds and not Stansted?'

'Because if Ryan's people are watching the airports, they'll probably be concentrating on Stansted, Gatwick and Heathrow. They won't be expecting us to go from Leeds.'

She looked at me, slightly surprised that I'd worked it all out.

'What happens when we get to Spain?' I asked her.

'I've got a flat there. It's in a little village called Tejeda, on the south coast of Andalusia. I bought it a few years ago.'

'In a false name?'

'False everything,' she said. 'It's completely safe. No one knows anything about it. It's where I go when I want to disappear for a while. My secret hideaway.'

'So this holiday you were talking about,' I said, 'the one you could have paid for twice over with the money you didn't get for my false ID . . .'

'I lied,' she said. 'The only thing that cost me anything was the flight.' She glanced at me. 'The rest of it was true, though. I *was* flying out today. I did *have* a flight.'

I smiled at her, hoping she couldn't see the truth behind my smile. Because the truth was – I was sick to death of lies. My lies, her lies, big lies, small lies . . . I didn't care what kind they were, I'd had enough of them. They made me think about things, and I didn't want to think about things.

'Are you all right?' Eddi asked me.

'Yeah . . . I'm fine.'

She gazed at me for a moment, then she nodded her head and turned her attention back to the road again. 'It'll just be for a while,' she said.

'Sorry?'

'When we get to Tejeda . . . I mean, we don't have to stay there forever. It's just a safe place to stay until we've worked out what's happening, and what we're going to do.'

'What *are* we going to do?'

'I don't know yet . . . I need to think about it.' She flashed a quick grin at me. 'That's why we're going to Tejeda.'

The BMW was a powerful car and it wasn't long before we'd left London behind and were speeding along the motorway through the heart of the country – Leicester, Derby, Nottingham. I'd never been up this way before, and although I couldn't see much in the passing darkness outside, everything seemed cold and ancient. The land-scape was darker, the night sky blacker. Even the lights of the passing towns seemed dimmer than the brightly lit towns of the south. The cities themselves were barely visible in the clouded night, they just glowed in the distance, like shallow nests of lights in the darkness. They looked as if they'd been there forever.

Another world, another time.

And as we purred along through the unfamiliar land-scape, I wondered if that's what I wanted – another world. Somewhere new. Somewhere different. Somewhere else.

Somewhere I could forget about things.

'How much do you know about mobile phones?' I asked Eddi.

'Why?' she said. 'What do you want to know?'

'Are they safe?'

'It depends . . . hold on.' She looked in the mirror and

pulled out to overtake a slow-moving car. Once she'd got past it and moved back into the middle lane again, she turned her attention back to me. 'What do you mean by *safe*?'

'If I called someone on a mobile phone and their phone was bugged, could the people who were listening in get a trace on my phone?'

Eddi looked at me, intrigued but slightly concerned. 'Would this be a landline you were calling?'

'Yeah . . .'

'From a prepaid mobile?'

'I think so.'

'And who'd be listening in?' She raised her eyebrows at me. 'I don't suppose it'd be Ryan, would it?'

I looked at her. 'I just want to call Bridget and Pete to let them know I'm all right. I haven't spoken to them since all this happened. I just want to tell them I'm OK. It'll only take a minute.'

Eddi looked away and stared through the windscreen, thinking about it.

I said, 'I don't even know if Ryan *is* tapping their phone –'

'He's bound to be.' She lit a cigarette. 'How long did you say you've been with Bridget and Pete?'

'Just over a year.'

'Do you trust them?'

'I don't know . . . I suppose so. They've always been really good to me.'

'How did they end up fostering you? Did it all go through the usual channels?'

'Yeah, as far as I know. They've been fostering for years. The kid they had before me was with them for ages.'

'So there was nothing unusual about it?'

'Like what?'

'I don't *know*, Robert. At the moment, all I know about any of this is what you've told me – you woke up in hospital and you had something inside you, or Ryan was *putting* something inside you, and now he's got everyone looking for you, and people are dying all over the place . . .' She paused, taking a drag on her cigarette, then she leaned down, stabbed it out in the ashtray and blew out a long stream of smoke. 'All I'm trying to do,' she said, 'is work out what the hell it all means – what was inside you, who put it there, why they put it there.' She looked at me. 'We need to know if anyone else was involved.'

I stared through the windscreen for a moment, remembering my own doubts about Bridget and Pete. I still didn't want to believe they had anything to do with all this, and from the way Ryan had spoken about them at the hospital – as if he'd never heard of them before – I was fairly sure they *didn't* have anything to do with it.

But it still wasn't impossible.

'I don't know if Bridget and Pete are involved,' I said to Eddi. 'I don't *think* they are . . . I mean, I can't think of anything unusual or suspicious about them. They just seemed quite nice, you know? They were good to me and I liked them. That's why I want to call them. And anyway, if you think about, it doesn't really matter whether they're involved or not.'

'Why not?'

'Because if they are, they'll act as if they're not when I call them. And if they're not . . . well, it won't make any difference, will it? As long as I don't tell them where we are or anything, and my call can't be traced, it doesn't matter if anyone's listening in or not.'

Eddi didn't speak for a moment, she just sat there in silence – chewing on her lip, thinking things through. After a while she said, 'It depends what kind of tracking equipment Ryan's people have got. If they've got the very best stuff, which I think they probably have, and they're expecting a call to a particular number, and the call comes in from a landline, they should be able to get a trace on it almost immediately. If the call comes in from a prepaid mobile, though . . . well, they'll still get a trace on it, but it'll take them a while to get a location, especially if the mobile isn't registered. And even when they *do* get a location, it won't be very accurate.'

'So,' I said, 'if we had a prepaid mobile that wasn't registered, and I used it to call Bridget and Pete, what's the worst that could happen?'

'Ryan would eventually find out that you made the call from somewhere between Nottingham and Leeds.'

'And that's it?'

'Yeah.' She glanced across at me. 'Go on, then. Make your call. There's a couple of phones in the side pocket of my rucksack. Use the Nokia.'

'Are you sure?' I said, smiling at her.

She shook her head. 'Just do it . . . before I change my mind.'

I reached over to the back seat and started going through the pockets of her rucksack. It had lots of pockets, but I couldn't find any phones. I looked round at Eddi to ask her which pocket they were in, but she was having a bit of trouble with a lorry we were overtaking – it kept speeding up and swaying into our lane – so, rather than disturb her, I just turned back to the rucksack, opened it up and started digging around inside. There was a full carrier bag packed at the top of the rucksack and it was hard to find anything without moving it. I pulled it out and put it down on the seat, and then the car lurched slightly and the bag flopped over to one side . . . and a pile of £50 notes slid out.

I stared at them. I'd never seen so much money in all my life. And there was more inside the bag too – lots more. The whole bag was packed full of notes – fifties, twenties, euros . . . all banded up in grubby little stacks.

'Shit,' I whispered.

'What are you doing?' I heard Eddi say.

I glanced up and saw her watching me in the rear-view mirror. Her eyes were cold and steely.

'Sorry,' I spluttered, 'I couldn't find the phones . . . I was just looking . . . I didn't mean to –'

'The phones are in the side pocket with the little red zip,' she said calmly. 'Make sure you put all the money back.'

I scooped all the spilled cash back into the bag, stuffed the bag into the rucksack, then found the side pocket with the little red zip and pulled out a polythene bag full of phones. There were three of them: two Motorolas and a Nokia. I picked out the Nokia and settled myself down in the seat again.

Eddi glanced at me for a second, then looked away.

'Is that all your money?' I asked her.

'What do you mean? Does it all *belong* to me, or is that all I've *got*?'

'Is that all you've got?'

'It's all the *cash* I've got, yeah.'

'How much is it?'

'Just over ten grand, including the euros.' She nodded at the phone in my hand. 'Make your call. And keep it short.'

I couldn't remember the number for a moment. I sat there staring at the phone in my hand, trying to think, trying to picture the number – my *own* telephone number – then I gave up thinking and let my thumb do it for me. Thumb-memory. It worked. My thumb punched in the number and I put the phone to my ear.

For a couple of seconds, I felt really weird – anxious, excited, afraid, uncertain. I didn't know who was going to answer the phone or what I was going to say to them. I was hoping it'd be Bridget, but even if it was . . . I still didn't know what I was going to say to her or what she was going to say to me. I didn't even know if she'd *want* to talk to me.

But I needn't have worried.

The phone didn't ring.

It didn't do anything, just hissed emptily. A ghostly electric sound.

'No answer?' asked Eddi.

'No nothing,' I said, holding the phone to her ear to let her listen.

'Maybe you got the wrong number,' she suggested. 'Try it again.'

I tried again, keying in the number slowly and carefully, but when I put the phone to my ear, the emptiness was still there.

'Here, let me try it,' said Eddi. 'What's the number?'

I passed her the phone and told her the number. As she punched it in and held the phone to her ear, I quickly reached into my pocket, pulled out one of Ryan's business cards and placed it on the seat beside my left leg, out of Eddi's sight. I glanced across at her. She was listening hard to the phone.

'Anything?' I asked her.

She shook her head. 'Are you sure it's the right number?'

'Yeah.'

'It hasn't been disconnected or anything?'

'It was fine when I left home on Monday. What do you think it means?'

She shook her head again and passed me back the phone. 'I don't know,' she said. 'I don't know what it means, but I don't like the sound of it.'

I looked down at Ryan's business card and started to punch in the number.

Eddi glared at me. 'What are you *doing*?'

Ignoring her, I quickly keyed in the last two digits and put the phone to my ear.

'Give me that!' she said, grabbing for the phone.

I leaned away from her and switched the phone to my left ear, keeping it out of her reach.

'*Robert!*' she hissed.

But it was too late. The number was ringing. I put my finger to my lips and held up my hand to Eddi – keep quiet. She thumped the steering wheel with her fist and stared angrily at me.

The phone answered on the second ring.

'Hello, Robert.'

At the sound of his voice, a wave of nausea welled up inside me. I breathed in slowly and swallowed it down.

'Ryan?' I said.

'How are you, Robert?'

His voice was calm and confident.

'I'm all right,' I told him.

'That's good.'

I could hear the clean smile in his voice. I could see his silver eyes. I could picture him – dark suit, white shirt, coal-black hair . . . sitting at a desk in a basement office. The office was white. White walls, banks of computers and phone equipment, wires, cables, flashing lights. Maps on the wall. Pins in the maps.

'Where are you?' Ryan said.

'Where are *you*?'

He laughed quietly. 'I'll tell you if you tell me.'

'I don't think so.'

Rapid metallic clicks sounded on the line, like a cogwheel. In the background, I could hear a thin and distant whine.

'Where's Morris?' Ryan asked me.

'Who?'

'What have you done with him?'

'I haven't done anything.'

Ryan sighed. 'You're in a lot of trouble, Robert.'

'I know.'

'Tell me where you are. We can talk about it.'

'We can talk about it now.'

'OK, if that's what you want.'

'Are you tracing this call?'

'You're on a mobile. You're safe enough for now.'

'How do I know you're not lying?'

'You don't.'

I thought about that for a few moments, trying to work out if he *was* lying or not, but there was no way of telling from his voice. It was nerveless, expressionless, empty.

'Where are you?' I asked him again.

'Why do you want to know?'

'Tell me where you are or I'll hang up right now.'

He didn't say anything for a while. I waited, staring straight ahead. I could feel Eddi watching me, silently urging me to end the call, and I didn't want to look at her. I wanted to concentrate on Ryan. I didn't think he'd tell me where he was, and even if he did, I knew he'd probably be lying. But I didn't really care. I just wanted to see what he said.

'I'm in London,' he said eventually.

'No, you're not.'

'Why should I lie?'

'Whereabouts in London? What's your address?'

'I can't tell you that.'

'Why not?'

He sighed. 'We're in Queen Anne's Gate, SW1.

'What number?'

'We don't have a number. It's just a building, an office block —'

'What do you do there?'

'Work.'

'What kind of work? What do you do?'

'We find things.'

'What kind of things?'

'Things like you.'

'Who's *we*? Who do you work for?'

'Robert, listen –'

'What do you think I am?'

'What?'

'What do you think I *am*?'

'What do you mean?'

'You know what I mean.'

'I'm sorry, Robert. I don't know what you're talking about.'

'Yes, you do.'

He paused for a moment, then said, 'Are you with someone?'

'Look,' I told him, 'I don't know anything about any of this. Do you understand? You *think* I do, but I don't. I don't know anything about it.'

'You don't know anything about what?'

'Everything, anything . . .' I closed my eyes for a moment and tried to think. I wanted to ask Ryan what he knew about me – what I was, what I was made of, where I came from – but I couldn't just come out and say it, not with Eddi listening.

'Robert?' Ryan said into the phone. 'Robert . . . are you still there?'

'What was that thing inside me?' I asked him.

'Sorry?'

'Inside me . . . what is it?'

'What are you talking about?'

'Just tell me.'

He sighed again, this time with something that sounded like honesty. 'You're not making sense, Robert. I think you're a bit confused –'

'Where's Bridget?' I asked him.

'Bridget's fine –'

'*Where* is she?'

'I don't know . . . I expect she's at home. Where else would she be?'

I felt Eddi's hand on my arm then and without thinking I glanced across at her. *No more*, she mouthed at me. *End the call now* . . .

I shrugged her hand off my arm and turned my attention back to Ryan.

'Why did you kill him, Robert?' he said.

'What?'

'Why did you kill him?'

'Who?'

'Dr Casing.'

'Oh, yeah,' I said, 'I read about that in the papers. Very good. By the way, he's a professor, not a doctor.'

'He was a doctor.'

'He's a professor. Kamal told me. A consultant surgeon. Gastroenterologist.'

'Who's Kamal?'

'I know what you're trying to do.'

'I'm not trying to do anything. I just want to help you. Look, if you give yourself up now, a good solicitor will get you off on a manslaughter charge. You'll get ten, fifteen years at the most. You'll probably be out in half that. But if you keep on running, you're only going to make things worse for yourself. You can't run forever, Robert. We'll never stop looking for you. And wherever you go, we'll find you.'

'Do you think I'm *stupid*?'

'No.'

'What's the matter with you? This is *me* you're talking to. Robert Smith. I was there, in the hospital. You don't have to make up stories for me. I was *there*. I know what happened. And I know what'll happen if I give myself up. I *know* what you'll do to me.'

'And what's that?'

'You'll cut me open. You'll lock me up.'

'Why would I want –'

'Tell me what you look like.'

'What?'

'Tell me what you look like. Describe yourself.'

'Why?'

'You're not Ryan.'

'Of course I am.'

'What do you look like?'

'Robert –'

'What do you *look* like?' I was shouting now.

'I'm tall,' Ryan said calmly. 'Six feet and a bit. Black hair. Grey eyes.'

'Grey?'

'Yes.'

'What's your ID number?'

'One one nine, one two, one two.'

'Are you a policeman?'

'No.'

'Describe what happened.'

'When?'

'At the hospital.'

'You know what happened.'

'I know. I want you to tell me.'

'You attacked Dr Casing with a scalpel –'

'Don't be ridiculous.'

'It was –'

'You're not Ryan. Let me speak to Ryan.'

'Look, Robert, I'm sure you didn't mean to do it. It was a mistake. You're under a lot of stress. I understand that –'

'You don't understand anything.'

'Robert –'

'You weren't there. You don't know anything about it. You don't know why Ryan wants me. You don't know what he knows, what I know. You don't know –'

'You're not human.'

His words froze me.

You're not human.

I stared through the windscreen, not knowing where I was for a moment. All I could see were lights – orange lights, white lights, red lights . . . streaming through the darkness, like liquid, like metal . . . like tiny stars. I kept looking. Mesmerized.

You're not human.

Did he really say that?

I tried to think, to put things in order. One . . . two . . . three . . . four . . . five . . . put them in a line, one thing after another. Things that happened. Things that happened. Sounds, movement, words, feelings, intent.

I couldn't think.

'We'll find you, Robert,' Ryan said distantly. 'Wherever you go, whatever you are, we'll find you.'

I shut off the phone.

My stomach hurt.

I stared at the lights in the darkness.

*

Have you ever seen inside yourself? Do you *know* what's in there? Think about it. Imagine it. You don't know what's under your skin, do you? You *think* you do. You *think* you've got all the usual stuff – heart, lungs, stomach, liver – but how do you *know*?

You don't.

You see pictures in books, pictures on TV. You read about stuff. And you just assume that's it. Guts, blood, bones, organs – that's what you are. But you don't know anything about it. You don't know if it's really there. And even if it is, you don't know how it works.

You don't control it.

It controls you.

18

I couldn't do anything for a while. Couldn't speak, couldn't move, couldn't think. All I could do was sit there in silence, staring blindly through the windscreen at the never-ending streams of light – orange, white, red, silver – pulsing like stars in the darkness. Like liquid, like metal, like countless glimmering particles . . .

'Robert?'

. . . like strings of stars, like crystalline compounds with radiating shards.

'Robert?'

I blinked my eyes and looked at Eddi.

'Give me the phone,' she said firmly.

'Uh?'

'The phone.' She held out her hand. 'Give it to me.'

I passed it over. She checked the connection was cut off, then pressed a few buttons and glanced at the display. As I watched her, I could feel things coming back into focus again. Eddi, the car, the motorway, the lights . . . the lights were just lights. Headlights. Tail-lights. Motorway lights. I breathed in and rubbed my eyes.

My belly still hurt – a deep, distant ache.

I breathed out, wincing slightly.

'Are you all right?' asked Eddi.

'Yeah . . . yeah, I'm all right.' I looked at her. 'Look, I'm sorry –'

'You should be,' she said. 'That was just stupid . . . ringing Ryan.' She shook her head. 'Stupid beyond belief. What did you think you were *doing*?'

I shrugged. 'I don't know . . .'

'You don't *know*?'

'I had to speak to him.'

'Why?'

'To find out . . . I had to find out . . .'

She sighed and shook her head again. 'And what did you find out? What did he tell you?'

'Not much . . .'

'Well, there's a surprise.'

'He was trying to confuse me. He was trying to make me believe his lies . . .'

'Of *course* he was. What did you expect him to do? He's not going to tell you the truth, is he? He wants to unbalance you, get you confused. He wants you to make a mistake.' She looked at me again. 'This is big stuff, Robert. Whoever these people are, and whatever it is they want from you, they won't stop at anything to get it.' She glanced at the phone in her hand, turned it off, wound down her window, then looked back at me. 'So, no more stupid phone calls – OK?'

I nodded.

She looked in the rear-view mirror, waited for a car to pass by in the outside lane, then looked in the mirror again. Another brief pause, then she switched the phone to her right hand and quickly dropped it out of the open window.

I heard a faint clatter of shattering plastic, and when I looked over my shoulder I saw the remains of the phone disappearing under the front bumper of an articulated lorry.

Eddi wound the window back up and carried on driving.

For the rest of the journey, Eddi asked me questions and I tried to answer them. She asked me what happened at the hospital again; I told her. She asked me to describe the thing I'd found inside me; I described it. She asked me about Ryan, Casing, Morris, Kamal; about Bridget and Pete, and my other carers; about my schools and the Homes I'd stayed in. She asked me about my childhood, my memories, my life.

I did my best. I tried to think about it. I tried to remember the first few years of my life, but I didn't know if the things I remembered were part of my life or just part of a story.

'All I really know about anything is what I've been told,' I explained to Eddi. 'I was told I was abandoned at birth. I was told I was looked after by the nurses at the maternity hospital. I was told they named me Robert. And I was told that when I left the hospital I went to live with a couple called Smith, but I don't remember anything about them.'

'Nothing at all?' Eddi asked.

I shook my head. 'I was just a baby. I can't remember anything – no faces, no voices, no sense of place. I don't even know how long I was with them. I can remember most of my other carers . . . not in any detail or anything, but I sort of remember bits of them. You know, bits of houses, bits of faces, bits of times . . .'

'But nothing about the Smiths?'

'No.'

It was strange, trying to think about it. I knew that I had *been* a child. I could remember growing up, getting older, getting bigger. I remembered getting feelings that I'd never felt before.

I *had* grown up.

'What did Ryan say?' Eddi asked me.

'Sorry?'

'On the phone . . . what did Ryan have to say?'

'About what?'

'Anything . . .' She glanced at me. 'Why did you ask him what he thought you were?'

'Did I?'

She nodded. 'You said to him, "What do you think I am?" You asked him that twice.'

'Oh, yeah . . .' I shook my head, as if it was nothing. 'I was just letting him know that I'm not an idiot. You know, like, what do you think I am – stupid?'

'Right . . . so this was when he was trying to make you believe his lies?'

'Yeah, I suppose.'

'And what about anything else? Did he tell you anything at all?'

'Not really . . .'

'What about when you asked him where he was?'

'He said he was in London – Queen Anne's Gate, sw1. I think he was probably lying.'

'Queen Anne's Gate?'

'Yeah.' I looked at her. 'Do you know it?'

'The Home Office is in Queen Anne's Gate.'

'What does that mean?'

'I don't know.' She shrugged. 'It could mean anything.

He could have been lying, in which case it means nothing. Or he could have been telling the truth, which could mean he works for the Government.'

'Why would he tell me the truth?'

'To make you go looking for him. He tells you where he is, you go looking for him, he's waiting for you. He'll have cameras, guards, people on the street watching out for you. You wouldn't stand a chance.'

'Not even if you were with me?'

She smiled. 'What do you think I am – stupid?'

We finally got to Leeds around ten o'clock. The rain had started falling again and the city streets looked cold and hard in the night. I was tired and hungry. I wanted to know when we were going to stop, and where, but I couldn't be bothered to ask. I'd had enough of talking. I was sick of the sound of my own voice. So I just sat there and watched the streets pass by.

We drove on, following the signs to the airport. After a while, I began to see the flashing lights of low-flying aeroplanes in the distance up ahead. As the airport got closer, I could hear the drone of planes flying over us, and I started to feel the reality of what we were doing, and where we were going. We were leaving the country. *I* was leaving the country . . . with a girl I hardly knew. I was going somewhere else, with someone else, and I didn't know how I felt about it.

Then Eddi started slowing the car, and I looked out and saw that we were turning into the courtyard of a hotel . . .

And I started feeling another reality.

*

There was only one room available – an executive double.

'It's quite expensive, I'm afraid,' the woman at the reception desk said. 'But it's all we have left at this time of night. If you'd booked earlier –'

'We'll take it,' Eddi said, passing her a credit card.

While the receptionist pressed buttons on her keyboard and Eddi filled out a form, I picked up a *Daily Mirror* from the desk and started flipping through it. I couldn't find anything about me – no photographs, no stories, no lies.

'Thank you, Mrs Rogers,' the receptionist said to Eddi. 'You're on the second floor. Through the doors, down the corridor, the lift's on your right.'

I folded the newspaper under my arm and we took our bags up to the room.

'You don't *look* like a Mrs Rogers,' I told Eddi as she opened the door.

'Don't I?'

I shook my head. 'I knew one once. She was a cleaner at one of my Homes. A dumpy little woman with a big hairy mole on her face. Everyone called her Kenny.'

'Why?'

I shrugged. 'I don't know.'

We went inside and Eddi locked the door behind us. It was a big room – double bed, loads of cupboards, plasma TV, fridge, armchair, desk, settee. The bathroom gleamed with chrome and glass, and there were two white bathrobes laid out on the bed. I watched Eddi as she went over to the window and pulled back the edge of the curtain. We were at the front of the hotel. I could see headlights streaming on the road outside. I glanced at the bed, wondering what I was wondering, then I turned on the TV and started clicking through the channels.

'Is there anything in the newspaper about you?' Eddi asked.

'I couldn't find anything.'

'Check the news channels,' she said, nodding at the TV. 'See if there's anything about Morris.'

While I searched through the channels, looking for Sky News or BBC 24, Eddi went over and picked up her holdall, then took it into the bathroom and closed the door. I heard taps running, zips unzipping, things rattling . . .

I turned my attention back to the TV. There was lots of news, lots of rolling headlines – murders, bombings, wars, disasters – but nothing about a dead man in a barn. I muted the TV and sat down on the bed. It was soft and comfortable. I gazed around the room . . . remembering another hotel room . . . another night. I put my hand inside my shirt and felt the scar on my belly. I looked down at the bite mark on the back of my hand. I rubbed my right arm where the bullet had grazed me. The wounds tingled slightly, but there wasn't any pain.

I glanced over at Eddi's rucksack, imagining the carrier bag full of cash inside. £10,000. It was a lot of money. I could live on that for a while.

I thought about it.

I could see myself getting up off the bed, picking up the rucksack, then quietly leaving the room. I could see myself doing it . . . walking down the hallway, down to reception, out into the cold rainy night. Getting in the back of a taxi, telling the driver to take me to . . .

Take you to where?

I closed my eyes.

I couldn't see anything.

When Eddi came out of the bathroom she was wearing a long woolly jumper, a pair of long woolly socks and not much else. Her skin smelled soapy and freshly washed, and she was drying her hair with a towel.

'Did you find anything about Morris?' she asked me.

'No.'

'I didn't think you would.'

'Maybe they haven't found him yet.'

'Maybe not . . . but even if they have, they'll probably try to cover it up. I doubt if we'll see anything about Morris in the news.'

She went over to the fridge, opened it up and looked inside. I was too tired to stop myself staring at her.

'Are you hungry?' she said.

'Starving.'

She pulled out a tray from the fridge, placed it on the floor, then emptied the contents of the fridge on to the tray and brought it over to the bed. There were crisps, peanuts, chocolate bars, cans of beer and Coke, little bottles of wine.

'Help yourself,' Eddi said, cracking open a bottle of wine. She took a long drink, opened up a packet of crisps and settled down on the bed beside me. I looked at her for a moment, watching her stuff a handful of crisps into her mouth, then I ripped open a Mars bar and got stuck in.

We ate in noisy silence – chomping and chewing, slurping and burping – until there was nothing left but wine and beer and a muesli bar. Eddi opened another bottle of wine.

'You want some?' she asked me.

I shook my head.

She drank half the little bottle in one go, then leaned back against the wall, crossed her legs and lit a cigarette. As she blew out the smoke, I could smell the sweet taste of wine on her breath, and for a moment it reminded me of when she'd drugged me – the whiteness, the fog, the helplessness. I tried to keep the memory from my eyes, but Eddi had already seen it.

'I know you can't forget what I did to you,' she said, 'but we both have to get over it. I'm not saying we have to trust each other –'

'I know,' I told her. 'It's all right . . . it just came back to me for a moment, that's all. It's not a problem.'

She nodded. 'I still don't understand how you managed to wake up.'

'I know . . . it happened at the hospital too.' I looked at her. 'Maybe it's got something to do with what they were doing to me.'

'What do you mean?'

'I don't know . . . that thing inside me. I mean, whatever it was, it had to do *some*thing. It had to have a purpose. And it was inside my body. So maybe it had some kind of physical effect on me . . . and somehow that made me less susceptible to the anaesthetic.'

'Yeah, but you didn't have anything inside you when I drugged your wine, did you? You'd already got rid of it by then.'

'Maybe the effects carried on after I'd got rid of it.'

'How?'

'I don't know.' I shrugged. 'I'm just thinking out loud.

226

I don't even know if that kind of thing's possible.'

'What about the scar on your stomach?'

'What about it?'

She looked at me. 'You only cut yourself open on Monday night.'

'So?'

'Well, it's a bit quick for a scar to form, isn't it? I mean, I know I've only seen it once and I don't know what's normal anyway –'

'What do you mean – *normal*?' I said. 'What are you trying to say?'

'I'm not trying to *say* anything –'

'I've always healed quickly,' I told her. 'Look.' I showed her the bite mark on the back of my hand. 'See? That's healing too. And you *know* when that happened.'

'I'm not *doubting* you, Robert,' she said. 'I'm just trying to work out what this thing inside you could be . . . what it could have done to you . . .' She shook her head. 'You started it anyway.'

'Started what?'

'The idea that it might have some kind of physical effect on you. It was your idea, not mine.'

'Yeah, well . . .'

'I'm just trying to find some answers, that's all. I'm just . . .'

'Just what?'

She smiled at me. 'I'm just thinking out loud.'

We looked at each other for a moment, and I wondered what she was thinking. Did she believe me? Did I believe her? Did we both think we were fooling each other?

She smiled again, then leaned over and reached for an

ashtray on the bedside cabinet. As she lay there, stretched across the bed, stubbing out her cigarette, her jumper rode up, revealing the still-moist skin of her half-naked body. I couldn't help staring at it for a moment, but then I forced myself to look away, not wanting to think about what it was doing to me . . . certain things, uncertain things. Skin and bone, flesh and blood . . . carbon, metal, plastic.

It was all too complicated.

Eddi sat up straight again and drained the bottle of wine. 'It sort of makes sense,' she said.

'What does?'

'This thing that was inside you . . . I mean, it *could* be some kind of experimental technology, some kind of microchip that works inside a human body. It could do all *kinds* of weird stuff. It's not impossible. And if Ryan and his people *are* experimenting with it, it'd make sense for them to use someone like you as a guinea pig.' She looked at me. 'You've got no family, no one to look out for you. They can move you around, put you in different situations. They can have people watching you all the time. And if there's ever a problem with anything, they can make sure you're alone when they fix it.'

I stared at the bed, thinking hard, trying to untangle the truth from the lies. Eddi could be right. What she was suggesting *did* make sense – to both of us. To her, it was a possible solution to what she thought was the truth. And to me, it was a possible solution to what I *knew* was the truth. And somewhere between the two possibilities – or maybe somewhere *within* them – there was another possibility: the possibility of me finding out my truth without Eddi finding out that hers was a lie.

'What do you think?' she asked me.

I looked at her, too tired to think any more. 'Yeah,' I said, 'it's possible.'

Some time around midnight, Eddi started getting ready for bed. She called down to reception for a four-thirty alarm call, set the alarm on the TV and went into the bathroom to clean her teeth. I didn't know what to do. I just sat there, looking at the walls, not daring to think. I knew what I *wanted* to do, but I knew that I couldn't. I wasn't normal, was I? I wasn't *human*, for God's sake. How could I even *think* about that? Of course, I hadn't been human the night before either. But I'd still ended up in Eddi's bed. That was different, though. I was drunk then. I was drugged. I didn't know what I was doing . . .

'Did you say something?'

I looked up suddenly at the sound of Eddi's voice. She'd come out of the bathroom and was jamming a chair up against the door. She glanced over her shoulder at me. 'I thought I heard you say something.'

'No . . . I was just . . . I was just thinking . . .'

'Yeah, well, we'd better get some sleep. We need to get going at five tomorrow morning. Five thirty at the latest.' She came over to the bed and stood in front of me. 'Are you going to sit there all night?'

I smiled, trying to hide my embarrassment, and got to my feet. While Eddi started clearing away all the crisp packets and empty bottles from the bed, I went over to a shelf by the door and lifted off a spare duvet and some pillows. I carried them across the room and dropped them on the settee.

'What are you doing?' Eddi said.

I turned and looked at her. 'I was just making up a bed . . .'

'What for? There's a bed right here.'

'Well, I just thought . . . you know . . .'

'Oh, don't be stupid.' She shook her head. 'What's the matter – don't you trust yourself? Or is it me you don't trust?'

'No, it's not that . . . it's just . . .'

'Look, if it's me you're worried about, you can forget it. Even if I wanted to do anything, I'm too tired. And if you don't think you can control yourself . . . well, you can leave that to me.' She stared at me, waiting for me to say something, but all I could do was stare back at her. 'I haven't got time for this,' she said, turning to the bed and throwing back the duvet. 'It's up to you, Robert. Sleep where you want.' She got into bed and pulled up the duvet.

I stood there for a few moments, wondering what it was that was beating so hard inside me, then I went to the bathroom. I washed, peed, cleaned my teeth. I sat on the edge of the bath and took off my shoes and socks. I stood up and took off my shirt and trousers. Then I turned round and looked at myself in a full-length mirror on the back of the door. My eyes looked tired. My hair was blond and unfamiliar. My skin was scarred. Stomach, arm, hand, arm. Scalpel, scalpel, teeth, bullet. The scars were ghost scars – thin and white, barely visible. Like threads of see-through plastic.

My reflection shimmered . . .

I didn't want to look at it any more. I opened the door, turned out the light and quietly went over to the bed. I climbed in, careful not to make any noise, switched off the light and lay down with my back to Eddi. The pillows were soft and cool, the sheets crisp and clean – it felt like heaven. I stretched out my legs and tried to relax.

'See?' Eddi said quietly. 'It's not so bad, is it?'

'Very nice,' I muttered.

We lay there in silence for a while. I could hear Eddi breathing, a whispered rhythm of sighing breaths, and I could feel her body moving as she breathed in and out . . . her chest rising and falling, her hair stirring faintly on the pillow . . .

I could feel the heat of her presence.

It was hard to ignore.

But I had to. So I just lay there in the darkness, keeping perfectly still, trying not to think of anything.

Empty your head, I told myself.

You need to rest.

Go to sleep.

Just close your eyes, forget about Eddi, forget about everything, and go to sleep.

I closed my eyes.

And I started thinking about things . . .

I opened my eyes again.

'Are you asleep?' I whispered to Eddi.

'Yeah . . .' she mumbled.

'Sorry,' I said.

'What is it?'

'Can I ask you something?'

'What?'

'It's about Curtis . . . John's brother. Your ex-boyfriend –'

'I know who Curtis is. What about him?'

'Was he taken into care at the same time as John?'

She didn't answer immediately. She just lay there, not moving, not saying anything. I waited, listening to her breathing. Her breaths weren't so steady any more. Eventually she said, 'Curtis was thirteen when they took him and his brother away. I suppose John would have been about nine or ten at the time. They kept them together at first – a few months in a Home at Southend, then a year or so with a foster family in Basildon. I'm not sure where they went after that . . .'

I waited for her to go on, but she didn't. 'John told me what happened,' I said. 'You know, with his dad and everything.'

'Curtis never talked about it.'

'Their dad used to abuse them . . . you know, mess about with them. Really nasty stuff. And he was always beating the shit out of them too. John showed me his scars once.'

'Yeah, Curtis had them all over his back. Cigarette burns.'

'John told me that his mum knew all about it, but she never did anything.'

'Yeah, well . . .' Eddi said quietly. 'Sometimes it's hard to do the right thing. Even when you know something's wrong, it's not always easy to stop it.'

'Is that how it was with you and Curtis?'

Eddi went quiet again, and I thought for a moment she wasn't going to answer me, but finally I felt her stir and she let out a sigh. 'He was all right at first,' she told me, 'but then he started getting a bit weird . . . you know, wanting to do all this kinky stuff, then getting mad at me when I wouldn't do it . . .' She sighed again. 'The first time he beat me up, I thought he was going to die of shame afterwards. He was crying and sobbing, begging me to forgive him, promising me he'd never do it again . . .'

'But he did?'

'Yeah, it just got worse and worse. Even when I *did* do what he wanted me to, he'd still find an excuse to hit me. And the worst thing was, I just put up with it. Probably like his mother used to put up with his father. I just kidded myself that somehow it was all OK – he didn't mean it, he loved me really . . . all that kind of shit.'

'Is that why you grassed him up?'

'Yeah . . . it was the only way I could think of to get him out of my life. I just couldn't put up with it any more. He was killing me. Every day, he was slowly killing me. So I set him up, ratted him out . . . and I made sure the police had everything they needed to send him down. And they did. If he hadn't got himself killed in some dumb prison fight, he'd still have another five years to serve.'

Neither of us said anything for a while. We were both still lying with our backs to each other, both still alone in the darkness. I wondered if I ought to do anything, or if Eddi might want me to do anything – say something, comfort her, ask her how she felt about things. But the silence seemed to be enough. It didn't feel awkward or empty. It felt OK.

So I just left it there.

After a while, Eddi's breathing gradually slowed into the steady rhythm of sleep, and I closed my eyes and tried to join her. I emptied my head. I tried to forget everything. I tried to sink down into the darkness. But, whatever I tried, it just didn't work.

I couldn't sleep.

I couldn't stop thinking.

As Eddi lay sleeping beside me and the night traffic murmured on the road outside, my thoughts kept flashing on and off – black and white, red and silver, this and that . . .

This?

Or that?

Normal/abnormal?

Human/unhuman?

Animate/inanimate?

Conscious/unconscious?

Living/dead?

Fleshmetalplasticcarbonelectricchemical . . . ?

Heartmachine?

Brainmachine?

Truthliestruthliestruthliestruth . . . ?

Some time in the early hours of the morning, Eddi started twitching and whimpering in her sleep. I lay there listening to her, but as the whimpering became louder and her head started flinching from side to side, I sat up and looked down at her. She was all scrunched up – her eyes clamped shut, her limbs drawn tightly to her body – and she kept making strange little movements with her hands, kind of pawing at her face, as if she was trying to get rid of something.

I watched her, wondering what she was dreaming about. Terrible things? Terrible places? Morris? Curtis? Me?

I knew I ought to wake her up, but I didn't have the courage. So I just sat there watching her, waiting for her to kill the dream, and gradually she began to calm down.

The twitching eased off, her body relaxed and her whimpers slowly faded away. It took a while, but eventually she was quiet again.

I looked at the clock on the bedside table.

It was four o'clock in the morning.

There was no point in going to sleep now.

I sat there and waited for the alarm to go off.

19

The roads were quiet when we left the hotel in the morning, and we got to the airport with plenty of time to spare. Eddi parked the BMW in the long-stay car park, paying for thirty days, and we caught the courtesy bus to the terminal. As the bus drove out of the car park, I saw Eddi glance back at her car. I could tell by the look in her eyes that she didn't think she was going to see it again.

It was still only five forty-five when we got to the terminal, but it was already surprisingly busy. Lots of people, lots of noise, lots of movement. There were queues all over the place, people milling around, policemen with guns, announcements blaring out every few seconds . . .

I said to Eddi, 'I've never been in an airport before.'

She looked at me. 'What – *never*?'

I shook my head. 'I've never been on a plane. Never been abroad. I was supposed to be going on holiday next year with Bridget and Pete –'

'Don't say anything,' she said, cutting me off.

'What?'

'When we're checking in . . . don't say anything. Just keep your mouth shut and leave everything to me. If anything goes wrong, we just turn round and walk away.

We don't run, we don't panic. We just casually walk back the way we came. All right?'

'Yeah . . .'

'And keep your eyes open. I don't think anyone's going to be looking for us here, but it's best not to take any chances. Have you got your passport ready?'

'It's in my pocket.'

'What's your name?'

'Robin Ames. What's yours?'

'Jennifer Nelson. And if anyone asks, when we get to Malaga we're hiring a car and driving to Fuengirola. A friend of ours owns a villa there. We're staying for two weeks. Our friend's name is Elizabeth Hunt.'

'And she's got a brother called Isaac.'

Eddi gave me a look. 'Like I said, just keep your mouth shut and leave everything to me.'

Nothing went wrong at the check-in desk. We showed our passports, the check-in girl looked at them and asked us where we were going. Eddi told her. She tapped her keyboard, checked our bookings, asked us how many bags we had. Eddi gave her the holdall. She weighed it, put some stickers on it, asked a few questions. And that was about it. She gave us our boarding passes, told us which gate to go to and wished us a pleasant flight.

Easy.

The next bit wasn't so easy.

I followed Eddi across the airport and we joined the queue to get through the security gates. As the queue shuffled forward, I looked around at the other passengers, trying to work out what was going on . . . and after a while I got it. And that's when I started worrying. There was an archway at the end of the queue where a man was checking everyone's boarding passes, and beyond the archway there was another short queue, and at the end of that queue . . .

'Is that a metal detector?' I whispered to Eddi.

She nodded. 'You have to take off your jacket and remove any metal items from your pockets – keys, phones, stuff like that. You put them in a tray and they go through the X-ray machine with your bag, then you walk through the metal detector.'

Shit, I thought. How am *I* going to get through a metal detector with what's inside me? Filaments, wires, living metal. The shadows of silver bones . . .

'What's the matter?' Eddi asked me.

I leaned in close to her and spoke quietly. 'What if I've got another microchip inside me? It might set off the metal detector.'

She looked at me, then whispered back, 'You said there *wasn't* another one.'

'No, I said I didn't *see* another one. That doesn't mean it's not there. For all I know, there could be dozens of them.'

The queue shuffled forward again, and as we shuffled with it, I looked up and saw that we were almost at the archway now.

'What am I going to *do*?' I whispered to Eddi.

'I don't know . . . we can't leave the queue now. It'll look too suspicious. They've already seen us whispering. You'll just have to carry on and hope for the best.'

'Hope for the best?'

'If they're only computer chips, there won't be much metal in them anyway, so they probably won't set off the detector.'

'Yeah, but what if they do?'

'Tell them you broke your arm and it had to be set with a metal plate.'

'They might want to check it –'

'Boarding pass,' she hissed. 'Give him your boarding pass.'

I smiled at the man in the archway and gave him my boarding pass. He studied it, stared at me, then passed it back and ushered me through. I waited for Eddi, then we joined the queue for the X-ray machine and started shuffling forward again. There were only a few people ahead of us, so there wasn't time to do anything now. Not that I knew what to do anyway. What *could* I do? I couldn't run. I couldn't hide. I couldn't change anything.

'Take off your jacket,' Eddi told me.

I removed my jacket and searched through my pockets, but I didn't have anything in them. I watched the people in front of us putting piles of stuff in a plastic tray – keys, phones, coins, jewellery – and I watched the security guard place the tray on a conveyor belt and slide it into the X-ray machine, then I watched the people walk through the metal detector. Nothing happened. Nothing beeped. They started collecting their bags and stuff from the conveyor belt.

And then it was our turn.

Eddi was behind me, so I went first. I gave the security man my bag and my jacket. He put them on to the conveyor belt and asked me if I had a mobile phone. I shook my head and he waved me towards the metal detector. And I knew I couldn't hesitate now. The security guard on the other side was looking at me, nodding at me to come through. I couldn't hesitate. I couldn't think about what I was, what I was made of, what was going to happen to me when the alarms went off. I couldn't think about anything. I just had to take a deep breath, compose myself and walk straight through . . .

So that's what I did.

Holding my breath, trying to look normal, trying to ignore the sickening fear in my belly . . . I just walked straight through.

And nothing happened.

No beeps. No alarms. No nothing.

I've thought about it since, trying to work out how I got through without setting off any alarms, but I still don't really know. One possible explanation is that whatever's inside me simply wasn't recognized by the metal detector. There are all kinds of metal and they don't all show up on a metal detector. Calcium, for example, the stuff of human bones. Calcium is a metal. And human bones don't show up on a metal detector. Another possibility is that I was protected by the shield inside me – that hard pliable shell that Casing had noticed when he cut me open . . . the seal beneath my skin, the flexible hinge . . . the thing that made my X-rays look normal.

Unless, of course, I *am* normal.

Physically normal.

But mentally abnormal.

But I know that I'm not.

I've seen what's inside me. I've touched it. Sniffed it. Tasted it. I still don't know what it is, but I know it's there, and that's all I *can* know.

Once I'd got through the metal detector, everything suddenly caught up with me – the lack of sleep, the fear, the panic, the momentary belief that everything was coming to an end – and my consciousness seemed to switch off. It was as if I'd been holding everything in, holding myself together, and now that I didn't have to any more, there was no longer any need to think.

No need to be aware of anything.

No need to be anything.

I vaguely remember following Eddi down a series of corridors, showing my passport to someone, then sitting down in some kind of waiting area . . . but it all seems clouded in a haze of numbness. I was there, but I wasn't really *there*. I don't recall anything about getting on the plane, and all I can remember after we'd boarded was sitting down and asking Eddi how to put the safety belt on, and then I closed my eyes and went to sleep.

20

I was still fast asleep when the plane landed at Malaga, so I have no recollection of the flight at all. One minute I was sitting on a plane in Leeds . . . the next thing I knew, Eddi was nudging me and telling me to wake up and I was opening my eyes to a whole new world. The plane had just stopped in the parking area, so there wasn't a lot to see, but I could still feel the difference. Different skies, different light, different air. Everything felt different. And new.

It felt good.

'All right?' Eddi asked me.

'Yeah . . .' I said sleepily. 'I think so.'

'You were dreaming,' she said.

'Was I?'

She smiled. 'Twitching like a puppy dog.'

'I didn't embarrass myself, did I?'

'In what way?'

'I don't know . . . sometimes you do embarrassing things when you're asleep, don't you?'

'What, you mean like drooling and farting, mumbling to yourself, saying things you shouldn't say . . . that kind of thing?'

'Yeah, that kind of thing.'

'No,' she said, smiling again, 'you didn't embarrass your-self.'

Although I'd already started feeling good about being in a different place, it wasn't until we'd stepped off the plane and were walking along the airport tarmac that the full effect of it really hit me. The smells, the sights, the sounds. The people. The feel of the place. The warmth. The dryness. The clarity.

It was amazing. I felt like a bright-eyed kid in a toy shop, gazing around in wonder at everything.

There was a mountain in the distance.

I'd never seen a mountain before.

There were clear blue skies.

White buildings.

Winter sunshine.

I didn't feel tired any more.

We didn't have any trouble getting out of the airport. After we'd collected Eddi's holdall from the baggage claim, there was a quick passport check, and that was it. No problems at all. We found the exit and went outside and Eddi lit a cigarette.

It was hard to believe it was the end of November. The skies were cloudless, the air was warm, people were dressed in T-shirts and shorts.

I felt a bit overdressed in my plain black suit – uncom-fortable and hot. I looked over at Eddi. She'd put some of her studs and rings back in, and she was wearing strappy leather sandals and a sheer white cotton dress. As she stood there smoking her cigarette, the hazy winter sunlight cut straight through the dress, revealing the pale silhouette of her body. She didn't look overdressed. Hot, maybe . . . but not overdressed.

'Am I all right like this?' I asked her.

'Like what?'

'The suit . . . it doesn't look too out of place, does it?'

She looked me up and down. 'No . . . it looks good. You look fine. We'll get you some new clothes in Nerja.'

'Where?'

'Nerja . . . it's the nearest town to Tejeda.' She put out her cigarette and picked up her bags. 'Come on, we'd better get going.'

We walked from the airport to a car-hire place and half an hour later we were racing along a pale dusty road in a little black open-top Jeep. The road ran alongside the sea, and as the warm air rushed through our hair I could smell the scents of the ocean – salt, sand, freshly cooked fish. The sea was bluer than anything I'd ever seen before – a smooth blue sparkle, shining in the sun, like a silver-rimmed slice of perfect blue sky. There were mountains in the distance, unfamiliar plants and trees, flowers and birds. There were white stone houses clinging to the flanks of earth-coloured hills.

We didn't speak for a while. There was no need to say anything. We just drove on in contented silence – past small towns and villages, past beaches and tourist resorts, over stone bridges, through long dark tunnels that cut through the hills. And the further we went, the more I liked it. The dusty brown earth, the greys and the greens, the hillside orchards, the cooling blue sea. The quiet simplicity of whiteness.

It was fine. Everything was fine. Even the traffic was enjoyable. The sound of the passing cars, the kids on their scooters and motorbikes, smiling and laughing and beeping their horns.

It was all right.

For the first time in ages, I felt OK.

'It's beautiful, isn't it?' said Eddi.

She was right. It was beautiful.

It was almost beautiful enough to make me forget everything.

We got to Nerja around midday. It's a small coastal town, about thirty miles east of Malaga, wedged between the Mediterranean and the Sierra de Tejeda mountains.

'It gets a bit touristy during the summer,' Eddi told me, 'but it's not too bad. There aren't too many pubs and fish-and-chip shops yet.'

We dropped the Jeep off at a car-hire office, then walked into town and found a taxi rank.

'*Al Tejeda, por favor,*' Eddi told the driver as we got in the back.

He glanced at us in the rear-view mirror, then nodded his head and pulled away.

It wasn't far to Tejeda.

A few miles out of Nerja, we turned off a roundabout and started heading up a steep winding lane into the hills. It was a treacherous road – tight bends, no markings, no barriers – but the taxi driver didn't seem to notice. He just kept his foot down and drove. I didn't like looking down at the steep rocky drop below us, so I kept my eyes on the hills. Although the rocky slopes were mostly dusty and barren, they were dotted here and there with little oases of colour – whitewashed houses with flowered gardens, holiday villas, bright-blue swimming pools glinting in the light. There were cacti too – broad-leaved giants with vicious-looking spines – and orchards of leafless fruit trees. I breathed in. The windows of the taxi were open and I could smell the hillside air. It smelled sweet and earthy, ancient and dry.

After twenty minutes or so, the taxi veered off the road and headed down into a shallow valley. Up ahead, I could see a quiet little village nestling in the foothills of the mountains, overlooking the sea.

'Is that it?' I asked Eddi. 'Is that Tejeda?'

She nodded.

I gazed around as we entered the village. It had steep cobbled streets, little shops, pretty white houses, a small stone church.

It had a silence.

An emptiness.

A feeling of home.

'¿A dónde?' the taxi driver asked Eddi.

She told him where to go, and a few moments later he pulled up at the side of the road and we both got out.

'Gracias,' Eddi said, handing him some euros.

He took the money and drove off, and Eddi started leading me down a narrow cobbled lane. There were white terraced houses on one side of the lane and a brick-walled orchard on the other. The houses were old and higgledy-piggledy. Wooden shutters on the windows, flowers and vines tumbling from balconies.

'What do you think?' Eddi asked me. 'Do you like it?'

'Yeah,' I said, 'it's really nice.'

She took a key out of her pocket and stopped outside one of the houses. 'Here we are,' she said, unlocking the door. 'I'm on the top floor.'

We went inside. The hallway was cool and scented with flowers. There were pictures on the wall, religious ornaments, porcelain statues lined up on a shelf. At the foot of the stairs, a tinny little motorbike was propped up against the wall. As Eddi closed the front door, an old woman appeared at the end of the hallway. She was dressed all in black and she had a large white dog at her side.

'*Hola, Maria,*' she called out to Eddi. '*¿Como está usted?*'

Eddi smiled and waved at her. '*Bien, gracias, Señora Garcia. ¿Y usted?*'

The old woman smiled and shrugged.

Eddi looked at her dog. '*Hola, Chico.*'

The dog barked once.

Eddi touched my arm and looked at the woman again. '*Este es mi amigo, John Martin,*' she told her.

The woman nodded at me.

I smiled.

The woman said to Eddi, '*¿Cuanto tiempo se queda aquí?*'

Eddi shrugged her shoulders. '*No sé . . .*'

The old woman stood there nodding for a few moments, then she smiled again, mumbled something to her dog, and they both shuffled off to wherever they'd come from.

'That's Lola Garcia,' Eddi explained as we went up the

stairs. 'She lives here with her daughter and son-in-law and their three kids. They're all right. They keep themselves to themselves.'

'Did she call you Maria?

'Yeah, that's who I am when I'm here – Maria Lombard.' She looked at me. 'I told Lola your name was John Martin.'

'Why?'

'I don't know,' she shrugged, opening the door to her flat. 'Just habit, I suppose. Why tell the truth when it's safer to lie?'

'So I'm John Martin?'

'Sorry – it was the first name that came into my head.' She grinned at me. 'You can call yourself Johnny if you want.'

'Thanks.'

The flat was about the same size as the one in Finsbury Park. It had the same number of rooms too – a large front room, a kitchen, two bedrooms, a bathroom – but that was as far as the similarities went. This flat wasn't darkened with heavy black curtains, or crowded with computers and TV screens, it was light and spacious, and somehow it felt more natural. It had stone-tiled floors, whitewashed walls, a large wooden fan on the ceiling. There was a high window at the far end of the front room, and through the window I could see the ocean glimmering brightly in the distance.

Eddi switched on the fan and opened the window. The fan whirred slowly, purring gently in the afternoon silence, and I could feel the cool breeze on my skin. I looked at Eddi. She was standing at the window, staring out to sea, lost in thought. I went over and stood beside her.

'Are you all right?' I said.

'Yeah . . . just a bit tired, that's all.'

'It's been a long couple of days.'

She nodded. 'There's still a lot to do.'

'Yeah, I suppose . . .'

She carried on staring into the distance for a while, then she stretched her neck, rubbed her eyes and turned to look at me. 'We can do this, Robert. We can find out what's been happening to you. We *have* to. I mean, we can't just run away from it all, can we?'

'No,' I agreed.

'It's too big to run away from. These people, Ryan and the rest of them, whoever they are, they're not going to give up. Wherever we go, they'll find us in the end. The only choice we have is to find out who they are, and what they've done, and what they want –'

'And then what?' I said.

'Sorry?'

'When we've found out all this stuff, what are we actually going to *do* with it?'

She stared at me. 'I don't know yet . . .'

I shook my head, realizing the truth of it: there was nothing we could do. Whatever we found out, whether it was Eddi's truth or mine, I could never be normal again. I could never be Robert Smith. I could never be anything except what I was. And what kind of future was that?

Eddi put her hand on my shoulder. 'Look, Robert,' she said, 'all we can do is take things one step at a time. We're safe here for the moment. We can take it easy for a while, get some rest. We can get on with things without having to look over our shoulders all the time. So we might as well enjoy it while it lasts. And, in the meantime, I'll start looking into things. I haven't got as much access to information here as I had in London, but I've got a laptop and an untraceable Internet connection, and I know a few tricks . . . I should be able to find out something. But there's no point wondering what we're going to do with it until we know what it is. So let's just wait until then – OK?' She gave my shoulder a squeeze. 'Don't worry, we'll think of something. Trust me.'

I smiled at her. 'I thought you said we couldn't trust each other?'

'I was lying.'

We didn't do much for the rest of the day. Eddi showed me around the flat, letting me know where everything was – food, towels, sheets, toothbrushes, all that kind of stuff. She gave me keys to the flat and the front door. She showed me how the shower worked, and the TV, and the fan, and she told me not to bother looking for a phone, because there wasn't one.

'Do your mobiles work here?' I asked.

She shook her head. 'We're not going to use *any* phones here. It's too much of a risk. We don't use mobiles, we don't use payphones . . . we don't call *anyone* – OK? We just keep quiet and sit tight.'

I nodded.

She looked at me for a moment, making sure that I was taking her seriously, then she led me into the smaller of the two bedrooms and started showing me where I could put my stuff.

'There isn't much room, I'm afraid,' she said. 'I haven't

really got round to sorting it all out yet. I was going to get some more furniture and make it into a proper little guest room, you know . . . but then I realized there wasn't much point because I wasn't going to have any guests.'

'It's fine,' I told her, looking around the room. There was a single bed, a wardrobe, a wicker chair by the window. Bare floorboards. A cooling silence. I could hear the sound of little kids playing in the street outside, and from somewhere in the distance, the carefree strumming of a guitar. They were good sounds. Safe sounds. 'It's fine,' I told Eddi again. 'Really . . . it's great.'

'Are you sure?'

'Yeah, absolutely.'

We smiled at each other for a moment, neither of us sure what else to say, then Eddi nodded at me and said, 'Well, I'll leave you to it, then. I'm going to take a shower and get unpacked. I'll see you later, OK?'

'Yeah, thanks.'

She looked at me for another second or two, then turned round and left.

Later on, Eddi took me for a stroll around the village. It didn't take long, as there wasn't much to stroll around – just a main street, called San Miguel, a few little side streets and a churchyard square at the end of the village.

'It used to be a fishing village,' Eddi told me, 'but I don't think there's many fishermen left any more. Most of the villagers either work in Nerja or they hire themselves out as labourers with the companies that renovate old farmhouses in the mountains for holiday villas.'

'It's not a tourist place, then?'

'Not really . . . you get a few day-trippers from Nerja sometimes, and there's a big festival here in summer that brings in the crowds, but it's pretty quiet most of the time. That's why I like it.'

We went into a little shop and bought some provisions – bread, ham, cheese, cigarettes, water, wine – then we wandered back through the village, just ambling slowly in the afternoon sun, and returned to the flat.

It was strange, the two of us being together . . . doing normal things together – walking, talking, passing the time. I just wasn't used to it, I suppose. I wasn't used to being with someone else. Not in this way anyway. I'd kind of got used to being with Bridget and Pete, but that was different. Being with them had been simple. They were my foster parents and that's all there was to it. No questions, no doubts, no uncertain feelings. But this – me and Eddi . . . well, I still didn't know what it was all about. Why were we together? Why was she with me? Why did I feel comfortable with her when there was nothing to feel comfortable about?

Lies.

Awkwardness.

Deception.

It was strange.

But somehow it didn't feel wrong.

After we'd eaten, Eddi opened the wine and poured herself a large glass. She asked me if I wanted to join her, but I told her I was too tired.

'Are you sure?' she said. 'It'll help you to sleep.'

'I don't think I need any help, thanks.'

'Suit yourself.'

She spent the rest of the night drinking wine and smoking cigarettes and tapping away at her laptop, while I just sat there watching satellite TV. I wasn't really watching it, I was just staring at the pictures on the screen. Trying not to think about anything. Trying not to wonder . . .

A few hours later, Eddi came over and sat down beside me. She'd got through at least two bottles by now, maybe more, and it showed. Her eyes were glazed, her body was swaying, her breath was smoky and sweet.

'I'm going to bed now,' she said, trying to focus her eyes. 'I need some sleep.'

'OK,' I told her.

'If you want anything . . .' she started to say, then she paused, closing her eyes and rolling her head. 'God,' she muttered, 'I've had it. I think I'd better go.'

She tried to stand up, pushing herself up from the settee, but almost immediately she sat back down again and slumped against me. As her head rolled sleepily on to my shoulder and I felt the touch of her breath on my neck, I forced myself to get to my feet and help her up from the settee.

'Sorry,' she mumbled as I guided her across to her bedroom. 'I didn't mean . . . I wasn't . . . I'm sorry . . .'

'Here we are,' I said, opening her bedroom door. 'Are you going to be all right now?'

She let go of me and stood swaying in the doorway. 'Yeah . . .' she said, smiling crookedly. 'Yeah, I'm all right, thanks . . .'

'No trouble.'

'I'm going to sleep.'

'Good idea.'

She looked into my eyes, blinked a couple of times, then stepped up and kissed me on the mouth. It wasn't a long kiss, but it was more than just a goodnight peck, and it felt so indescribably good . . . like I was burning, melting, floating, falling . . . like nothing else could ever feel this good. And if she hadn't stopped when she did, if she hadn't touched her hand to my face, looked me in the eye and gently stepped away . . .

I don't know what would have happened.

But she did stop.

'Goodnight, Robert,' she said.

I couldn't speak. I just nodded.

She smiled again, not quite so crookedly, then went inside and closed the bedroom door.

The air was warm and heavy in my room and my breath felt like lead in my lungs. The stillness was suffocating. I went over and opened the window, and then I just stood there for a while – breathing in the cool mountain breeze, listening to the night, gazing out at the endless black sheen of the sea. Lights were flickering somewhere in the distance and I wondered what they could be. Fishing boats? Fireflies? Travellers in the dark?

The words of a song came softly into my head.

> Then the traveller in the dark
> Thanks you for your tiny spark;
> He could not see which way to go,
> If you did not twinkle so.

Twinkle, twinkle, little star,
How I wonder what you are.

I took off my shirt, sat down in the wicker chair and waited.

Some time later, when all I could hear was the muffled sound of Eddi's drunken snoring, I took the endoscopy video out of my rucksack, padded quietly out of the bedroom and went into the front room. I waited a moment, listening hard, then – satisfied that Eddi was still fast asleep – I put the video into the VCR, sat down on the settee and picked up the remote.

Twinkle, twinkle, little star . . .

I had to see what was inside me again. I didn't *want* to see it, but I had to make sure it really was there, that I hadn't imagined it. I knew I hadn't. I was *sure* I hadn't imagined it . . . but that kiss, the way it'd made me feel . . . I hadn't imagined that either.

Can a machine feel that good?

I listened to the silence again. Faint sounds of the night were drifting in through the open window – insects chirping, the soft sigh of the wind, a motorbike droning away in the distance – and from across the room I could hear the quiet buzzing of a solitary fly. I stared at the blank television screen, the remote in my hand, my thumb hovering over the PLAY button . . .

'Twinkle, twinkle,' I muttered to myself, 'let's see what you are.'

I took a deep breath and pressed PLAY.

*

It was all still there. The things I didn't understand, the black things, the grey things, the shadows of silver things. Dulled white, shining dark. Like metal, like plastic. Tubes, patterns, circles and waves, tiny asymmetrical grids . . . I'd thought it might have been easier to face this time, not so much of a shock, but it wasn't. In fact, if anything, it was even harder, because this time there was no doubt that what I was seeing was me. I *knew* it. It was me. All of it – the thin gauzy membrane, the blackened chamber, the filaments, the struts, the crystals . . .

Inside me.

The wrong-coloured liquids, milk and oil, shimmering like mercury. The brown of something alive. Shreds of whiteness, flecks of red, a heart of pulsing stars . . .

It was all still there.

Of course it was.

It had always been there.

And it always would be.

I sat there for an hour or so, replaying the tape over and over again . . . watching the things inside me . . . watching the machine . . .

Watching myself.

My self.

When I couldn't bear to watch it any more, I took the video out of the VCR, turned off the TV and went back to my room.

It was two o'clock in the morning.

I got into bed, turned off the light and wished I could cry.

21

The next few weeks seemed to pass really quickly. We didn't really do anything, and nothing much happened, but somehow the days and nights just came and went and we gradually fell into a routine. We'd get up whenever we woke up. I'd go to the shop for bread and milk. We'd eat breakfast together, drink coffee, sit around talking for a while. In the afternoons, we'd go for a walk together – around the village, down to the beach, up into the mountains. Occasionally we'd get on Eddi's motorbike (the tinny little thing I'd seen in the hallway), ride into Nerja and spend a few hours wandering around the shops. But most of the time we didn't bother leaving the village. We'd sleep for a time in the late afternoon/early evening, then Eddi would start tapping away at her laptop, looking for anything that might help us find out what had happened to me. While she was working, I'd watch TV or read a book, or maybe go out for another short walk, then at eight or nine in the evening, Eddi would stop working and we'd go out together for something to eat.

We ate in the same place every night, a little restaurant called El Corazón. It was situated on a hillside lane that looked down over San Miguel, so you could either eat inside or sit out on the balcony and watch the world going by on the street down below. That's where we always sat. Eating and drinking, talking quietly, gazing down at the gentle bustle of village life – families going out together, young men on horses, old men on donkeys, kids on scooters and motorbikes, boys and girls, doing their thing.

We didn't really talk about much.

Eddi rarely said anything about how she was getting on with her research, and I didn't ask. Sometimes she'd ask me specific questions about Ryan or Casing or Kamal, or the non-existent microchip, and sometimes she'd ask me for details about my past – names, addresses, dates – and I'd try to help her if I could, but a lot of the time I couldn't.

'It's not that I can't remember anything,' I told her once, 'it's just that the memories are all mixed up because I kept getting moved around so much. This Home, that Home . . . schools, foster parents . . . it's hard to remember how it all fits together.'

'I know what you mean,' Eddi said. 'My family moved around a lot when I was a kid.'

'Really?'

She shrugged.

I looked at her, waiting for her to go on, but she just sat there smoking a cigarette and staring into the distance.

'Why did your family keep moving around?' I asked her.

She shrugged again. 'It was just a work thing . . . my father's job . . . you know . . .'

'What did he do?'

She looked at me, and I got the feeling that she didn't

really want to talk about it, but she didn't want to explain *why* she didn't want to talk about it either.

She took a drag on her cigarette. 'My father was an officer in the Army,' she said reluctantly. 'His job took him all over the place – Germany, Cyprus, Hong Kong, Belfast – and wherever he went, he took us with him.' She sighed. 'I didn't even know where I was half the time.'

'Who's *us*?' I asked.

'Me and my mother.'

'No brothers or sisters?'

'No.'

'Is your dad still in the Army?'

She shook her head. 'Both my parents were killed in a car crash when I was twelve.'

'Christ . . . that must have been hard for you.'

'Yeah, I suppose . . . but I was only a kid at the time, and we were never really that close as a family. My father was always working, my mother was always just waiting for him to come home . . . I mean, they didn't treat me badly or anything, they were just a bit . . . I don't know. They didn't show much affection.' Her face hardened at the memory. 'They weren't exactly the most *loving* parents in the world.'

'What happened to you after they died?'

'Not much.'

'Who looked after you?'

'I went to live with an aunt in Guildford.'

'Then what?'

'I grew up,' she said simply.

I looked at her. 'What do you mean?'

She shrugged again. 'I just grew up, you know . . . went

to school, got into trouble, got thrown out, moved to London when I was sixteen . . .'

She started talking about something else then, and I knew she wasn't going to tell me anything else about herself, so I didn't bother asking. And, besides, I wasn't really sure whether I believed any of the stuff she'd told me anyway. I don't know why I doubted her story. There was just something about it, something about the way she'd told it . . . it just didn't feel right.

The odd thing was, though – it didn't seem to matter. It was as if whatever we'd both been before, whatever we'd done – real or imagined – that was all gone now. It was history. It didn't mean anything to *us*. We were here now, and now was all we had.

So, most of the time, that's all we talked about – now, today, tonight, maybe tomorrow.

Every night, after we'd eaten, we'd sit in El Corazón for a while – Eddi drinking wine and smoking cigarettes, me drinking Coke or water – and then we'd wander back to the flat. As soon as we got in, Eddi would open a bottle of wine and roll a joint (she'd bought some grass in Nerja), and then she'd sit with her laptop for the rest of the night, drinking and smoking until she could barely see any more, and eventually she'd stumble off to bed.

At first, I wasn't quite sure what to make of it. After she'd gone to bed, I'd sit there on my own, wondering if she'd been like this before – getting whacked out of her head every night – or if it was something new. And if it *was* something new, why was she doing it? Was it anything to do with me? Was she scared, addicted, troubled by nightmares? I didn't know, and after a while I realized it was pointless even thinking about it. She did it, and that was that. And it wasn't as if it was a problem anyway. She didn't lose control or anything. She just got a little bit quiet and sad . . . a bit distant, a bit lost.

There weren't any more kisses.

After we'd got back from El Corazón one night, instead of getting straight to her laptop, Eddi said she wanted to talk to me. It was some time around the middle of December by then and the days were beginning to get cooler. It was still fairly warm most of the time, but as the nights closed in and the winds blew down from the mountains, the temperature began to drop.

'Let me just put a jumper on,' I told Eddi.

When I came back, she was sitting on the settee with a glass of wine in one hand and a sheet of paper in the other. A joint was smouldering in an ashtray on the arm of the settee. I went over and sat down next to her.

'I got an email from Bean,' she said, passing me the paper.

I looked at her for a moment, then turned to the printout.

they come rnd ur plce yday, I read. *3 sutes 1 ldy 2 bill. gry merc & blk trnst nos blkd out. smashed n & serched 4 hrs. fprints all knds. took ur pcs & stuff. crimtaped ur flt*

I had to read it twice before I understood it. I read it again, just to make sure, then I passed it back to Eddi.

'What are you going to do?' I asked her.

'Nothing,' she said. 'The flat's clean. The computers are wiped. The hard drives are gone. They won't find anything about this place.'

'But they know who you are now.'

'Yeah . . . they know who I am.'

'And they'll know you're with me.'

'Probably.'

'So what does it all mean?'

She drank some wine and took a deep drag on the joint. 'It means,' she said, blowing out smoke, 'that I can't go back to my flat. And, unless we get something sorted out, I can't go back to England either. They'll be looking for me now. Even if they don't know about Morris, they'll have found out enough about me to put me away for something – fraud, deception . . . whatever.'

'If Ryan knows you're with me,' I said, 'he's not going to let anyone put you away.'

She looked at me. 'No . . . you're probably right. If what I've found out about him is true . . .'

'What? What have you found out?'

'Nothing.'

'Nothing? But you just said –'

'That's it, that's the whole point – there's nothing *to* find out. Nothing about Ryan or Hayes or Morris, nothing about Casing, nothing about Kamal . . . there's no trace of them anywhere. Even if Ryan's people are using false names, I should have found something . . . but I didn't. I couldn't even find anything on Bridget and Pete. There's no trace of *anything* anywhere. I've gone through everything – hospital records, your records, fostering records. School records. Police records. Births, deaths, marriages. I've searched newspaper archives. I've hacked into national security systems, biomechanical companies, computer companies, government offices.' She picked up her glass, took a long drink and relit the joint. 'There's nothing there, Robert. No facts, no information, no hints, no rumours . . . no nothing. And that's frightening, because there's always *some*thing. No one can hide everything. But, somehow, that's what they've done. The only other explanation is that none of it ever happened. There *is* no Ryan, no Casing, no Robert Smith. There never was a man called Morris . . .' She paused again to stub out the joint and then she just sat there for a while, staring silently into the ashtray, her eyes unblinking. I waited for her to go on, but when she still hadn't said anything after a minute or so, I couldn't wait any longer.

'It *did* happen,' I said quietly. 'Ryan *does* exist. So do I.'

'I know,' she muttered, still staring at the ashtray. 'That's the trouble . . . I know it all happened, I know it's all real . . . it's just . . .' She shook her head. 'This is bigger than I thought, Robert. *Much* bigger. These people – Ryan and the rest of them, whoever they are – they can wipe people out. Erase them. They can make things disappear.' She looked at me. 'Do you realize how *impossible* that is these days? You'd need access to everything – the media, the law, the state. You'd need limitless power, money and resources . . . legal *and* illegal. Shit, you'd need to be some kind of *god*.' She shook her head again. 'We can't go up against Ryan. We can't do *anything* with him. It's probably best if we don't even mention his name.'

She lit a cigarette and poured herself another glass of wine, and we both just sat there for a while, not saying anything.

The flat was quite cold now. The window was open and

I could feel the night air tingling on my skin. I watched clouds of cigarette smoke drifting across the room and out through the window, and I wondered why I didn't feel too bad. If Eddi was right – and there was no reason to think she wasn't – then I should have been worried. If Ryan and his people were that powerful, we didn't stand a chance. We couldn't fight them, we couldn't deal with them, we couldn't face up to them. This wasn't a Hollywood film, this was the real world. And in the real world, the little guys *don't* beat the big guys. It just doesn't happen. So why wasn't I worried? If we didn't do anything about Ryan, I'd never find out what I was, or why I was here, or where I came from . . . I'd never find out anything. Which should have worried the hell out of me. But, for some weird reason, it didn't.

'What do you think we should do?' I asked Eddi.

'I don't know,' she sighed. 'I really thought I could get somewhere with this. Find out what it means, find out who's behind it, then work out what to do . . .' She stared at the floor, slowly shaking her head. 'I thought I could do it,' she mumbled to herself, 'I honestly thought I could do it.'

'It's all right –'

'No, it's not,' she said sullenly. 'It's *not* all right.'

'Why not?'

'Because . . .'

'We're safe enough here, aren't we?'

She shrugged.

I said, 'Do you think Ryan will find us here?'

'I don't know . . . maybe, maybe not. But that's not the point. The point is . . .' She sighed heavily. 'We can't stay here forever.'

'Why not? I mean, if we start running again, that's just going to make it easier for them to find us, isn't it? We'll be seen more, we'll have to get a car, stay in hotels . . . we'll be leaving a trail. But if we stay where we are, there's no trail to follow. And we're more likely to notice if anyone starts snooping around.'

'What about money?'

'What about it?'

'We can't live without money, Robert.'

'We've got some money . . . well, *you've* got some.'

'It won't last forever.'

I looked at her. 'I thought you said you had some more?'

'I have . . . but I can't get to it from here. I mean, I *could* get to it, but that'd mean going into a Spanish bank and filling out lots of forms, and then the Spanish bank would have to contact various banks in England, and they'd want to see proof of ID, which would mean lots of different IDs, and they'd need an address . . .' She shook her head. 'I could probably work out a way to do it, but it's just too much of a risk. There's too much information involved. Too many uncertainties.'

'Yeah, well,' I said, 'it's only money.'

She laughed coldly. 'Only money?'

'We'll manage.'

'Yeah? And how are we going to do that?'

'I don't know . . . we could always find some work –'

'Work?' she said, horrified. 'I'm not *working*. Christ . . . I know things are bad, but they're not *that* bad.'

'We'll have to do something when your money runs out.'

'Yeah, well, if *you* want to get a job, that's fine. But

don't expect me to. There are better ways to make money than working.'

I looked at her. 'Like what?'

'I don't know,' she said, avoiding my eyes. 'I'll think of something . . .'

'You're not going to try selling me out again, are you?'

Her head snapped round. 'What?'

'Joke,' I said, smiling.

She glared at me. 'There's nothing *funny* about this, Robert. We're in the shit. There's nothing to *smile* about.'

I shrugged. 'We're still alive, aren't we?'

'Yeah, for now . . .'

'We've got food, shelter, a nice place to live. The weather's good . . . Christmas is coming.' I grinned at her. 'It could be a lot worse.'

'It could be a lot better too.' Her face was still grim, but her voice had lightened a little. She didn't sound quite so forlorn.

'What are you missing?' I asked her.

'What do you mean?'

'From before . . . I mean, what did you have before that you haven't got now?'

'Money,' she said.

'Apart from that.'

She shrugged. 'I don't know . . . I had my cars, my flat, my work. I had a *life*.'

'What about friends?'

'I had *friends*,' she said defensively. 'I knew *lots* of people . . .'

'Yeah?'

'Well, all right . . . they weren't exactly friends. But it

266

was hard . . . doing what I did. I couldn't let anyone get too close. And I didn't want to anyway . . . not after Curtis.' She drank some more wine, puffed on her cigarette, then leaned down and put it out in the ashtray. 'I suppose you're right,' she sighed. 'It wasn't really much of a life.' She looked at me. 'But neither is this.'

'It's better than being dead.'

She stared at me for a moment, her face empty and still, then her mouth started twitching, her eyes lit up and she began to laugh. It was a good laugh – giggly and uncontrollable, like the carefree laughter of a child – and it made me feel good to hear it.

As I lay in bed that night, thinking about all the stuff we'd been talking about, I still couldn't understand why I didn't feel too bad about things. Eddi was right – there *wasn't* anything to smile about. I was on the run, I was an outlaw, I wasn't human. That wasn't good. I didn't know what I was, and I might never find out. That wasn't good either. And Eddi? Yes, I liked her, and I liked being with her, and that *was* good. But I still didn't trust her. I might have been smiling when I'd asked her if she was going to sell me out, but that didn't mean I didn't have my doubts.

Because I did.

They were there all the time:

Why was she with me?

What did I mean to her?

Did she think I was worth something?

Maybe she *was* going to sell me out to Ryan, or blackmail him.

Or maybe she was going to sell my story to the

newspapers – GOVERNMENT EXPOSED IN ROBO-KID EXPERIMENT HORROR. Or, THE MACHINE WHO LOVED ME: MY NIGHTS OF PASSION WITH A TEENAGE ANDROID.

Or maybe . . . maybe she *worked* for Ryan. She'd been with him from the start. She was part of the whole damn thing. And now she was just studying me, observing me, analysing me. Testing me – my behaviour, my reactions. She wasn't searching for information *about* Ryan every night, she was reporting back to him. Telling him what I'd done and what I'd said . . . how much I'd eaten, how often I'd smiled. And one day the observation period would end and I'd go to sleep at night and wake up the next morning with a gun in my face . . .

It was possible, wasn't it?

Everything was possible.

It was even just possible that she simply *liked* being with me.

22

On the Thursday before Christmas Day, I woke up around ten o'clock, put on a dressing gown and shuffled out to the bathroom. When I came back, Eddi was waiting for me in the front room. She was fully dressed, which at ten o'clock in the morning was unusual for her, and she seemed a bit anxious.

'Hey,' I said. 'You're up early.'

'Yeah . . .'

'Are you all right?'

'I'm fine.' She put her hands in her pockets. 'Listen, Robert . . . you know we were talking about making some money . . . ?'

'Yeah.'

'Well, I've been thinking about it. And I know how I can make some.'

'How?'

'I know some people . . . well, I don't actually *know* them, but I know where they are. I'm going to see them today.'

'What people? What do they do?'

'They're dealers.'

'Drug dealers?'

'Yeah, they're kind of middlemen. They don't sell in small quantities, but they're not quite wholesalers either. They're sort of somewhere in between. They'll give me a decent price and I should be able to make a good profit.'

'Hold on a minute –'

'If I don't do it now, Robert, we won't have enough cash left to make it worthwhile.'

I stared at her. 'Why didn't you tell me about this before?'

'Because I knew you wouldn't like it and you'd probably try to stop me.'

'I *don't* like it. It's a stupid idea. What if you get caught?'

'I won't. I've done it before. I know what I'm doing.'

'Yeah, but what about –'

'I'm not going to listen to you, Robert. If you say another word, I'm just going to walk out the door. I'm doing this – OK? I've made up my mind and that's all there is to it. Now, do you want to know where I'm going and when I'll be back, or do you want me to just walk out the door?'

I looked at her, not knowing quite what I was feeling. I suppose I was angry with her for not telling me. And maybe I was a bit upset that she hadn't asked me if I wanted to go with her. But mostly, I think, I was just scared that she wouldn't come back.

'Where are you going?' I asked her quietly.

'Granada. It's about forty miles north of here.'

I nodded. 'Are you going on the bike?'

'Yeah, it shouldn't take too long. I just need to find the right people, then make the deal. With a bit of luck, I might even get back tonight. If not, it'll probably be some time tomorrow.'

'What should I do if you're not back by tomorrow?'

'Nothing. If it looks like it's going to take more than a few days, I'll get a message to the Garcias.' She smiled at me. 'I'll be back before Christmas, I promise – all right?'

I shrugged.

'One more thing,' she said. 'If anything happens while I'm away . . . I mean, if anyone comes nosing around or anything, there's a gun in the bottom drawer of my bedside cabinet.'

'*What?*'

'A pistol. It's fully loaded, the safety catch is on. All you have to do is turn the safety to "off" and it's ready to fire.'

I stared at her. 'You've got a *pistol* in your bedside cabinet?'

'I got it when I first came out here,' she explained. 'I was on my own. I thought it'd be a good idea . . .'

'You could have *told* me.'

'Why?'

'Because . . .'

'Because what?'

I shook my head. 'You just should have told me, that's all.'

'Yeah, well, I'm telling you now. It's there if you need it.'

'Thanks,' I said sarcastically.

She stood there for a moment, looking at me as if I was a spoilt child, then she picked up her coat from the settee and started to leave. I watched her go, suddenly feeling stupid. I was stupid, she was stupid. This was stupid.

'Eddi?' I called out.

She stopped at the door and turned round.

I smiled at her. 'Be careful.'

She smiled back. 'You too.'

'*Hasta luego.*'

'Yeah,' she said. 'See you later, Robert.'

She opened the door and went out.

It felt really strange, being on my own again. I hadn't been on my own for a long time and I'd kind of forgotten how it felt. And I still couldn't remember now. Because things were different now. I was different. So being on my own felt different. And as I walked across the empty flat towards Eddi's bedroom, it suddenly dawned on me that whatever I was now, and whatever that meant, I'd never know again how it was to *not* be like this. Whatever I was now, that's what I was.

Eddi's pistol was exactly where she'd told me it'd be – in the bottom drawer of her bedside cabinet. It was an automatic, just like Ryan's, only this one had a slightly longer barrel and an ivory grip. I thumbed a little catch and the magazine slid out. Sixteen bullets. I replaced the magazine – *snick* – and stared at the gun in my hand.

Why hadn't she told me she had it?

And why tell me now?

Why?

I sat down on her bed and looked round the room, wondering what else she might be hiding from me. I'd only been in Eddi's room a couple of times before, and even then I'd never stayed long, so it felt quite odd to be sitting there on my own, casually looking around at her things. This was her space, her private place. It wasn't meant to be seen by anyone else.

The room was a mess. Clothes were piled all over the floor, the bed was unmade. There were empty wine bottles and cigarette packets, overflowing ashtrays, a dressing table strewn with make-up things. The air smelled of stale smoke and nightmares.

I opened the top drawer of the bedside cabinet. Inside it was a little bag of grass, a packet of cigarette papers and a Bible. I took out the Bible, flipped through the pages, then put it back in the drawer.

'Paradise,' I muttered.

And for a sickening little moment, I thought I was still there. The Paradise Hotel, the hotel room, the pistol, the Bible, the endoscopy video in the VCR . . . I was still there. I'd never left. I was still drunk, still bleeding, still sitting on the bed, still staring at those unbelievable images on the screen . . .

'Shit,' I said, shaking the thoughts from my head.

I didn't want to be there. I didn't want to *go* there. If I started thinking about what was inside me, I'd start thinking about cutting myself open again and I didn't want to do that.

I rubbed my eyes, put the pistol back in the drawer and started searching the room.

I didn't *like* doing it – poking around through Eddi's things – but I knew that I had to. If I didn't, my fears and doubts about her would just keep growing, eating away at me like a cancer. Why *was* she still with me? What *did* I mean to her? Had she *really* gone to Granada?

I had to know.

I had to *try* looking for answers.

I just *had* to . . .

I nearly changed my mind. As I crouched down beside her dressing table and started rummaging around through the drawers, the *cheapness* of what I was doing lurched up inside me and filled me with a dirty shiver of guilt. It was a cold and sickening feeling, and it was almost enough to make me stop.

Almost, but not quite.

I closed my eyes, shook off the shiver and carried on searching.

I didn't find anything in her bedroom. No secrets, no mysteries, no shocks, no answers. I didn't find anything anywhere else either. Bathroom, kitchen, front room . . . drawers, cupboards, cabinets. I looked everywhere. Nothing. The only place I didn't look was her laptop. Not that I didn't try. But when I opened it up and turned it on, the first thing it did was ask me for a password. I thought about taking a guess, but I knew it was pointless. Eddi wasn't stupid enough to use a password that I could guess. And I was pretty sure that if I started putting in loads of wrong passwords, the computer would tell her about it the next time she logged on. And then I'd have a lot of explaining to do . . .

So I just gave up.

Now that I'd done what I had to do, but still hadn't found any answers, I wasn't sure how to feel. Should I feel good because I hadn't found anything bad, or should

I feel bad because I hadn't found anything good?

Or should I just feel ashamed of myself?

Or scared?

Or stupid?

Or lonely?

As I sat by the window and watched the night come down, I tried not to feel anything.

Around seven in the evening, I went out to get something to eat. I didn't feel like going to El Corazón on my own, so I thought I'd just get something from the shop and take it back to the flat – bread and cheese, bacon, ham . . . something like that. The shop was at the church end of San Miguel, so it didn't take long to get there. It was a dark little place, cool and shady, and it sold just about everything you could ever want – food, drink, cigarettes, stamps, postcards, beach balls, newspapers, toys. It was owned and run by the Valdez family, and when I went in, Señor Valdez himself was sitting behind the till, writing something on the back of an envelope.

'*Buenas tardes, John*,' he said, looking up. '*¿Qué tal?*'

'*Bien, gracias*,' I told him.

'*Bueno.*' He smiled. '*¿Qué deseas?*'

I asked him in my clumsy Spanish for some bread, ham and cheese (*pan, jamón y queso*). He scuttled around the shop, picking it all out for me and packing it into a paper bag, then I paid him and left.

It was a nice clear evening, the sky bright with stars, and it felt good to be out and about. So instead of heading straight back to the flat, I decided to take the long way round – down San Miguel, across the church square, then up through the narrow side streets to the other end of San Miguel.

I'd been in Tejeda for almost a month now and the locals had got used to seeing me around. Most of them seemed to know my name – John Martin – but they didn't seem too bothered about knowing anything else about me. No one ever asked me what I was doing here, or who I really was, or where I was from. I suppose they just assumed I was with Eddi, or Maria as she was known to them. And that was fine with me.

As I ambled along that night, chewing on a crust of bread, I was constantly nodding at passers-by, exchanging a few words, smiling and waving at the old men and women who sat in their doorways watching the world go by. It felt good. Like I belonged here.

And I'd never felt that about anywhere before.

Just as I was leaving the square, a voice called out from behind me.

'Hey!' it said.

It was a man's voice, not harsh or loud, but full of confidence. It was the kind of voice that's used to telling people what to do. I froze for a moment, and in that moment everything suddenly came back to me – what I was, what I was doing . . . hiding, running, living a lie . . . I hadn't forgotten any of it, I'd just let it sink down into a place where it wasn't killing me all the time. But now it was back, the cold reality of it all: nothing was normal, nothing was safe, everything was a fragile sham.

'*Un momento, señor*,' the voice said. '*Quiero hablar con usted.*'

I wasn't sure exactly what he was saying – something about wanting to talk to me – but at least I knew he was Spanish now, which probably meant he wasn't one of Ryan's people. I didn't know that for sure, though, and as I slowly turned round, still chewing on a piece of bread, I wished I'd brought Eddi's pistol with me. But then, when I saw who it was, I was glad that I hadn't. The man standing in front of me, with his hands on his hips, was León Alvarez, the local police officer. I didn't really know him, but I'd seen him around the village before. He never seemed to do very much. He'd just drive into the village, hang around for a while, chatting and laughing with the locals, then he'd drive off back to wherever he came from.

'*Hola*,' he said to me now. '*¿Eres Juan, no?*'

'*¿Cómo?*'

He smiled at me. '*¿Juan? ¿Juan Martín?*'

'*Sí*,' I told him, glancing at the pistol strapped to his belt.

He nodded his head. '*Lo he visto en El Corazón con Maria. Ella es una buena, muy hermosa.*'

I shrugged, showing him that I didn't understand. '*No entiendo*,' I said. '*No hablo mucho español.*'

'You are English, yes?' he asked me.

'*Sí.*'

He smiled again. 'I speak English.'

'*Bueno*,' I said.

He gazed at me for a moment, still smiling, then he raised his chin and looked around the courtyard, pretending to check things out. There wasn't anything to check out, of course – he was just reminding me that he was a policeman. I watched him, wondering what he wanted with me. Did he know anything? Was he after anything? Or was he just nosing around?

'You with Maria,' he said, turning back to me. 'Señorita Lambarda.'

'Lombard,' I corrected him.

'It's what I say. You with her?'

'Yes.'

He nodded. 'She's good lady. Very fine.'

'Yes . . . yes, she is.'

He sniffed and hitched his belt. 'So . . . Juan . . . you OK? You like here?'

'*Sí*,' I told him, '*es muy bien.*'

'*¿Cuánto tiempo se queda aquí? ¿Está usted de vacaciones?*'

'*¿Cómo?*'

'How long you stay here?'

'*No sé.*' I shrugged. 'I don't know . . . Maria's working . . . writing . . .' I raised my hands and wiggled my fingers, miming someone tapping at a keyboard. 'She writes,' I explained.

'Ah . . .' he said. 'And you – you also write?'

'No . . . no, I don't write.'

'You do nothing?'

I shrugged.

He smiled again. 'You want work?'

'Work?'

'*Sí* . . . work, *trabajo* . . . a job.'

'What kind of job?' I asked him.

He told me that his brother, Jorge, who I'd seen a few times in El Corazón, had just bought up a load of old farmhouses in the mountains and was about to start reno-

278

vating them, turning them into luxury holiday villas, and he was looking for labourers. It was easy work and easy money, León told me, rubbing his thumb and forefinger together. Cash. When I told him that I didn't know anything about construction work, he just laughed and told me not to worry.

'You carry bricks,' he shrugged, 'paint a wall . . . no problem.'

I thanked him for the offer and told him I'd think about it . . . and that was it. End of conversation. That was all he'd wanted to talk to me about – did I want to do some work for his brother? As he said goodnight and walked off across the square, I realized that I was sweating. My palms were moist, my back was clammy and cold with sweat, and I was starting to shiver in the chilly night air.

Across the square, León was getting into his police car. He started it up, looked over at me and waved, then drove off up San Miguel.

'See you, León,' I muttered to myself. 'Thanks for scaring the hell out of me.'

23

Eddi didn't come back that night. She didn't come back the following day either, and by Saturday afternoon, Christmas Eve, I was starting to get really worried. I'd checked with the Garcias downstairs to see if Eddi had left them a message, but they hadn't heard anything from her, and now I didn't know what else I could do. She could be anywhere – in a prison cell, in a hospital. She could have crashed her bike in the mountains. She could be lying dead in the hills somewhere. She could have been arrested. She could have got into some kind of trouble with the drug dealers . . .

Or worse . . .

There *were* no drug dealers. Never had been. It was all a big lie. She'd just gone, left me, ridden off to somewhere else. Another town, another country. Maybe she had another flat somewhere? Maybe she'd gone back to England? Maybe she'd done a deal with Ryan and was telling him all about me right now?

I still didn't have any answers.

All I could do was wait.

So I sat by the window and waited.

*

The time passed slowly – hours, minutes, seconds . . . all the time in the world – and inside my head, a thousand things floated and feathered together. The silence of the flat, the emptiness, the bright blue sea in the distance. Eddi's eyes, jewels of the ocean . . . her lies, my lies . . . her absence.

Desires. Wishes.

Memories . . .

I remembered a birthday party . . . or was it a Christmas party? I seemed to remember a fat man in a cheap red suit. How old was I? I had no idea. Over five, under ten. A child. There was a long table and benches. Jellies, music, paper plates, plastic cutlery, bowls of boiled sweets. Orange juice in beakers, coloured balloons . . .

No, it wasn't Christmas. The fat man in a cheap red suit was just a fat man in a cheap red suit. It wasn't Christmas. The room was cold. The walls were painted toilet-green. There were high windows with latched openings, long hooked poles leaning in the corner. Scary poles. And sounds. I remembered sounds: kitchen sounds, the babble of children eating and drinking, excited voices, laughter. Most of all, though, I remembered myself concentrating on a door at the end of the room. Waiting for it to open.

Please open.

Please come in.

I don't know who I was expecting. I had no one.

It was some time in the early evening when I finally heard the sound of Eddi's motorbike buzzing away in the distance. I held my breath and listened hard. The sound was getting louder, getting closer. With a pounding chest,

I opened the window and leaned out, hoping desperately that I wasn't mistaken . . . and I wasn't. It was Eddi. She'd already turned the corner at the top of the street and now she was heading down towards the house – the motor-bike chugging and coughing, grey exhaust smoke trailing along in its wake. Eddi looked up as she pulled in at the side of the road, and I smiled and waved at her. She waved back, but her face wasn't smiling. She looked tired. Worn out and dishevelled. She didn't look happy.

But I didn't mind.

She was here. She'd come back. That was all that mattered.

I ran downstairs to meet her.

She hardly said a word until we were back in the flat, and even then I had to wait until she'd been to the bathroom, changed her clothes and poured herself a large glass of wine. It was a strange kind of silence, and I couldn't work out what it meant. I'd never seen her like this before. She seemed angry, but angry in an odd kind of way. Angry and sad, perhaps. Or angry with something she didn't understand. I watched her, waiting, as she drained the glass of wine in one swallow, then topped it up, drank some more and lit a cigarette. She breathed in deeply, blew out a long stream of smoke, and then finally she turned her head and looked at me.

'Are you all right?' she said.

I nodded. 'I was worried about you. I was beginning to think you weren't coming back . . .'

She gazed at me for a moment and I thought she was going to say something else, but her lips couldn't seem to

282

form any words. She opened her mouth, blinked her eyes, then looked away and stared at the floor.

'What is it, Eddi?' I said. 'What's the matter?'

She didn't answer me, she just shook her head and carried on staring at the floor. I realized then that she was crying. As I moved up closer to her, I could see the tears dripping from her face to the floor.

'Eddi?' I said quietly.

She looked at me, her face drained and pale. 'It all went wrong, Robert,' she said tearfully. 'Everything went wrong . . . they robbed me . . .'

'Who robbed you?'

She couldn't speak any more, she was crying too much. I took the glass and the cigarette from her hands, placed them on the table and put my arms around her. She stiffened for a moment, but then she just let herself go – burying her face in my chest, wailing and sobbing, letting it all pour out.

She cried for a long time.

Every now and then she'd try to speak, but she was too breathless and hysterical to make any sense. And when I tried to tell her that I couldn't understand what she was saying, she didn't seem to hear me. So I just held her in my arms, letting her do whatever she wanted, until eventually the tears began to dry up and she fell into an exhausted silence.

By the time she'd calmed down enough to tell me what happened, the sun had gone down and the evening sky was already bright with stars. I closed the window and we sat down together on the settee.

*

She'd got to Granada without any problems, she explained. It had taken her a while to track down these people she knew about, but eventually someone had given her a phone number and she'd called the dealers and set up a meeting.

'It all sounded fine,' she told me. 'They couldn't see me until eight the next evening, so I booked into a cheap hotel for a couple of nights. I was going to do the deal, stay another night in Granada and come back this morning.'

'So what went wrong?' I asked.

'I don't know . . .' She shook her head. 'I don't know if the dealers stitched me up, or the people at the hotel, or if it was just bad luck . . .' She paused to light a cigarette. I noticed that her hands were shaking.

'What happened, Eddi?' I said.

She swallowed hard. 'I met the dealers, we did the deal . . . everything seemed perfectly all right.' She looked at me. 'It was cocaine . . . really good stuff. I could have made a fortune out of it. God, I was so *pleased* with myself . . .' She shook her head again. 'They were waiting for me when I got back to the hotel.'

'Who was waiting for you?'

'I don't know . . . three guys. They were in my room. As soon as I opened the door, they just grabbed me and dragged me inside . . .' She was staring straight ahead now, lost in the memory, and I could see the fear in her eyes as she relived the moment. 'I couldn't do anything, Robert . . . it all happened so quickly. I didn't know what was going on.' She wiped her eyes. 'One of them held a knife to my throat, another one snatched the bag of coke . . . and then they just ran. It was all over in seconds . . .' She paused, trying

284

to control herself. 'Christ . . . I've never been so frightened in all my life . . .'

Her voice trailed off and I felt her shiver.

I took hold of her hand. 'It's all right . . . you're all right now.'

'I was just so *scared*,' she whispered. 'I couldn't *do* anything. After they'd gone, I just stood there, snivelling like a little kid. . . God, I felt so *pathetic*.'

I squeezed her hand.

She looked at me, her eyes filling with tears again. 'I wanted to come home . . . but it was dark . . . I would have had to ride through the mountains at night.' Her lips started quivering and she lowered her eyes. 'I was so *scared*, Robert . . . I just wanted to come *home* . . .'

'It's all right,' I said gently. 'It's over now. You're safe –'

'No, it's *not* all right,' she sobbed. 'I was stupid . . . everything I did was stupid. I should never have gone there in the first place. It was a stupid idea. Now we haven't got any money at all –'

'It doesn't matter.'

'Yes, it does.'

'No, it doesn't.'

She looked at me, getting impatient. 'It does.'

I smiled at her. 'Doesn't . . .'

'Does,' she said, smiling now through her tears.

I felt something inside me then, something I'd never felt before. A feeling that somehow the world had just shrunk and everything there was – the skies, the mountains, the stars, the sea – everything was right here, right now. Inside me, inside this room, inside this silent white cube. This was the world and that's all there was.

Just me and Eddi.

Sitting on a settee.

On a starlit Christmas Eve.

'I really missed you,' I said to her.

She smiled. 'I missed you too.'

Later that night, as we lay together in her bed, our nakedness bathed in the light of the moon, I couldn't help wondering about what we'd just done. I didn't want to think about it, I didn't want to think about anything. I just wanted to lie there and smile. But I couldn't. I couldn't stop thinking about myself – my self, my body, my skin, my flesh. My workings. The physical things. The glistening sweat on my skin. The excitement, the arousal, the love, the sex. My feelings. My actions. My liquids . . .

The sex.

How did it happen?

How did it work?

What had actually happened inside me . . . inside Eddi? What had passed between us? Were we making something together? Was it possible?

Was it *right*?

I had no way of knowing.

And I think it was then that I began to realize that I didn't really care any more. Whatever I was, whatever was inside me, there was nothing I could do about it. I knew it was there and I knew I'd never be able to forget it, but what could I do? I couldn't do anything. So why bother trying?

I functioned as a human.

I looked like a human.

I thought and felt like a human.

Did it matter that I *wasn't* human?

No.

What did it matter what was inside me? As long as it worked, and as long as it didn't stop me from being myself, who cared what it was?

I looked down at Eddi. She was snuggled up warmly in the duvet, her sleepy eyes fixed on mine. Through the open window, I could hear church bells ringing. Eddi smiled at me and draped her arm over my chest.

'Happy Christmas, Robert,' she whispered.

I nodded, smiling at her.

I was either too happy, or too sad, to speak.

24

In some ways, nothing really changed after that first night together. We still did the same things, went to the same places, lived the same simple lives. Our daily routine didn't change. Our nights were different, of course. Our nights were very different. There was no sense of awkwardness or embarrassment after that first time, it all felt perfectly natural. We didn't need to talk about it. We both just knew that we'd be sleeping together from then on, and we both just got on with it. And it was wonderful – like Christmas Eve every night. Fabulous, strange, exciting, unknowing . . . sometimes a bit frightening, and still very confusing. But mostly just wonderful.

The other thing that changed, though – and this was the thing that meant the most – was the closeness between me and Eddi. It's hard to describe what it was like, and I don't know how much it had to do with the physical closeness we'd found, but after our first night together it felt as if an invisible barrier that had been keeping us apart had suddenly been taken away. We were *close* now – whatever that means. We were together.

I'd never known that with anyone before. And, just like everything else, it felt really strange – to feel that close to another person, to be almost at one with someone else, but still be yourself. To still have your secrets and your lies, and the things you can't say . . . to live every second of every day wondering what would happen if the only other person in the world could see inside you and see what you really are . . .

I tried not to think about it.

Eddi hadn't taken all her money to Granada, so we weren't completely broke. But the few hundred euros she'd left behind didn't last very long and by the beginning of March we'd both got ourselves jobs. I started working for Jorge Alvarez just a few weeks after Christmas. I'd never had a job before, and it took me a while to get used to it, but after the first few weeks or so I felt as if I'd been doing it forever. I'd get up early in the morning, ride Eddi's motorbike up into the mountains, then spend the day with a few other locals working on some old farmhouse – knocking down walls, painting, tiling, a bit of plastering sometimes. We'd stop work around two or three, then I'd get on the motorbike and ride back home again. The job didn't pay very much, but it was cash in hand and it was just about enough money to live on.

It was still quite a struggle for a while, though – trying to get by, living from day to day, having to count every euro we spent – and it didn't really get any easier until Eddi got herself a job as a waitress at El Corazón. I knew she didn't like it. She didn't like wearing the uniform, she didn't like having to be *nice* all the time and she didn't like working the long hours – five days a week, from 11 am till 2 pm, then from 7 pm till one in the morning.

But she didn't complain.

Her days off were Wednesday and Sunday, and mine were Saturday and Sunday, so we didn't have nearly as much time with each other as before. But we could still share those lazy afternoons together, and there were always the long hot nights . . .

And that was more than enough for me.

It was a life.

We even started going to church every Sunday, which was extremely weird for me, because I'd never been in a church before. In fact, the whole thing was extremely weird. It all started on a bright Sunday morning in May, when Eddi suddenly decided that she wanted to go to Mass. We were still in bed at the time, and we'd stayed up late the night before, so I was still feeling tired and sleepy.

'Robert?' she said. 'Did you hear me?'

'What?'

'I want to go to Mass.'

'You want to what?'

'Go to Mass . . . you know, Mass . . . the church . . .'

'What are you talking about?'

'Church, Robert . . . I'm talking about going to church. I'm Catholic. I used to go to church all the time when I was a kid.'

'Yeah, well,' I said, looking at her, 'you're not a kid any more, are you?'

She punched me on the arm. 'Come on, get up. I want to go to church.'

'OK,' I said, rolling over, 'have a nice time. I'll see you later.'

Without another word, she got out of bed, yanked the sheet off me and stood there waiting for me to get up.

'All right,' I groaned, 'all right.'

She wore a plain black dress, the only one she had that was long enough to cover her knees, and she made me put on my suit.

'It's too hot for a suit,' I complained.

'You're going to church,' she said. 'You wear a suit. And make sure you comb your hair.' She smiled at me, gently shaking her head. 'Look at you . . .'

'What? What about me?'

She laughed quietly. 'Have you seen yourself recently?' She nodded at a full-length mirror on the wall. 'Take a look.'

I turned and faced the mirror. At first, I didn't under- stand what she was talking about. All I could see was myself, the same person I saw whenever I looked in the mirror . . . but then it suddenly hit me. All at once, I was seeing myself as someone else might see me – a tallish young man, his skin tanned brown, his hair long and dark, his body lean and muscled. I stared at myself, feeling strangely embarrassed.

I looked like a man.

The streets were busy when we left the flat. Everyone was going to church. They always did. Families, couples, big kids, little kids . . . all dressed up in their Sunday best: the women in long skirts and hats, the men in sombre suits. The sun was shining, the church bells were ringing, everyone was smiling and talking to each other. It felt pretty good . . .

Until we went inside the church and the service began. That's when it got really weird.

I just didn't understand it – the strange sense of doom, the sinister rituals, the mad ideas and the fancy clothes. It all just seemed so ridiculous. God, Jesus . . . bread and wine, death and glory . . . I mean, I didn't really *mind* any of it, and I actually quite liked all the stuff that went with it – the sounds, the smells, the music, the colours, the candles, the baubles, the strangely bewitching words . . . *this is my body, this is the cup of my blood* . . . I didn't mind it at all. I just found it incredible that anyone could actually *believe* it.

It was also quite weird being surrounded by so many men in dark suits. No one normally wore suits in the village – it was too hot most of the time and there was simply no reason to wear one anyway – so I just wasn't used to seeing them, and I'd kind of forgotten how much they reminded me of Ryan and his people. But now the memories were coming alive again. And as I sat there in the church, listening to the priest droning on about sacrifice and resurrection, I found myself gazing around at the rows of dark-suited men, looking for anything that felt out of place – the wrong kind of eyes, the wrong kind of face, the wrong kind of feeling . . .

I didn't see anything I didn't want to see, but I still didn't like it. The memories, the fears, the shadows of shadows . . .

Ryan.

The past.

Ghosts.

I didn't want to think about ghosts and shadows. I just wanted to *be* here – sitting with Eddi in a small stone church on a Sunday morning in Tejeda.

Nothing else.

Afterwards, when we got home, I asked Eddi if she'd enjoyed herself.

'You don't go to Mass to enjoy yourself,' she told me, going into the bedroom to get changed.

I followed her into the bedroom. 'No? What's it for, then?'

'I don't know . . . it's just church. You know, going to church . . .'

'Do you believe in any of it?'

She started to take off her dress. 'When I was a little girl at convent school,' she told me, 'I used to confess to sins I hadn't committed. We all did. We used to talk about it all the time, telling each other what we'd confessed to the priest.' She looked at me. 'We were only little kids . . . we were too young for sins. But we were all too scared not to confess to any. So we made things ups – I stole some sweets from the shop, I had wicked thoughts, I said a bad word to Sister Mary.' Her face darkened for a moment, her eyes lost in the memory, then she shook her head, dismissing it from her mind, and she turned back to me and smiled. 'The way I look at it, I'm still in credit when it comes to sins. I spent so many years atoning for imaginary ones that now I can commit them for free.' She stepped out of her dress and came over to me. 'Do you want to share one with me now?'

I looked into her naked blue eyes. 'I don't believe in sin.'

'That's all right,' she said, unbuttoning my shirt. 'You can leave all the believing to me. I've got more than enough for both of us.'

25

Every year, in the first week of June, the villagers of Tejeda hold a festival in honour of their patron saint, La Virgen de las Maravillas. The celebrations last for four days, starting on the Friday and building up over the weekend until the festival reaches its climax on Monday night with a grand procession through the streets.

Jorge Alvarez told me all about it. He was a member of La Cofradía, the local brotherhood that organized the procession. His brother, León, was a member too . . . and his father, and his grandfather, and most of his uncles and cousins. This year, though, Jorge was one of the *costaleros*, the men who carried the image of the Virgin through the streets, and he was really excited about it. It was a huge honour apparently. And in the weeks leading up to the festival, he didn't talk about anything else. In fact, he talked about it so much that by the time the festival finally started I was pretty excited myself.

I didn't go to work on the Friday, and I wasn't planning to go back until the following Wednesday or Thursday, but Eddi had to work over the whole weekend. She didn't want to, but the festival was a big event, and people came from miles around to see it, so the restaurants and bars were always really busy.

'I can't get out of it, Robert,' she told me on the Friday afternoon. 'They want all the waitresses on duty over the whole weekend.'

'Every night?'

'Yeah . . . I'll probably get a couple of afternoons off, and I might get to see some of the procession on Monday –'

'Can't you tell them you're sick or something?'

She shook her head. 'It's the busiest time of the year . . . the money they make over the next few days is enough to get them through the winter. They need everyone they can get. It wouldn't be fair if I didn't help out.'

'Yeah, I suppose . . .'

'You can still go to everything . . . you'll enjoy it.' She smiled at me. 'It's the *Reina da la Feria* tonight. You can watch the Queen of the Fair being elected.'

'Yeah?'

'I think there's fireworks too.'

'Pretty girls and fireworks, eh?' I nodded thoughtfully. 'I suppose I could *force* myself to enjoy it.' I gave her a sad-looking smile. 'Of course, it won't be the same without you.'

'Yeah, right,' she grinned.

So I spent most of that night on my own, just wandering around the village, enjoying the celebrations. It would have been nicer if Eddi had been there, but I still had a pretty good time. The streets were crowded, the night was warm and the whole village was alive with colour and sound. Music was playing everywhere – guitars, trumpets, singing and dancing – and a lot of the locals had dressed up for the night. There were handsome women in brightly coloured frocks, men in white shirts and neckerchiefs, dancers in sequinned gowns, musicians in wide-brimmed hats. There were old people gathered in doorways, watching the tourists taking their pictures, while others looked on from upstairs windows. There were young people looking for fun – boys and girls, men and women – their eyes alight in the heat of the night. Candles were burning, drinks were flowing, the restaurants and bars were full . . . and I was just strolling around on my own, soaking it all up. I watched the festival streetlights being switched on. I watched the crowning of the Queen of the Fair. I watched the firework display. I listened to the music of the Alalba orchestra. And then, as midnight approached, I made my way up to El Corazón, found myself a table at the back and waited for Eddi to finish work.

It was gone two o'clock by the time we got home and Eddi was so exhausted that she didn't even want a drink. She just got undressed and fell into bed, and within seconds she was fast asleep.

The next day, Saturday, I met her after work in the afternoon and we went to a children's funfair together. There were clowns and magicians, stalls and rides, a DJ playing records. All the little kids were dancing around like lunatics, shouting and jumping and singing along . . . it was really good fun. But Eddi was tired, so we didn't stay long. When we got home, she went back to bed and slept until the early evening. I woke her up around six, made us both something to eat and then it was time for her to go back to work again.

'Are you sure you can manage this?' I asked her. 'You don't want to wear yourself out.'

'It's all right,' she said, stifling a yawn. 'I'm just not used to it.' She smiled and blew me a kiss. 'I'll see you later – OK?'

I stayed at home for an hour or two, then I went into the village and watched a dance performance in the square. After that, I listened to a band playing flamenco music for a while, but I couldn't really enjoy it. I was worried about Eddi. She looked so tired . . . and she'd been really quiet that afternoon. So, just like the night before, I headed back to El Corazón and stayed there for the rest of the night.

Eddi seemed a lot better on Sunday. She was still a bit quieter than usual, but she didn't look so tired any more, and she didn't have to go into work until eight o'clock that night, so we had the whole of the day to ourselves. It was a beautiful day – a brilliant blue-sky Sunday – and we had a beautiful time together. A quiet walk on the beach in the morning, a sleep in the afternoon, then in the early evening we went to church and watched a flower offering to La Virgen de las Maravillas. Although Jorge had told me that the Virgin was the patron saint of the village – the Virgin of the Wonders, or Our Lady of the Wonders – I still didn't really understand what it was all about, so I had no idea *why* she was being offered flowers, and neither did Eddi. But it didn't really matter. It was a nice thing to watch. Lots of colours, lots of flowers, lots of pretty lights. And as we left the church and headed back home, a glorious red sunset was spreading across the sky. It was a beautiful way to end a beautiful day.

'It's the last day tomorrow,' Eddi said as we started walking back to the flat. 'One more night and that's it.'

'Until next year.'

'Yeah . . .'

I looked at her. 'Do you think we'll still be here?'

'I don't know . . . maybe.' She carried on walking in silence for a while, but I could tell she was thinking about something. I kept quiet and waited. Eventually she looked at me and said, 'Would you mind if we were still here next year?'

I shook my head. 'No, I wouldn't mind. I like it here.'

She smiled. 'Me too. I think I could . . .'

'What?' I said as her voice trailed off. 'You think you could what?'

'Nothing,' she said hesitantly. 'I just meant that . . . you know, I could live here . . . with you. I mean, I think we could live here. That's all I meant.'

I looked at her. She seemed slightly embarrassed, as if she'd said something she hadn't meant to say. But it wasn't an awkward embarrassment. In fact, there was something almost radiant about it – her shining blue eyes, her pale skin glowing in the light of the evening sun. She was everything that's beautiful.

'I finish at nine tomorrow,' she said.

'Sorry?'

She smiled at me. 'Everyone's going to the procession, so the restaurant's closing early. I'll be finished by nine o'clock. You can come and meet me and we can watch the procession together.'

*

299

Something happened to me then. As I looked at Eddi, trying to speak, something was happening . . . some kind of feeling, somewhere inside me. I didn't know what it was. It was as if all my emotions – whatever they were – had suddenly gone into overload. The worst terror, the greatest joy, the deepest sadness, the most violent hatred . . . everything there ever was. It was all there, all in a single moment. And although I was feeling it now, I somehow knew that it came from another time, a time when everything would come together – the past, the future . . . the beginning, the end. Everything that would ever be.

It was all there.

I could feel it coming.

And I couldn't do anything about it.

26

When I got to El Corazón at nine o'clock on Monday night, Eddi had already changed out of her waitress uniform and was waiting for me on the balcony outside the restaurant. She was wearing the white cotton dress that she'd worn when we'd first arrived in Spain, and it looked even better on her now than it had done all those months ago. It somehow seemed to look different too. And I suppose, in a way, it *was* different. Back then, it had just been a dress. But now . . . well, now it was more than that. It was part of our lives. Part of our history. It was part of *us*.

'You look beautiful,' I told her.

'So do you.'

As we kissed each other, I heard whistles and cheers from inside the restaurant, and when I looked over Eddi's shoulder I saw the smiling faces of the rest of the staff – the chef, the barman, the restaurant owners.

'Just ignore them,' Eddi said, grinning at her colleagues. 'They're jealous.'

Although the procession hadn't started yet, San Miguel was already packed with people, so instead of fighting our way through the crowds, we decided to stay where we were and watch the celebrations from the balcony. It was a warm sultry night and the air was cooler on the terrace, and as the procession would pass directly beneath us, we wouldn't have to stretch our necks to see anything.

'Do you want something to eat?' Eddi asked me as I pulled up a table to the edge of the balcony.

'I'm all right, thanks.'

We sat down.

She said, 'How about a Coke or something?'

I shook my head. Eddi smiled at me, then turned her attention to the street down below. The festival was beginning to reach its peak now and people were starting to parade down San Miguel in advance of the main procession. There were men on white horses, people in costumes and masks, children with candles and sparklers. There were drummers, clowns, musicians, dancers. The wine was flowing, the music was whirling, the whole village was coming to life. And as Eddi sat there watching it all, and I sat there watching her, I could see the simple joy in her eyes. She looked fresh and happy . . . relaxed and untroubled.

She looked alive.

'Are you sure you don't want anything to drink?' she said, turning to look at me. 'I can get us some coffee if you want.'

'I'm fine,' I told her. 'What about you? Don't you want any wine?'

'I don't think so.' She smiled. 'Not tonight.'

When the main part of the procession finally appeared, the bustling noise of the street quickly faded into a reverent hush and the crowds were suddenly still. At the head of the procession was the image of the La Virgen de las

Maravillas. Set upon a wooden cradle – which Jorge had told me was called a *paso* – the beautifully painted statue was carried high on the shoulders of the *costaleros*, and as they passed by beneath us, I could see the pride on Jorge's solemn face. It was a wonderful sight. The intricately carved cradle was decorated with candles and flowers, and as it moved gracefully through the crowded street, heading for the church, the Virgin's pale luminescence shimmered softly against the clear black sky.

This is Tejeda, I thought to myself. This is the village, the world. This is everything. There doesn't have to be anything else.

As the crowds followed the procession down to the church, we stayed on the balcony and watched the rest of the celebrations from a distance. This was the climax of the festival, when the statue of the Virgin was returned to her church, and the *paso* was put away until the same time next year. The rituals began with the *costaleros* lifting the *paso* up to the sky, then lowering it again, then lifting it again, and lowering it again . . . and as this went on there was music playing, dancers dancing, a choir singing . . . and the villagers and the tourists were all gathered round the courtyard, clapping and cheering, their shadowed faces flickering in the candlelit darkness. After a while, the church doors were opened and the *costaleros* began swaying in time to the music, rocking the *paso* to and fro, moving the Virgin towards the church, then away from it . . . then towards it again and away from it again . . . until finally they started carrying the statue into the church. They moved sedately, like mourners carrying a coffin. When they were halfway through the church doors they stopped . . . and started moving back out. Then they stopped again and started moving back in . . . and then out again . . . and in . . . and out . . . and in. And all the time, the choir sang on, their angelic voices drifting up into the night . . .

It was mesmerizing. And as I sat there watching the rituals and looking around at all the people, I started getting that feeling again – the feeling of another time, a time when everything would come together – and just for a moment I wondered if that time was now.

The music had stopped. The Virgin had been returned to her church and the doors had finally closed. The air was silent and still. I looked at Eddi. Her eyes were fixed on mine and she was smiling at me like I'd never seen her smile before.

'We don't have to say anything, do we?' she said quietly.

I smiled back at her. 'About what?'

'Us . . . you and me . . . you know, how it feels . . .'

'No,' I told her, 'we don't have to say anything.'

'Good,' she said, still smiling. 'Because I think I might start crying if I tell you how I feel right now.'

Just then, a firework fizzed up into the sky from the church square. We both looked up as the bright white trace climbed higher and higher into the darkness, whistling faintly in the clear night air, and then suddenly the sky exploded with a massive burst of blinding colours, and almost immediately a thunderous boom ripped through the night. As the starburst sky crackled and hissed, and the boom echoed dully around the hills, I looked across at Eddi again. The sparkled night was shining brightly in the blue of her eyes, like coloured stars floating in the sea, and as she leaned across the table and took my hand, I could feel myself drowning.

We sat there looking at each other for a long time, smiling

like fools in our own tiny universe, neither wanting nor needing to be anywhere else.

It was a moment I'll never forget.

The fireworks were still going off as we left the restaurant and started walking back to the flat, and the streets were beginning to get busy again. The Virgin was back in her church, the serious business was over, and the crowds were moving back into the village to make the most of the last few hours of the festival. Everyone was drinking, laughing, singing and dancing . . . it looked as if it was going to be a long and noisy night.

But I wasn't really there.

As we walked the streets, hand in hand, I was lost in my head, trying to work out what to do. I didn't *want* to do anything. I just wanted to be happy . . . and I was . . . I *was* happy. I'd never felt so good in my life. But that was it: my life. My life was a lie. *I* was a lie. Whatever Eddi felt about me and whatever I felt about her . . . whatever we had together . . . it was all made worthless by that one big lie.

She didn't know what I was.

How could I be happy with that?

How could I live with it?

How could I let *her* live with it?

I couldn't. Not any more.

But what could I do?

The question kept spinning around in my mind, getting bigger and bigger all the time, until eventually it blocked out everything else and there was nothing left inside my head but the echoing sound of those four simple words:

What can I do?

What can I do?
What can I do?

As we turned off San Miguel and headed down the cobbled lane towards the flat, I knew there was only one answer. I had to tell Eddi the truth. It was the only way. I had to tell her everything. And if she didn't believe me, I'd have to show her. I'd have to cut myself open and let her see the truth for herself. Whatever it took, she had to know what I was.

And then . . . ?

I didn't know what would happen then. She might be horrified, repulsed, disgusted. She might hate me for lying to her. She might just walk out and leave me. But whatever happened, and however she felt, at least there'd be no more lying. And then maybe, just maybe, everything might be OK. We might even have a future together.

A true life.

We'd reached the house now, and as Eddi got out her key and unlocked the front door, I looked at her and smiled. She looked back at me for a moment, then put her arms round my neck and kissed me.

'It'll be all right,' I said.

'What will?'

'Everything.'

She smiled. 'I know.'

The house was quiet inside. The Garcias were probably still at the festival, and I guessed that Chico, their dog, was cowering in the dark somewhere, scared into silence by the fireworks. The booms and crashes of the fireworks were still thudding away outside as we headed up the stairs, and even in here I could smell the faint drift of gunpowder smoke in the air.

'What do you think about looking for somewhere else to live?' Eddi asked me as we reached the landing. 'I mean, I really like it here, but it'd be nice to get a bigger place eventually. You know, somewhere with a bit more room.' She put her key in the door. 'I'd have to get a different job, I suppose . . . something that pays a bit more.' She pushed open the door, then paused, smiling at a sudden thought. 'Hey, maybe we could get a car as well . . . a nice little Jeep or something. What do you think?'

'Sounds good to me,' I said as I followed her into the flat. 'As long as you're paying for it . . .'

As soon as I shut the door behind us, I knew that something was wrong. The lights were off, so I couldn't see anything . . . but I didn't have to see it to know it. Something was different, something had changed . . . and then it dawned on me. It was the darkness. Even with all the lights turned off, the flat was never as dark as this. The window was always open, the curtains never closed . . . there was always a hint of light from somewhere, even on the darkest of nights. And tonight the sky was ablaze with fireworks.

'Hold on, Eddi,' I started to say, 'I think there's –'

Eddi gasped, a short intake of breath, and the sound of her shock cut through the blackness. The lights suddenly snapped on and there was Ryan – sitting in the armchair with a gun in his hand, his silver eyes fixed on me.

'Hello, Robert,' he said. 'You're a hard man to find.'

27

It took me a moment to realize that Ryan wasn't alone. It was a long moment, a moment I'd always known was coming, and now it was here – the time when everything came together: the past, the future . . . the beginning, the end. This was it. Me and Ryan. This was everything. And for a second or two, that's all there was – me and Ryan, his eyes, his gun, the whirling blackness inside my head. There *was* nothing else. No sound, no movement, no thoughts, no sense. Nobody else existed.

But then Eddi spat out an angry curse – '*Shit!* Get *off* me!' – and a massive firework flashed and boomed in the sky outside, and suddenly my head was clear. I could see all around me. I could see that Eddi had been grabbed from behind by the woman called Hayes, and that Hayes was holding a gun to her head. And I could see two men in suits, one on either side of me, both of them carrying pistols. One of them, the one on my right, was the bull-headed man from the hospital basement, the man whose nose I'd broken. Cooper. The other one I'd never seen before, but he looked just as mean as his partner.

'Lock the door, Kelly,' Ryan told him.

Kelly locked the door.

I glanced over at Eddi. Hayes still had hold of her, and I could see the anger and shock in Eddi's face, but she wasn't struggling. She was just standing there, looking at me, her eyes calm and steady. She was letting me know she could deal with this . . . *we* could deal with it.

'Are you all right?' I said to her.

She nodded.

I looked back at Ryan. He was watching me, studying me, his silver eyes glinting dully in the cold white light. He seemed older than I remembered – older and greyer, his face lined with tiredness. He looked like a man who'd come a long way.

He glanced over at Hayes and nodded his head. Hayes let Eddi go, but kept the gun on her.

'Sit down over there,' she told her. 'On the settee.'

Eddi stared at Hayes for a moment, then she walked over to the settee and sat down opposite Ryan. Hayes went over and stood behind her. Eddi glanced over at the bedroom door, then quickly looked away again.

Ryan smiled at her. 'If you're thinking of going after your gun, Miss Ray, I'm afraid we've already removed it.' He showed her the pistol in his hand, letting her see that it was hers. 'Anyway,' he continued, 'it's nice to meet you at last, Eddi. Do you mind if I call you Eddi? Or would you prefer Maria? Or Jennifer, or Sheila . . . ?'

Eddi said nothing, just stared at him.

He gazed back at her for a while, then he looked up at me. 'How much does she know, Robert?'

'Why don't you ask her?' I said. 'She's sitting right in front of you.'

'I'm asking you – how much does she know?'

'I know everything,' Eddi said to him.

Ryan ignored her, keeping his eyes on me. 'It must have been very hard for you, Robert, living a lie all this time. It must have taken a lot out of you.' His eyes narrowed. 'Or maybe it wasn't so hard? I suppose it all depends on whether or not you have any human feelings – contrition, remorse . . . empathy.' He smiled again. 'Do you have any feelings, Robert? Does it work like that?'

I could feel Eddi looking at me now, her eyes filled with questions, and I wanted to look back at her and say – I was going to tell you, honestly. I was going to tell you tonight. I was going to tell you *everything* . . .

But it was too late for that now. It was too late for everything.

'Eddi doesn't know anything,' I told Ryan. 'She doesn't have anything to do with this. Why don't you just let her go?'

Ryan said nothing.

'If you let her go,' I said, 'I'll cooperate with you. I'll talk to you . . . I'll tell you everything I know. I'll do whatever you want.'

Ryan smiled and shook his head. 'You're going to do whatever we want anyway, Robert. We don't need your cooperation. And, besides, Miss Ray has valuable information about you . . . *intimate* information, if your shared bedroom is anything to go by.'

'What are you?' Eddi spat at him. 'Some kind of pervert?'

He still didn't look at her, he just carried on staring at me, and I could tell that Eddi was about to snap. He was treating her as if she didn't exist, and she just couldn't stand it any more.

'No, Eddi –' I started to say.

But she'd already started to lunge at Ryan, leaning forward and trying to snatch the pistol from his hand. Ryan barely looked at her. He just sat there and watched as Hayes reached out, grabbed Eddi by the hair and yanked her back into the settee. Eddi twisted round and swung her fist at Hayes, but Hayes just leaned back and dodged it. In the same movement, she grabbed Eddi by the hair again and slammed her head against the back of the settee. The blow wasn't hard enough to knock Eddi out, but it was enough to knock the fight out of her.

There was nothing I could do. Kelly had got hold of me as soon as he'd seen Eddi going for Ryan, and now both men were holding me by the arms, stopping me from moving.

'Eddi!' I called out, straining to get to her. 'Eddi . . . are you all right?' She was slumped on the settee, dazed and groaning, holding her head in her hands. 'Eddi!' I yelled again, screaming like a madman. '*Eddi!*'

'She's all right,' Ryan said dismissively. 'She's not hurt.'

I glared at him. 'You're dead if she is.'

He stared at me, a slight smile playing on his face. I stared back at him for a moment, then turned away and gazed over at Eddi again. She'd stopped groaning now. She was just sitting there, perfectly still, her eyes fixed coldly on the curtained window behind Ryan. Blurred flashes of distant fireworks were showing through the curtains and I could still hear the booming crashes echoing around the village, but it all seemed a long way away now. It was out there, and out there was a different world.

'All right,' I heard Ryan say, 'let's get this done.'

I looked over at him. He'd got up out of his chair and was talking to Hayes and the two men. 'And remember,' he said, 'I want them both alive, but don't take any chances. I'd rather get them back dead than not get them back at all. OK?'

His colleagues nodded.

'Right,' said Ryan, 'you know what to do. Let's do it.'

Across the room, I saw Hayes take a hypodermic syringe from a metal case, and almost immediately I realized that Kelly was holding a syringe too. As he raised it to the light and tapped the barrel, Cooper grabbed me tightly round the chest, pinning my arms to my sides. I didn't do anything for a moment, I just stood there, feeling the power of his arms. But when I looked over at Eddi and saw Ryan holding her down and Hayes leaning over her, preparing to stick the needle in her arm, I suddenly went berserk – screaming and yelling, trying to break free, kicking out at Cooper, stamping on his feet, hurling my head back at him . . . I did everything I could to break his grip, but he barely even flinched. He just stood there like a rock, his arms wrapped tightly round my chest, squeezing the life out of me. I couldn't move. Couldn't do anything.

Over at the settee, Ryan had grabbed Eddi's wrist now and Hayes had the tip of the needle pressed against her arm. As I yelled out desperately again – *'No!'* – Eddi's head suddenly lurched forward and she heaved, as if she was going to be sick. Hayes instinctively jerked away from her, but Ryan barely moved. As Eddi gulped and heaved again, Ryan kept hold of her and looked coolly at Hayes.

'Do it,' he told her.

'She's going to throw up,' Hayes said.

'Just do it.'

Eddi was pale now, her face dripping with sweat. 'Oh, God . . .' she groaned. 'I need the bathroom . . . I'm going to . . .' She retched again, this time lurching towards Ryan. He flinched slightly, keeping out of her way, but he still didn't let go of her.

'Come *on*,' he said to Hayes. 'What are you waiting for?'

'Sir,' Hayes said calmly, 'I think we should let her use the bathroom. If she's sick when she's unconscious, she might choke on her own vomit.'

Ryan thought about it.

'We want her alive, sir,' Hayes reminded him.

He gave it some more thought, then nodded. 'All right . . . take her to the bathroom. But leave your gun here and don't let her out of your sight.' He let go of Eddi and took Hayes's pistol. Hayes put the syringe back in the metal case, dropped the case in her pocket, then helped Eddi to her feet and started walking her to the bathroom.

Ryan looked over at me.

Cooper was still holding me, and Kelly still had the syringe in his hand, but they'd both been too distracted by Eddi throwing up to do anything. Now they were looking at Ryan, wondering what he wanted them to do.

Ryan sat down on the settee.

'Sir,' Kelly said cautiously, 'do you want us to –'

'Not yet,' Ryan said. 'Just keep hold of him.'

'Sir,' Kelly nodded.

Ryan took a handkerchief from his pocket and wiped a fleck of liquid from his sleeve. He folded the handkerchief back into his pocket, then slowly looked over at me. 'What's the matter with her?' he said. 'Is she ill or something?'

'There's a bug going round,' I heard myself say.

'A bug?'

I nodded. 'A virus or something. It's the festival – it brings in a lot of outsiders. You know how it is, they come down here and spread their germs all over the place . . .'

I couldn't believe what I was saying – the banality of it, the calmness of my voice. It was ridiculous. My life was falling to pieces. Cooper still had hold of me, crushing my arms to my sides. I was about to be drugged and kidnapped, and Eddi . . . I didn't know *what* was happening with Eddi. And yet, here I was, chatting away to Ryan as if he'd just popped round for a cup of tea. It was madness.

'What about you?' Ryan said to me. 'Have you got this bug?'

'I don't get ill.'

'No,' he said, 'I don't suppose you do.'

I smiled at him. 'How did you find me?'

'Sorry?'

'How did you know I was here?'

He glanced over his shoulder, wondering about Eddi and Hayes, then he turned back to me. 'A couple of British tourists staying in Nerja,' he said. 'They saw you, remembered your face from the newspapers, informed the police.'

'How did you know where I lived?'

'We didn't. We had to ask around.'

'Who did you ask?'

'Does it matter?'

'Not really.'

I looked at Kelly. He was just standing there, staring at the floor, holding the syringe in his hand.

I turned back to Ryan. 'You realize that whatever's in that syringe, it's not going to keep me out for long.'

'It doesn't have to,' he said. 'Before we leave here, you're going to be tied up so tightly you won't even be able to blink.' He looked at me. 'You know this is all for your own good, don't you?'

'Really?'

He nodded. 'You don't know what you are, Robert. We know that. Over the last six months we've taken your life apart – dissected it, examined it, analysed it. We've checked out all your Homes, your carers, your schools. We've investigated your teachers, your social workers, the children you grew up with. We've studied your files, your medical records, your therapists' reports. We've talked to people. Watched people. Followed people. We've studied your endoscopy video a thousand times. We've analysed every trace of forensic evidence we could find – blood, hair, skin . . . everything.' He shook his head. 'But we still don't know what you are. The only thing we know for certain is that you don't know what you are either. No one does.' He stared at me. 'You can't spend the rest of your life like that, Robert – not knowing what you are, or where you came from, or why you're here.'

'Why not?'

'Because –'

'Sir?' Kelly said.

Ryan looked up and saw Kelly staring at something behind him. Ryan paused for a moment, then slowly started turning his head to see what Kelly was looking at . . . and suddenly he froze. Eddi was standing behind him, pointing a pistol at his head.

'Give me the gun,' Eddi said coldly, holding out her hand. 'And the one you took from Hayes.'

Ryan smiled at her. 'You're very good, Miss Ray, I'll give you that.' He glanced at the pistol in her hand. 'I searched your bathroom twice . . .' He looked back at Eddi. 'Where was it?'

'Just give me the guns,' she said.

He shook his head. 'I'm afraid I can't do that.'

'I'll kill you if I have to,' she warned him.

'I'm sure you will. But then Kelly will have to shoot you, which will inconvenience us a little, but we'll still have Robert.' He shrugged. 'And that's all that really matters.'

Eddi's eyes flicked over at Kelly. He'd dropped the syringe and pulled out his pistol and was holding it down at his side. He didn't move as Eddi looked at him, he just stood there, perfectly still, staring blankly into her eyes.

'You see, Miss Ray,' Ryan continued, 'it's not that I don't value my own life, because I do, but sometimes we have to think of the bigger picture. And Robert here . . .' He gazed over at me. 'Well, Robert could be the biggest thing the world has ever seen.' He looked back at Eddi. 'You have no idea what you have loved, do you, Miss Ray?'

Eddi's lips moved, but she couldn't say anything. She stared silently at Ryan for a while, then her head turned slowly and she looked over at me. As she gazed into my eyes, everything else disappeared. I knew that Cooper was still holding me, and I knew that Ryan and Kelly were still watching our every move, but just for a moment they didn't exist. The only life in that room was the life that burned in Eddi's blue eyes as they stared into mine . . . trying to see inside me, trying to understand . . . and for a fraction of a second, I think she *did* understand. I might have been fooling myself, trying to see what I wanted to see, but in that moment, I truly believed that Eddi knew everything. She'd seen inside me. She'd seen what I was, and why I'd kept it from her, and she'd forgiven me.

'Now,' Ryan said.

In a blur of speed, I saw Kelly raise his arm and level his pistol at Eddi. I lunged desperately at him, dragging Cooper with me, and we both crashed into him just as he fired the gun. As Kelly grunted and staggered sideways, Cooper twisted me away from him and threw me to the ground, but even as I was falling I could see that Eddi hadn't been hit. She'd already spun away from Ryan and now she was facing Kelly – her eyes calm, the pistol gripped in both hands. She fired off three quick shots – *bangbangbang* – and I saw Kelly's head jerk backwards . . . and then it happened.

Bang.

Another shot.

Flat and dull.

Final.

It came from the other side of the room.

And I knew what it meant. The silence, the stillness. I could feel it screaming inside me as I lay there on the floor, staring in terror, waiting for the gun smoke to clear. I knew what I was going to see.

*

She was sitting on the floor with her legs buckled under her, leaning crookedly against the wall. Her hands were crossed over in her lap, her fingers curled like a sleeping child's. Her eyes were open, staring blindly, and a thin trickle of blood was seeping from the bullet hole in her head.

I wanted to cry. I've never wanted to cry so much in my life. But I couldn't. All I could do was stare at her.
My Eddi . . .
I stared at her for a long time.

Something left me then.
Something drained away.

When I finally got to my feet and looked over at Ryan, he was still sitting on the settee, still holding the gun he'd shot Eddi with, still looking calm and serene. As we gazed into each other's dead eyes, I knew what I had to do.
I looked round the room.
Kelly was lying dead on the floor, his gun-shot head ringed with a pool of darkening blood. Flies were already gathering at the edge of the crimson pool. I watched them for a moment, wondering if they knew what they were doing, then I looked over at Cooper. He was standing with his back to the wall, pointing a gun at me. His eyes were dark and angry. He wanted to kill me.
The ceiling fan whirred.
The air smelled of death.
Fireworks crackled faintly in the distance.
I started walking across the room.

318

Ryan watched me. I saw him glance over at Cooper and shake his head, then he looked back at me again. I walked past him and stopped in front of Eddi. For a moment I just stood there, looking down at her . . . her beautiful face, her pale white skin, her hands, her hair, her fading blue eyes. It was all nothing now. She was nothing.

She wasn't Eddi any more.

She wasn't anything.

I knelt down beside her and gently adjusted her dress. It had ridden up over her thighs when she'd fallen. As I smoothed it down over her legs, a drop of blood dripped from her head, spotting the sheer white cotton. I stared at the small red stain for a moment, then I reached out slowly and touched it with the tip of my finger. The blood was cold and sticky.

I licked it from my finger.

She was in me now. She was with me forever.

I leaned over and kissed her cold lips.

I closed her eyes.

I licked my finger again and wiped the trickle of blood from her forehead.

Then I ran my bloodied fingertip down my face – once, twice – from the corner of each eye to the corners of my mouth, painting my cheeks with tears of blood.

I turned to Ryan. 'I can't cry,' I told him. 'Something happens to me. The doors close, the lights go out. I disappear.'

He looked at me, but said nothing.

I reached over and picked up Eddi's pistol from the floor.

'Don't do it, Robert . . .' I heard Ryan say.

I looked at the gun in my hand. It was smaller than the one she'd kept in the bedside cabinet, and I wondered briefly where she'd hidden it and why she'd never told me about it . . .

It didn't matter.

I stood up, holding Eddi's pistol down at my side, and turned to face Ryan. He wasn't pointing his gun at me, but it was in his hand and his finger was poised on the trigger.

'You might as well put the gun down, Robert,' he said calmly. 'It's not going to do you any good. If you so much as think about using it, Cooper's going to shoot you.'

I turned and looked at Cooper. He hadn't moved. He was still standing there with his pistol levelled at my head and I didn't doubt that Ryan was right. The big man was just waiting for an excuse to pull the trigger.

'It's all right,' I said, smiling at him, 'it's over now. You can relax. I'm not going to do anything.'

Cooper didn't react for a moment, he just kept on staring coldly at me, and then I saw his eyes flick over at Ryan. It was no more than a momentary glance, a quick look of uncertainty, but that was all I needed. I raised my arm and shot Cooper twice in the chest. He managed to fire back at me, but he was already staggering by then and the shot went harmlessly into the ceiling. I watched as he fell to the floor, waited until he'd stopped moving, then I lowered the pistol and turned back to Ryan.

The pistol in his outstretched hand was aimed directly at my head.

'Don't make me do it, Robert,' he said carefully. 'Don't

make me pull the trigger. I don't want to, but I will. I swear to God . . .'

I looked at him for a long time, staring down the barrel of his gun, gazing into his silver eyes . . . letting him think whatever he wanted to think. I didn't care any more. I dropped my pistol to the floor, turned my back on him and walked down the hall to the bathroom.

'Robert?' he called after me. 'What are you . . . ? Robert?'

I ignored him and went into the bathroom. Hayes was lying face down on the floor with the hypodermic needle stuck in her neck. I squatted down and checked her pulse. She was still alive.

I stood up and looked in the mirror. The blood-streaked thing looking back at me wasn't a face. It was just a thing . . . a thing of skin and bone. Lips, teeth, eyes, blood-red tears . . . the shape of a skull.

Nothing.

I opened a cabinet above the sink and took out a razor blade.

When I went back into the front room, Ryan was still sitting on the settee. He'd picked up my pistol and placed it next to his on the cushion beside him. I knew he still had another one in his pocket, but it didn't matter. Nothing mattered any more.

I sat down in the armchair opposite him. 'Hayes is all right,' I said. 'She's not dead. Eddi just stuck the needle in her neck.'

Ryan nodded. 'I'm sorry about Eddi, Robert . . . I'm really sorry. It wasn't supposed to be like this.'

'You'll never know,' I told him.

He frowned at me. 'I'll never know what?'

I said nothing, just looked at him.

He shook his head. 'Listen, Robert . . . I know you don't want to believe me, but what I said earlier, about all this being for your own good . . . it's the truth. No one was meant to get hurt. We just want to help you.' He looked at me. 'Just give us a chance, Robert . . . listen to me. Let me explain who we are –'

'I don't care who you are.'

His eyes narrowed. 'But don't you want to know –?'

'I don't want to know anything.'

He leaned forward and looked me in the eye. 'We can find out everything about you, Robert. We can find out what you are, where you came from, why you're here –'

'I don't care why I'm here. I don't care about any of it – what I am, where I came from, who you are . . . none of it means anything. It never did.' I looked at him. 'It's time to end it now.'

'What?'

'I want to show you something.'

As I reached into my pocket and took out the razor blade, Ryan snatched up his pistol and swung it in my direction.

'What are you doing?' he snapped.

'Just watch,' I told him.

Holding the razor blade in my right hand, I clenched the fist of my left hand and held the arm out in front of me. I looked over at Ryan. He'd put the gun down now and was watching me intently. I pressed the razor blade into the fleshy part of my left arm and slowly drew it down. A thick red slice opened up, and I let the pain flood through me.

Don't think any more.

Just feel the pain . . .

Nothing else.

I stood up and walked over to Ryan. His eyes were transfixed, staring at the coloured liquids dripping from the gash in my arm. White blood, black blood, luminous silver blood. I stopped in front of him and held out my arm. He leaned forward and gazed curiously at the wound. I don't know what he saw – red things, pulsing things, the shadows of silver bones. I didn't care.

'Remember it,' I said to him. 'You'll never see it again.'

He looked up at me, started to say something, and I hammered my fist into his head.

I hit him hard enough to kill him. Bones cracked in my fist, and as he crashed down to the floor and collapsed, I thought for a moment that I *had* killed him. He was lying on his back, his arms and legs splayed out like the limbs of a broken doll. His eyes were closed. His mouth was half open. Blood and spit and bits of teeth were dribbling down his chin. The side of his face was misshapen – caved in and hanging down – and the skin around his jaw was turning black.

He didn't seem to be breathing.

I picked up Eddi's pistol and crouched down beside him. When I lowered my head to his, I could just make out a weak gurgling sound in the back of his throat.

He was breathing.

He wasn't dead.

I gazed into his face for a moment, wondering what lay beneath that tired grey skin. Bones and feelings. Blood and memories. Secrets, lies, big things, small things . . . ?

He'd never know.

I stood up and looked over at Eddi. She was still sitting there. Her eyes were still closed.

The fireworks had stopped now.

The room was cold and silent.

I looked down at Ryan again and levelled the gun at his head. I stood there for a long time, thinking of all the things he'd done – to me, to Eddi, to everything that might have been – and I came very close to pulling the trigger.

But I didn't.

Dying wasn't enough for him.

I wanted him to live – to live without ever knowing what I was. That was his death: to live without knowing.

I lowered the pistol and set about leaving.

There was nothing inside me as I moved around the flat, stuffing things into my pockets. I had nothing left. I was empty. Finished. Disconnected. Something knew what I was doing, and where I was going, and what I was going to do when I got there, but it wasn't me. I had no self any more. I wasn't Robert Smith. I was just a thing – looking for my passport, pocketing some cash, picking up the keys to Eddi's motorbike.

I didn't look at Eddi on the way out.

I couldn't look at her.

She wasn't there.

Nothing was there.

*

Downstairs, everything was quiet. No fireworks, no voices, no sign of the Garcias or Chico. I walked along the darkened hallway and opened the door to the Garcias' kitchen. Chico was lying dead on the floor, a bullet hole in the back of his head.

I closed the door and went back down the hallway.

I was nothing now. Timeless. Placeless. Thoughtless. My head was dead, the things inside it black and distant. Eddi Ray. David Ryan. Living things. Dead things. Robert Smith. The things I should have done, the things I shouldn't have done. The future, the past. Memories: a fat man in a cheap red suit, jellies, sweets, a long table and benches; the smell of disinfectant; the sound of laughter; faces, figures, unknown voices; childhood dreams of whirling winds, whirling waters, spinning me round and round, sucking me down into the darkness . . .

The past . . .

The future.

Now.

I was empty.

I was just whatever I was, wherever I was – an empty thing in an empty house, walking slowly down an empty hallway . . . opening the front door, looking around, gazing up at the clear night sky . . .

The stars were out.

Twinkling brightly . . .

I didn't stop to wonder what they were.

I went back into the house, wheeled out Eddi's motorbike, and rode off into the darkness.

Kevin BROOKS
Q & A

You've had lots of random jobs (crematorium assistant, refreshments vendor at London Zoo, civil servant). How did these experiences affect your writing?

It took me a long time to succeed as a writer and in the meantime I had to do lots of different jobs to earn money. But, although I hated them all, those experiences did give me an overwhelming desire to spend my life doing something that I actually like doing.

Also, those jobs allowed me to mix with lots of different people, classes and cultures from all over the country. Now, when I'm trying to write about particular characters or situations, I can go back and draw on those experiences. So although I didn't like doing those jobs at the time, they've actually come in quite useful!

What is your favourite book of all time?

I like crime fiction a lot and I also like westerns. Elmore Leonard's *Hombre* is one of my all-time favourites. It's a very simple book about a really cool half Native American, half white character. Also, I've always loved *My Side of the Mountain* by Jean Craighead George, which is about a boy who runs away from home and lives in the woods on his own. But truthfully, I really have too many favourites to pick just one.

Before you wrote you wanted to be a rock-star. How does music influence your writing?

I've taken a great deal from what I learned about writing songs and used it in my writing. For example, I use rhythm a lot. You can use the rhythm of writing to back up emotions, emphasize things and create moods without the reader being consciously aware you're doing it.

When I'm writing stories I'm always aware of the rhythm of the overall structure, but it goes right down to the level of specific sentences and individual words. I'll think about how many syllables a particular word has got in order to make it fit in with the rhythm of the sentence. Quite often I'm not aware of *how* it works – but I know if it's working or not.